Trust No-One

by

Grant Spencer

Book One

of the

Frank Tanner Series

A Grizzly Dare Publication

Grizzly Dare Books
London UK

British Library Cataloguing in Publication Data.
A catalogue record for this book is available
from the British Library

ISBN: 978-0-9567309-2-3

Edited by **Grizzly Dare**

Typesetting and Origination - Grizzly Dare

Cover Design Concept - Grizzly Dare

Cover Artwork, Website and Production Imagery - **Tommy Rocket**

Additional Artwork and processing by **Grizzle London** and **Grizzly Dare**

ACKNOWLEDGEMENTS

To those that know… remember this is fiction

Thanks to my *WW*ife Lucy, my confidante, my muse, my love; you are always by my side on the crazy paths I take you down

To all my family for the love and support and the roles you have played in my life

To my parents for allowing me to follow my dreams and join the Royal Navy, which has given me the experiences to base my story on

To all my friends, you have played a part in my life and within my stories

Those that edited reviewed and delivered honest, constructive criticism - whether I agreed or not, the truth matters

To my editor and the Grizzly Dare team, thanks for the diligent work - for the mentoring, proofing, editing and book design

To Ethan, Harrison, Alexandria, and Beau…
Never give up on your dreams

Chapter One

He felt the tension drain from him as Air Arabia flight G9201 landed at Al Fujairah International Airport and taxied to its delegated gate number. After a short wait, the airplane door swung open, and the passenger steps were in place.

Sergeant Andy Hunter was hit by the thirty-four-degree heat as he walked down the passenger steps to the tarmac. He could see the mirage of heat-ripples rising from the surface and felt the asphalt sticking to the soles of his boots as he walked. It was warmer than his previous destination, Tehran, the difference in the extra few degrees all the more apparent after his air-conditioned flight.

The skies were bright blue and cloudless, the sun warm on his face, and despite the gentle breeze he could feel the perspiration building on his skin. He smiled to himself; this was the start of a ten-day Rest & Recuperation period - R&R.

Hunter was looking forward to the simple pleasure of an ice-cold beer, his mouth watering at the thought.

The flight had been pleasant enough, only missing the drink he longed for. Air Arabia operated a strict alcohol-free policy on this particular route, a sacrifice he was used to while working in locations under the rule of Sharia law. He could refrain from certain pleasures to do the job he loved - he even respected the culture, but it didn't mean he had to agree with it.

Hunter had started his operational tour in Iran's capital four months earlier, deployed by the army as a HUMINT, a Human Intelligence Agent Handler, known as an Operator, conducting covert operations out of the British Embassy in Tehran.

Hunter ran various sources, another name for agents, trying

to keep one step ahead in the fight against terrorism.

He loved his job and the glint of danger that came with it.

Hunter passed through immigration and collected his luggage, before exiting the airport through the tinted glass doors. The combination of heat and sun returned, seeing a holiday feeling wash over him; Hunter started to relax a little.

Climbing into a taxi, it was a short trip to his hotel, the Palace Beach Resort Fujairah. He'd convinced his boss, Captain Dave Stones, to splash out on the 5-star hotel due to the intense workload he'd been conducting with one of his Covert Human Intelligence Sources - CHIS - codename 'Salamander'. Sources were given codenames to protect their true identities, usually associated to animals or precious metals, once they had even used the name of planets, the theme directed down from Command back in the UK.

He always thought Salamander was an apt name for this informant. Like the reptile, he had a long slender build and a permanent sheen over his skin - and similar to an amphibious nature, Salamander was able to move between his normal life environment to that of a covert source.

Hunter relaxed into the seat and revisited the meeting a few days prior.

He had built a good rapport since becoming Salamander's Handler and despite having some differences over the month or so prior, felt he'd developed the relationship sufficiently to make Salamander feel they were becoming friends.

The meeting had started well, Salamander had even asked what Hunter's plans were for his break, and Hunter, perhaps a little too smugly, had told him. Hunter had perceived his interest as a good sign, that despite all that had been happening, Salamander was engaging with him as a real friend would. Yet, just prior to Hunter leaving for his trip, Salamander had flipped into a completely different character and lost control.

It was like dealing with an entirely different-person. It had not been left on good terms and Hunter's report reflected as much, strongly recommending a two-week cooling off period with the source, which had been approved.

He pulled himself from his pondering and sighed. Hunter would deal with all of that when he returned to Tehran, right now he needed to forget the *money-grabbing snitch* and enjoy some much-needed downtime, and as the Ministry of Defence was footing the bill, he intended to make the most of it.

Chapter Two

A pristine road of tall palm trees and carefully manicured hedges delivered the taxi to the hotel entrance.

As Hunter observed through the window, a smile grew across his face, 'This is a bit of me,' he thought.

The Palace Beach Resort was a structure of pure white bathed in Middle Eastern sunshine, its bright glare so intense it felt like an interrogation light being shone directly into Hunter's face… It would not have been the first time.

The taxi circled a sculpture of twisted copper and bronze, the contemporary art resembling a flame, standing tall on an island at the front of the hotel. The modern structure stood several stories, double-breasted against the attractive entrance.

As the taxi stopped, the door was opened by an eager porter who then busied himself retrieving any luggage from the rear.

Hunter stepped out and looked up at the square-arch entry that rose above him displaying with pride the hotel's name in large golden letters, 'PALACE'.

He paid the driver and followed the porter through the large colonial-style glass wall that framed the doorway.

The attentive staff opened the doors, voicing native greetings as he approached.

Inside, the coolness of the air-conditioned foyer struck him, as if he'd stepped into a walk-in refrigerator - he closed his eyes, enjoying the moment after the stifling journey in the taxi.

The reception was as attractive, if not more so, than the outer building itself. The foyer was modern, clean cut and white. The high ceilings towered over green trees in large white pots, while comfortable royal blue armchairs dressed the space in groups of four, complete with courtesy table, each cluster sitting upon oversized rugs.

To the far reach, the floor-to-ceiling glass presented a pool area decorated in yet more palm trees, and just beyond, white sand lured guests toward the sun-kissed blue sea.

The porter led Hunter to the reception desk.

"Ahlan wa Sahlan," the local greeting of *welcome* was offered by a staff member wearing traditional Arab attire, who proceeded to check Hunter in with well-rehearsed efficiency.

Upon reaching his room, Hunter was pleased to find it comfortable and spacious with a luxurious feel. He opened the balcony doors and stepped out to take in the sea view and breathe in the warm salty air.

He returned to the coolness of the room intent on making a quick turnaround, with a shower to wash the travel off, before adorning a fresh set of civvies.

Soon after, he was in the elevator heading for the hotel bar.

Hunter ordered a Stella, 'Thank God they serve alcohol here,' he silently praised.

Hotels within the UAE had relaxed their Sharia law inside such complexes to be more westernised, encouraging more tourism to help grow their already booming economy. This also allowed Arab men to break the rules they lived by, and they were often found inside the hotels dabbling in various activities that would undoubtedly anger Allah.

The ice-cold beer was placed in front of him, and Hunter savoured the moment. He swooned at the condensation as it ran down the misty refrigerated glass. It had been several months since he'd had a drink, and right now this felt like a scene from a commercial. Unable to resist any longer, Hunter downed the drink in one motion, enjoying every drop like a bee collecting nectar from a flower. He felt the alcohol go straight to his head - it had certainly been a while.

He ordered another.

Hunter sipped his second beer and took in his surroundings. He liked to people-watch, a habit made all the more natural due to the nature of his job. He noticed a female guest sitting alone. She was a redhead, curvy, almost airing on the side of plump. She was absorbed within her laptop, likely here on business by the way she was dressed. She looked up and caught his gaze. Hunter smiled and held up his beer.

She rolled her eyes and returned to her computer screen.

'Snubbed,' he chuckled. In his younger bachelor days, he would have still made a move, the rebuke only encouraging him to pursue her, but not anymore, his thoughts turning instead to his fiancée and their unborn child.

At the time he met Zoe he wasn't looking for a relationship or to settle down, but from the moment they met they'd just clicked, and almost immediately after had become a couple.

When he wasn't deployed, they were inseparable, and within only a few short months had moved in together.

Life was good.

When she announced she was pregnant soon after, he was not impressed, but he'd forced a happy façade as he could see she was elated. At the time he thought about the dynamic change of lifestyle that was ahead of them, his self-interest warning how his freedom was surely to be stifled. It was a nagging notion that had seen Hunter keep his R&R plans to himself, and instead of baby-talk, shopping and baby advice, he'd instead come to Fujairah. It was selfish but he could live with it, and he found justification by telling himself he would learn to love being a family man once the baby arrived - but that until then, this could well be the last time he might relax by himself for the next few years.

He turned back to the bar catching the reflection of himself in the mirror, 'No wonder the redhead rolled her eyes,' he laughed inwardly to himself. His black hair and beard were unkempt, neglected over the past few months whilst he had been embedded in Tehran. Although this appearance allowed him to blend into the local Iranian population, it wasn't the cleanest of looks. There and then he could be mistaken for a tramp that should be sleeping on the bench out front rather than in his Deluxe Ocean View room.

Finishing his drink, he decided to get himself spruced up.

He headed to the reception when he was approached by a concierge who seemed almost a little too keen for comfort.

'Mo' as his name badge stated, most likely short for Mohammed, listened intently as Hunter enquired about a traditional barber. Hunter was quickly offered a seat on a plush royal blue armchair while Mo went to enquire on his behalf.

After ten minutes passed, with no sign of the eager Mo anywhere, Hunter assumed he'd been forgotten, but just as he was set to enquire elsewhere, the concierge returned with instructions of a recommended local place called, 'ATYAF Gent's Salon.' Mo informed Hunter he would call a taxi.

Hunter agreed to remain in the armchair until his lift arrived. He pulled out his iPhone to check his messages, and shortly after could see Mo approaching again. Mo was carrying a tray holding another ice-cold beer. He was going to object until Mo told him it was on the house as the taxi would be running a little late. Hunter would never refuse a free beer.

He placed the drink down and began texting Zoe.

He felt a twinge of guilt as he kept up the charade. In order to enjoy this trip, he'd told her he was still in Tehran, that the increased workload and some critical issues were preventing him from returning home.

He took no pleasure in lying to her, but felt he needed time alone before he would be anywhere close to the mindset of returning as a family man.

After a time, he glanced at his watch and near empty glass and was shocked to see forty-five minutes had passed. He finished the drink feeling a little lightheaded, the alcohol and situation with Zoe working quickly to cloud his mind.

He was set to postpone the venture and go rest in his room, when he saw Mo once again approaching.

The taxi had arrived.

Mo apologised for the delay and escorted him outside. Opening the rear door, Mo nodded to the driver as Hunter got into the back of the vehicle. It was a local style taxi, a faded yellow Toyota Camry with a token gesture TAXI sign on top. In an instant, Hunter found himself missing the hotel's air conditioning as the humidity set about its work to make him sweat. He could hear the car's air-con running, but it wasn't putting in much of a performance. Hunter tried to engage with the driver, informing him of where he wanted to go.

The driver raised a hand and grunted. Hunter assumed Mo had told the taxi company of his destination, the driver's dismissive nature not unusual in this part of the world.

The taxi made the short journey up the main carriageway before turning into the local streets of downtown Al Faseel.

Navigating between the dusty blocks made up of local small businesses and houses, it wasn't long before they pulled up outside ATYAF Gent's Salon.

The taxi driver muttered something.

Hunter looked at the meter and handed over one hundred Dirham, the equivalent of £20. The driver didn't seem interested in offering change, certainly taking advantage of Hunter's foreign appearance. Hunter let it go and stepped out, seeing the taxi quickly speed away down the street.

The salon was in a quiet part of town, near the end of a row of shops which all seemed to be closed. To the left of the barbers stood a food outlet - to the right what looked like a café. The front of the salon had a traditional Arabic feel, pale yellow render, with two mosque style arches along the front, one arch a window the other the door. The signage above had yellow writing displaying the name of the barbershop in Arabic, and underneath translated into English in white lettering set on a blue background. It looked small, clean, and tidy. Looking through the window, the shop appeared as empty as the streets surrounding it. 'Bit of a ghost town,' he thought, 'But never judge a book by its cover.' One thing Hunter had learned in his line of business was that often behind every dirty cover was a hidden gem or secret.

Unbeknown to Hunter, as he opened the door and walked inside… this would be the last secret he would ever uncover.

Chapter Three

Ahmad and Omar sat in their white Mitsubishi Pajaero. Although over ten years old it was still in good condition, the slight dent in its nearside rear quarter panel barely noticeable. With heavily tinted windows all round, it was a popular vehicle in this part of the world, and one in which it was easy to remain inconspicuous.

The 4x4 was parked at the roadside idling, its air conditioning running to keep its two occupants cool.

From one hundred metres they watched the man as he exited Al Fujairah International Airport - a male of average height and stocky build, in his late 30's.

Although the photograph they had was a little pixelated, the person now in front of them was recognisable to the picture on their dashboard. He looked scruffier than in the photo, his beard longer and bushier, his hair taking on a style of its own.

He walked towards the taxi rank.

They could tell he was military and would not have needed the previous night's brief to work that out. They'd followed his kind before and they all had a certain swagger about them, confident, strong, arrogant. They had despised this person before having laid eyes on him, now he was real and in front of them, their hatred swelled even more. Infidel!

They felt a twinge of adrenaline. Last night's meeting indicated their orders had come directly from the top level in Iran. Rumour had it, it was from Jafar Abdul Malik himself, the leader of their organisation - *Disciples of the Afterlife.* They, along with other disciples were to maintain visual contact with the target and track and report his movements.

This was nothing new, but for the first time, the group was asked to assess potential opportunities to be able to take out the target discreetly. Although they did not know why the organisation wanted this man killed, they were excited and nervous, this would be the first time they had been involved in such a serious undertaking.

Omar sat in the passenger seat, a hand resting on his Kalashnikov, hidden from view by his headdress scarf. As he watched the man he was struck by the thought, 'I could step out now and empty thirty rounds into him.' His time training in the desert dunes had illustrated he was not the best shot, but he knew the spread of the AK would likely cause fatal damage.

He eased his hand off the weapon and breathed, remembering his orders had stated discretion as a priority.

Ahmed and Omar were brothers. Orphaned at a young age, they were both loners, and apart from looking out for each other, they'd never really felt any real direction in life. That was until a guy they'd see in the barbers each week started talking to them, and after several conversations invited them to a meeting. 'Come and listen to the Elder speak,' he had smiled, 'Who knows, you might even find a purpose to your life.'

With not much else to do, they both went along and were shown down to the basement under the business premises.

Thirty people of various ages and backgrounds were in attendance that night, some of whom they recognised from around the area. They drank tea and met new people. Later that night, the head of the group had spoken in a manner that held their absolute attention. An elderly Arab, his words were resolute and convincing, his sentiment soothing and wise. They felt he could read their minds, preaching of finding a path in life, and how the life they were currently living was merely a stepping-stone to a better existence, an afterlife.

The hand both Ahmed and Omar had been dealt in life had seen their faith stray over the years, but they'd found a truth to the old man's words that saw them listen attentively. He had held up the Quran and spoke of how to achieve this heavenly honour, how to prove their worth to Allah and to the next world. His tone had intensified when talking about the non-believers who tried to silence the word of God, infidels that needed to be punished and did not deserve their current life let alone a glorious higher afterlife.

Ahmed and Omar had left that night feeling overwhelmed, trying to piece together what they had witnessed.

Upon leaving, they'd been quietly reminded by the man from the barbers, not to discuss the evening's events with outsiders as they too might want to suppress their cause.

Both Omar and Ahmed felt they had instinctively made a connection with people like themselves, and they in turn had reciprocated such attention. Life for them up until that night had been meagre, now they felt they were no longer alone, and if there was a chance of a better existence in the next life, well then fuck it, they were in.

Inspired by the Disciples of the Afterlife teachings, they had officially gone on to join the organisation.

Initiated as *disciples* they'd slowly built trust with the older members and since been tasked to follow several people, both local and Western.

Over the past six months they had met regularly with their new friends and brothers - never missing a single meeting. They were part of something and loved it, life was better.

They'd heard the disciples were growing in number, that word was spreading across the Middle East and beyond.

The message often preached by the Elder was, 'the Disciples of the Afterlife will soon make a statement to the world of infidels, a message that will make them stop and listen, while striking fear into their very existence.'

The message fuelled them both with excitement, and as they now observed the man walk towards the taxi queue, their anticipation only intensified.

The target climbed into the taxi and the car moved out into the flow of traffic. They already knew his destination and how long it would take to cover the short distance.

They joined the same traffic flow, keeping their distance, but with eyes on the vehicle at all times.

Omar removed his phone from his pocket and dialled.

"Marhaban," the voice answered, "Hello."

"On his way," Omar said simply.

"Allah Hafez," the voice replied, *May God protect you.*

"And you." Omar ended the call.

Traffic was light that time of day, and both vehicles soon left the airport complex and headed East along the E89 expressway. The road was wide and open. As they passed the University of Fujairah, Ahmed knew the quarry would not expect to be followed, but he slowed to allow a car to move in between them and the target vehicle. The taxi turned onto the E99 carriageway and headed North. As Ahmed followed, he looked right over the vast expanse of water, the Gulf of Oman.

It wasn't long before they passed the target's destination. Ahmed and Omar had driven this route several times for reconnaissance and knew the road layout would force the taxi past the hotel before backtracking. They continued in line of sight making the U-turn south down the E99. A few minutes later they were turning into the Palace Beach Resort Hotel. They parked under a shaded canopy to stake out the hotel entrance then watched as their target exited the taxi before being escorted into the building by a porter.

Neither of them knew how long they would have to wait, but they knew they could not miss the target if he left. They made themselves comfortable, Ahmed swallowing the bitter taste that formed as he looked at the lavish hotel…

'Palace of sins!' he thought.

Chapter Four

Mohammed spoke into his mobile phone, "Allah Hafez," before placing it back into his pocket. He felt a cold shiver move across him. He took a deep breath and grinned, it was his time to shine and do his duty as a disciple.

He never would have believed his path would lead to becoming a member of the Disciples of the Afterlife. He had only been officially part of the organisation for a month, but by regularly attending meetings he had made what he hoped, would be friends and brothers for life.

He thought back to when he was approached whilst working in the hotel lobby. An Arab dressed smartly in a white dish dashi wearing a red chequer keffiyeh, had signalled for his attention before ordering an iced tea. He'd asked if Mo could bring it to him pointing to a quiet corner of the lobby. Mo had thought nothing of it as his job was to keep the guests happy whether he liked them or not. The Arab man was polite, which made a change from the usual pompous clientele.

When Mo returned with the iced tea he was asked to sit. Mo had sheepishly looked around not wanting to get in trouble for being too familiar with the guests, then obliged. The Arab man started to talk with him asking Mo questions. He asked Mo if it felt degrading to serve these people who conduct sinful acts openly with no respect for their faith. Mo had at first been taken aback and admitted he had never really put much thought to it, how for the most part he simply drifted into work every day, then went home.

The Arab had continued, and the more Mo listened, the more he was drawn in. He remembered how the man seemed to understand him more than he did himself. The Arab had seemed pleased with many of Mo's answers and had invited him to a meeting later that evening, during which, he was told how his work in the hotel could have a truer meaning, a purpose, if he was willing to open his mind and listen, and not just be at the beck and call of these gluttonous hotel creatures.

Mo had attended the next meeting, and the next, and was soon feeling the passion of the speeches, the words spoken coursing through his veins. Not long after, Mo made what he deemed an easy decision - and became a disciple.

One evening at a weekly meeting, he was pulled aside by the Elder who led their organisation. Mo was asked if he would take on his first task, one of utmost importance to their cause that was to be kept confidential. He felt needed for the first time in his life, and responsible for making a difference. He'd found it hard to contain his enthusiasm - and now here he was, standing in the hotel foyer receiving the call, informing him how his integral part was set to begin.

All he had to do was watch the target and report back with updates. Mo relished the challenge, wanting nothing more than to prove himself to his fellow disciples and Allah.

Mo was in the lobby dealing with a customer when the target was led in by the porter. He quickly dealt with the client then assumed a position so he could watch the target from the other side of the room. After a short exchange with the reception staff, the target headed toward the elevator that whisked guests up to their rooms.

Mo watched the man enter the glass elevator and counted the levels as it rose smoothly, stopping at the third floor.

The target got out and he no longer had eyes on him.

Mo pulled out his phone and called the number he'd been given. It rang only once before it answered followed only by silence on the other end. "I can see the man; he has gone to his room, it's on the third floor." Mo stuttered nervously.

The receiver of the call hung up.

Mo returned the phone to his pocket, and upon realising he was sweating, told himself to calm down and not mess this simple task up.

He needed to find out what room the target was staying in.

Thirty minutes passed when the target presented himself again. He'd changed his clothes and his hair was wet, clearly from a recent shower. Mo moved across the room, watching as the man strolled to the bar area. He observed as the target ordered a drink - finishing the beer in one swift gulp.

He could hear the words of the Elder, 'The infidel must pay; he has already tried to infiltrate our ranks to silence us.'

Mo wasn't sure how much his part would earn a better place in the afterlife; all he knew was it added some welcome excitement to a mundane job.

As he noticed the target walking out of the bar, Mo approached him without thinking, his eagerness to prove himself all consuming. Mo stepped in front of him, "Salam Sir, can I help you at all?" The man seemed slightly put out at Mo appearing in front of him. "Can I help, Sir?" Mo repeated.

"Err, yes maybe," he responded in an English accent, "I'm looking for a traditional barber," the man pointed to his face in a circular motion, "Do you have one in the hotel or is there a local one nearby?"

Mo's chance to prove himself had arrived. He hoped he had not made a mistake by talking with the target, "Unfortunately, there isn't one in the hotel complex." Mo's mind was turning as to what to do, he'd not planned this out. Why didn't he follow orders and just watch and report? 'Yes,' he thought; 'I need to find time to report and accept any consequences.' With his decision made, Mo continued, "If you would like to take a seat, Sir, I can ask for a recommendation for you." He held out an outstretched arm towards one of the royal blue armchairs.

The man accepted and walked towards the seat.

Mo walked as calmly as he could to the staff areas behind the hotel. He found an empty meeting room and entered, closing the door behind him. Phone in hand, he redialled the number. Again, it answered on the first ring, followed by silence. Mo stammered, "I approached the man to ask if I....."

"You approached him!?" the voice interrupted angrily.

Mo started to panic, "I... I… thought I could find out what he was up to, I asked if I could help in any way," he added, "It's not unusual for someone in my role to make conversation with the guests."

"What did he say?!"

"That he is looking for a local barber, I said I would find a recommendation for him," still nervous Mo pressed on, "I didn't know if this would help, or what you wanted me to do?"

A long pause followed.

"Wait," the voice said and then there was silence.

The voice returned, "We will call back shortly, stay where you are." Mo was cut off.

He stood in the room wondering what he had done. Had he screwed up the one thing he'd been tasked to do - had his excitement got the better of him?

He sat staring at his phone.

Minutes later, his screen lit up and the phone vibrated. Mo answered, expecting to be chastised. The voice spoke, offering clear instructions on his next tasks. Mo listened carefully before acknowledging he understood the voice's demands. The call ended with words he did not expect to hear, "You have done well, Allah will be pleased."

Mo's new task was to find a way to keep the target in the lobby to give his fellow brothers time to organise the next steps, what these were he did not know, he was just determined to succeed in completing his part. He returned to the man still sitting on the chair engrossed in his phone.

"Sir, I have a highly recommend establishment which do traditional Arabic barbering, the full works," Mo announced, "ATYAF Gent's Salon, it's local and a short drive away. Would you like me to order you a taxi?"

The man seemed pleased and accepted his offer.

Mo walked away, 'I need to find a way to keep him occupied,' he thought, when suddenly an idea formed.

He headed to the barman to discover what the target had been drinking earlier. Moments later, Mo returned with a cold pint of Stella balanced on a tray.

As he approached, the man looked up and appeared somewhat surprised at seeing the drink on offer, but before he could speak Mo informed him it came with compliments of the hotel, due to a delay in securing the taxi. The man then happily accepted the gesture and returned to his phone.

From a distance, Mo monitored the target, ready to react if he needed to delay him any longer. He kept checking his watch. The minutes ticked by, and Mo started to feel nervous when he saw that nearly thirty minutes had passed. He looked at the man who was still distracted by his phone.

Mo almost jumped when his mobile phone vibrated.

He answered, the now familiar voice keeping the dialogue short, “The taxi is on its way.”

Mo looked to the man and then through the glass entrance, hoping the taxi would arrive soon. He had almost finished his task and now wanted nothing more than to hand the target over so he could finally relax.

When he saw a taxi coming towards the hotel entrance, Mo headed to the doors. He held a momentary glance with the driver, recognising the face, a fellow disciple.

Mo went to collect the guest. ‘Nearly finished,’ he kept rolling over in his mind. He escorted the target to the waiting car, nodding in acknowledgment to the driver as he opened the rear door allowing the target to climb in.

As the taxi drove away, Mo watched it disappear around the corner; his heart beating hard through his chest.

He turned and walked back into the hotel.

He checked his watch - three hours left of his shift.

He took a deep breath; noticing for the first time the wet patches that had formed beneath his armpits. Feeling exhausted from playing his double role, Mo wanted nothing more than to go home. He exhaled, and tried to ignore his growing concern on what would happen to the man.

Chapter Five

The Elder leading the Disciples in Fujairah sat in the basement below his food store business. He could not believe the fortuitous opportunity God had delivered, giving him the chance to prove his worth with what he had been offered. He beamed, knowing it was the time to act and not disappoint.

When he received the first call and listened to the disciple's report, he was raging, but it had eased as the conversation continued and opportunity presented itself. He knew his good friend Jafar Abdul Malik would be pleased, that this was to be the Disciples of the Afterlife's introduction to the world.

He was not aware of the whole story, just that a traitor had been discovered in the Tehran cell Jafar led, and this western infidel played a part in the treacherous violation of their organisation.

The Elder had known Jafar for many years; they fought together in the Iraq war under Saddam Hussein when the western coalition forces invaded in 2003.

Operation Iraqi Freedom the world's press labelled it.

Although neither of them was Iraqi, they shared a unified hatred of the West's arrogance in believing they had the power and the right, to dictate how other countries should be run. Western arrogance that fuelled many Middle Eastern men to take up arms against the invaders, especially when occupying their neighbouring homelands.

They had both been selected to work in a secret bunker complex twenty miles east of Baghdad. Jafar's background in Iran was as a biochemist, and his, an engineer. The regime had earlier recognised the importance of their skills and placed them together to work. They shared many things in common, both politically and religiously, and had soon become friends.

Their project was of high-level secrecy. They were to design and construct a biological weapon using various chemicals and toxins. They'd endured many setbacks trying to achieve this goal, a goal that would enable Iraqi forces to deliver vengeance on the enemy. They worked tirelessly, until eventually they were successful in delivering a poisonous weapon to be mass produced.

As time passed, they worked and waited in the bunker, until eventually, the realisation they were to be let down by the Saddam Regime became apparent - a regime that was to never authorise the use of such weapons.

Feeling angry and betrayed, they'd later witnessed as Iraq was overthrown by the collation forces, forcing them to exit the country acting as refugees.

They had remained friends ever since.

Observing their beliefs, outsiders might say they were too extreme, that they were not true believers - but when Jafar told him he was starting the Disciples of the Afterlife movement, he'd offered immediate support to help deliver the message. Now here he was, ready to make the first real strike for the cause. He had needed to act fast as he'd had little time to pull his resources together. He knew he must not fail, and more importantly, that he could not fail his friend. He'd called an emergency meeting in the basement of his shop, his devoted *cell* of followers having been on standby since last night's gathering. Only key people attended, but he'd also spread word to the disciples across Fujairah and the wider UAE - in which their numbers reached close to four hundred and fifty.

Most of the shops along his row were shut at this time on a Saturday. Over time he had convinced all the business owners on the same row, and most of their employees to convert and follow Jafar's organisation. It was a good pocket area for his cell headquarters, and they could go about their business without inference with eyes and ears everywhere.

The most important business in the row at this very moment was that to the side of his, ATYAF Gents Salon.

The owner Saad, a fellow Disciple, had been sitting outside the café next door, where he often drank tea after midday.

When called, he was prompt to arrive at the basement meeting. The plan was simple, the target was to be brought to Saad's salon, and there, he would have the blessing of conducting God's will. Saad accepted his calling.

The Elder had contacted Mo at the hotel with his new orders. So much could still go wrong. What if the target changed his mind? Would Saad have the courage to carry out the deed given to him by the Elder, by God himself?

Such thoughts had stopped him from contacting Jafar to update him with the exciting developments.

The Elder had sent his disciples to ensure the few open businesses in the row were shut, and the area be kept clear.

The thing he feared most were those with loose lips, people seeing and talking, the repercussions of which could bring unwanted attention to the area.

All that the small group gathered in the basement could do now… was take a moment for prayer.

The taxi was owned and driven by another disciple…

Saad opened ATYAF Gents Salon and waited.

Chapter Six

A bell rang, triggered by the frame of the glass door at ATYAF Gents Salon. Hunter walked inside leaving behind the mid-afternoon heat and the hum of the air conditioning unit mounted at the front of the building. He welcomed the coolness inside after his stuffy taxi ride. Inside, the space was longer than it was wide and styled in a basic fashion. The ceiling was slightly arched and decorated with simple white mosaic tiles, with two rows of strip lights covering the full length. The floor was a light grey marble effect, clean, smooth, easy to sweep the discarded hair away. To the left were three workstations each identified with a black leather and chrome traditional barber chair, each facing a large mirror mounted above mahogany-coloured units. The desktops displayed tools of the barber's trade, laid out like a surgeons table as if set to conduct an operation, while in the adjacent cupboards, arched openings allowed for leg room below. Dressed on both sides of the mirror the mahogany colour theme continued with shelves stretching up from the work surface to the ceiling, housing various arrangements of men's vanity products.

Men in the UAE were permitted to apply more effort into their appearance, unlike the women who remained hidden by the traditional Hijab leaving much to the male's imagination.

The opposite wall was dressed in more mahogany-effect panelling, with a few hooks for hanging the barber's cloaks and client's coats, next to which was a single chair for waiting customers, of which Hunter it seemed, was the only one.

A solitary local man faced Hunter as he walked in. He was shorter in height by comparison, and Hunter noted he was slightly rounded, the tightness of his throbe accentuating his belly. His white Taqiyah skull cap signified the man's Muslim faith, worn in acknowledgement to the belief that Muhammad always had his head covered, making it a recommended act for members of the religion to follow as a mark of respect.

Hunter noted the man's sandals left most of his feet on display, and mused on how irritating it must be having hair underfoot and stuck between your toes each and every day.

Hunter greeted the man but did not get much of a response, the barber choosing only to invite him to take a seat with an outstretched arm - directing him to take the middle chair.

Hunter smiled politely and walked across to take his seat.

Chapter Seven

Saad jumped when the bell rang and the target walked through the door. He had seen him arrive in the taxi, which had triggered a cold sweat across his body, and he felt his hands begin to shake. He told himself to breathe and control his nerves; this was his moment, his purpose.

He looked at the man standing in the doorway taking in the surroundings of his salon. He was taller than Saad, he looked strong and solid. This was the first time he had seen him, put a face to the name he had heard, he didn't know what to expect, but he felt nerves rising again at the sight of him.

He had been briefed along with the others that he had a military background; he could tell he would be a fighter.

Saad knew he needed to gain the advantage and once he was in the barber's chair he would be in control. He wanted it to be over already but knew he must wait for the right moment; he could not get this wrong and disappoint.

He offered the chair to the man, who moved across the room to take the seat. Saad swung the red and white chequered cape around the man's front in one fluid motion, pulling it up firmly around his neck and tying it at the back keeping it in place. Next, he neatly folded a paper towel and half tucked it between the cape and the neck, if anything Saad would remain professional, "What you like?" Saad asked in broken English.

The man made a circular motion to his face and smiled, a grin that Saad instantly hated.

Saad gestured to his own face, "Full treatment?"

The man nodded and put his thumb up in agreement.

'If only he knew what the full treatment included.' Saad

used the foot pump to raise the chair then walked to a sink to wet a towel which he placed in a steamer. He headed back to the man and reclined the chair allowing the back of his head to relax against the headrest. He applied oil to his hands, then standing behind, massaged the oils into the man's face and beard. He looked down to see the man smiling, eyes closed.

'I'm in control,' he voiced in his head, 'I'm in control.'

A few minutes later a buzzer on the steamer informed Saad the hot towel was at temperature. He wiped his hands to retrieve it before placing the towel across the front of the target's face, lifting his head, wrapping it securely around until it enclosed the man's face and head entirely.

The man let out a satisfied hum.

Saad looked at himself in the mirror, staring almost through his reflection, taken over by the moments that were to come.

He lowered his gaze to the infidel's exposed neck.

He was in complete control.

Saad's heart then skipped a beat as the bell rang out, and the door opened. Saad was expecting this man, but his arrival had still startled him all the same.

"Salam," the newcomer greeted as he turned to close the door and quietly lock it.

"As-salaam alaykum," Saad replied as calmly as he could.

The new addition to the salon stealthily reached up and lowered the roman blinds.

Saad's body and mind felt like it was about to melt from the emotion; his hand reaching into his pocket, feeling the grooved handle of the cutthroat razor.

Chapter Eight

The moment he felt pressure against his forehead and the cold blade on his neck, Hunter knew death had come for him. He cursed his lapse in focus. A moment ago, as the hot towel opened his pores, he had drifted into a world of relaxation. He hadn't even thought about his sense of sight being removed. The beers he had drank earlier were the first he'd had in some time, and he'd welcomed the haze as it washed away thoughts of Salamander, Zoe, and the baby.

Even when he heard the bell of the shop door and the exchange between the barber and who he believed to be another customer, Hunter had remained in a tranquil state.

All that worry and fear came rushing back a thousand-fold as his world switched to slow motion, every millisecond suddenly feeling like a minute. He felt the downward pressure applied as the blade severed his carotid artery, the warm sensation coating the exposed flesh as his blood pulsated out, the metallic smell hitting his nostrils through the towel.

As the blade opened his trachea, a gush of air escaped like a tyre deflating, his ability to scream disabled. The blade's journey ended with the separation of his jugular, the blood flowing easily through this unwelcome exit.

Hunter pulled the towel from his face, legs flailing, unable to stand. As he scrambled, he saw himself in the mirror.

The barber stepped away staring at him, his jaw dropping with a look of horror, intrigue, and cold satisfaction, his hands and the weapon dripping with blood.

Hunter was horrified by his reflection as he gripped at his own throat in an attempt to save his life.

His mouth was gasping, his natural instinct to find that elusive breath never to come. Eyes wide and bulging this would be the last image he saw. In his dying seconds , his thoughts returned to Zoe, the woman he loved but would never marry, their unborn child that he would never be a father to. He felt tears filling his eyes, and his vision started to blur and then fade. The final voice he heard was his own, “Why did you not just go home - you selfish bastard?”

Then there was darkness.

Chapter Nine

As he participated in yet another pre-deployment test, Colour Sergeant Frank Tanner considered if he was getting too old for such punishment. This was one of many that had to be passed to be allowed deployment on operations. Tanner was around 5ft 9" but what he lacked in height he made up for in width. He was broad, strong, and considered himself a tank. His head was shaved, not so much a fashion choice as his hair had given up on him several years ago. He sported a beard with several months of growth, standard practice before deploying to the Middle East as it helped operatives blend into the local environment when operating covertly, just enough that a passing glance would not warrant further investigation.

As one of the more senior people in the unit, or *old man* as the new generation coming through would say, he still felt he had a lot to offer - that he could keep up with the best of them. It was a matter of pride and respect.

He would never openly admit how he had to dig deep and put the extra *phys* sessions in to maintain his fitness levels, and with the added mixture of past niggling injuries, and years of battle tours, his *seniority* had started to take a toll.

He caught sight of the poster on the gym wall stating the mantra he had lived by for so many years…

'PAIN IS WEAKNESS LEAVING THE BODY!'

'Too bloody true,' he thought.

Tanner was part of an elite military intelligence unit that carried out covert operations both in foreign lands and on UK home soil. Globally running agents, or CHIS's, embedded in strategic positions such as terrorist cells, drugs and weapon smuggling networks and even politics - all with the aim of gathering high level intelligence. Sometimes it was operating an average person on the ground, as they too could assist the likes of Tanner find the bad guys that lurked in the shadows.

He had been in the Army several years before a Commanding Officer had recognised the raw skills he possessed and briefed him about this specialist unit. It had intrigued him, and felt like the next challenge in his career.

Soon after applying he attended pre-selection, which consisted of various tests not just about physical brawn but mental ability too. He was happy they had seen the required standards in him that saw him advance to the long, gruelling selection course to become an Advanced Operator known as a *Handler* on the intelligence circuit. Of the five hundred or so military personnel that put themselves forward to attend pre-selection each year, less than ten percent made it through to be *badged* as an advanced HUMINT Handler.

The Selection was several months of physical and mental testing with little sleep between learning and enhancing new crafts in weapons, tactics, unarmed combat, driving, and his main craft of handling CHIS's. This in itself was not something you could necessarily learn, you had to already have the natural ability to manipulate and mould people to your pleasing. To be able to befriend and remain emotionless in doing so was all part of your toolkit. To do what needed to be done no matter what.

Tanner had successfully joined the unit eight years ago, and was still doing, in his eyes, the best job in the world.

Now here he was with five team members conducting another pre-deployment programme, honing their skills and getting their fitness to peak readiness for the challenges ahead.

It was all about getting in the right mindset for the tour. As Tanner placed the dumbbells down, he felt a hand on his shoulder that told him it was now his turn.

One by one, as the instructor decides you are *fucked* enough, you'd be pulled out of the circuit you've spent the last hours enduring, involving weights, running, and anything else the evil trainer could think of to drain the body, and be forced into another challenge. Tanner was feeling it as he was led out of the gym to the squash courts, gulping down fluids before this next round of pain would begin. He knew what was coming, he'd ridden this rodeo many times.

As he approached the court the trainer pushed a gum shield into his mouth, which saw him struggle to breathe even more. He sucked in some breaths to get the oxygen into his blood, as the staff helped him slip on a pair of boxing gloves, the weight of which felt like they'd stretched his arms to the floor, walking like Darwin's pictorial theory of evolution.

The last thing Tanner heard as the instructor pushed him backward into the squash court was, "React to what you see!"

The problem being, you don't see it coming, even when you are expecting it. In the next moment, two of his oppo's from the unit, came bearing down on him fresh as daisies, fully padded up with one mission, to proceed in kicking the shit out of him. Tanner didn't have time to turn around as two padded bodies checked him at speed, sending him flying into the far wall of the court. Stumbling, he turned to face them.

They both came at him at once. The larger of the two, Ozzie, was six foot plus and had the weight to match, he leaned on Tanner pinning him to the wall. Jacko, the smaller of the pair delivered punches to his body, every strike feeling like a bat to the abdomen on an already exhausted frame.

Tanner managed to twist away from Ozzie's weight and move himself to the centre of the court creating space between them. Now it was time for the training to kick in.

Unlike the para's, the test isn't just about windmilling until you're the last one standing, you must find the next level. When all the odds are against you and you've nothing left to give, you need to still pull something out of yourself, to fight and survive, and show you have control over what you deliver, demonstrating unarmed combat training.

The attack continued, with Ozzie coming straight towards him. Tanner started to administer kicks to his lower leg area, if you can't walk you can't fight.

Jacko circled to come from behind, it was time to move again. With a step-through-kick to Ozzie's chest pushing him backward, Tanner moved into the vacant area and turned to face Jacko who connected him square in the face with a right hook, the glove squashing his nose instead of breaking it.

Tanner felt the warm blood run onto his lips followed by the taste of iron. As Jacko withdrew his punch Tanner managed to clasp both hands round the back of his neck, pulling Jacko into a barrage of knee strikes. Tanner felt like he was doing the Can-Can, before rolling Jacko's head around to the side, then throwing him onto the deck.

Tanner's gloves were getting heavier and heavier, every breath burning his lungs like a hot poker. A stitch in his side had now joined the party, and his legs were bringing the jelly.

Stepping into space, he turned to face the giant that was already on him, a quick movement, and he pushed him away giving him precious seconds to assess the situation.

Now they had both turned and come towards him at the same time. He could see them smiling, 'This is friendship,' he thought, well it was in the military. They would all be laughing about it together later. In Tanner's head he could hear his voice repeating, 'Don't get steered into a corner or you're fucked, and don't hit the floor or your double fucked!'

They hit him at pace, and he stumbled back. In a split second he regained his balance and continued the leg strikes whilst fending off blows from Jacko. Ozzie stepped back, his left leg not wanting to play anymore as he started to limp.

Pushing back on Jacko, Tanner created some air between them to throw some of his own punches, moving the fight back into the centre of the makeshift ring.

Tanner had served with Jacko in Afghanistan and Ozzie in Iraq, both decent guys you could have a laugh with. The unit was close-knit, brothers for life, everyone knowing and socialising with each other both in and outside of work.

As they were about to rush him again, the whistle blew to stop the session, but this didn't stop Jacko following through with a punch, laughing then sarcastically apologising.

You aim to survive the two minutes, and never to give up, but every minute felt like ten.

They all walked out together laughing and mocking each other as they went. Tanner's knuckles felt like they were dragging along the floor, his energy completely sapped.

Chapter Ten

Tanner walked out of the squash court feeling bruised and battered, his lungs burning. He was dripping with sweat as if he'd just stepped out of the shower, the red welts decorating his face courtesy of his unsympathetic oppos. He had been in their shoes several times, laughing and mocking his mates whilst using them as a human piñata.

The physical training instructor gave him a 'well done' smile as he pulled his gloves off and handed him some water. ‘Still got it,’ Tanner thought... ‘Just!’

Regaining his composure, Tanner saw the unit's Commanding Officer standing across the room looking at him. He was standing staunch upright, arms folded, wearing a rigid look on his face. Whatever was on his mind, it was not good news. Lieutenant Colonel Warren Gibbs walked to where Tanner was recovering, his faithful Border Terrier in tow.

“I take it you gave them a good seeing to in there?” he said, nodding towards the squash court.

“I eased off to give them a chance.” Tanner smiled. He respected Gibbs, the officers had to pass the same selection as everyone else and were expected to keep up that training undergoing the same rigid regimen. This way, all involved in the cause knew the man beside them would and could more than hold their own if the shit hit the fan whilst deployed.

The Boss was a quiet man, a composed thinker with a dry sense of humour. He had joined the army as an officer in the Royal Engineers before passing selection, and after a couple of tours, had been promoted to command the unit. On the social side, he was a family man, with a nice house out in the sticks.

Tanner had been invited around a few times for dinner - Gibbs loved to cook and he and Tanner would share a bottle of wine or three, and share pipedreams on how they'd make their millions from crazy ideas and inventions - though to this day, neither had followed through on any of them.

They were friends, brothers in arms.

"Grab a quick shower and come to my office," he said in a serious tone, which meant bloody hurry up.

After a quick shower, Tanner could still feel his clothes sticking to him, his clammy body yet to cool down. He knocked on the Commanding Officer's office door, *the Boss*.

"Come," the familiar voice instructed from behind the solid oak door, varnished and polished to a perfect sheen.

As he entered the office it felt like stepping back in time.

Tanner could never escape the feeling of nostalgia brought on by the smell of wood, leather, and the faint cigar odour. If he closed his eyes it took him back to his youth standing in his Grandfather Morris's study, the gentle giant of a man sitting in the corner, always with a smile and a lap to sit on. He'd died when Tanner was young, too soon, but some things you never forget, and would never want to.

The room was furnished with a sense of achievement.

On one side of the oak-panelled wall was an oil portrait of a historic army officer, his red tunic adorned with medals and a blue sash, striking a victorious pose hand on sword. A second painting was from a battle in the early eighteenth century depicting a cluster of uniformed men and horses in mayhem.

Between the paintings was a large print of the recently anointed, King Charles III, in all his military glory.

The furnishings crammed into the room consisted of a

green leather chesterfield sofa and an oak shelving unit displaying the Boss's awards, trophies, and photos of his military career. A large oak desk dominated the room, the Boss sitting behind it, with two chesterfield chairs facing him.

Also present, sitting in one of the chairs near the far window, was a man he had not seen before.

He displayed a presence of importance, but Tanner would make his own mind up on that. He had always been wary of a man in a suit that looked likely to cost more than what Tanner earned in a month. He oozed one of the MI's… the question was which, five or six? Either way, Tanner understood he too would be the bearer of bad news, as his sort usually were.

"Ah, Tanner, take a seat," Gibbs said, indicating the vacant chair. The unit operated on name terms to break the habit of using ranks when on the ground operating covertly.

In the Boss's office however, with an unknown guest, Tanner would show his boss respect.

"Sir," he responded acknowledging the invitation.

Tanner sat and looked around, the only sign of welcome was the Boss's dog 'Noodle' lying on the sofa, head up, tail wagging. It always made him smile, a man of Gibb's position with a little Border Terrier named Noodle.

"I'd like you to meet Mr Edward Boden," the Boss began.

Tanner nodded a greeting toward Edward.

"Mr Boden is one of our brothers from MI6."

'Hah!' Tanner acknowledged in his head. You could bloody copyright their image and sell it as a brand.

"What I am about to tell you cannot leave this office and is currently of the highest security level until further notice," Gibbs paused, "Unfortunately, a situation has occurred in Al

Fujairah, involving one of our handlers. Linked intelligence, picked up by one of our submarines in the Persian Gulf, was passed to MI6 via Northwood. That is why Mr Boden is here."

Indeed, this wasn't good news. "As far as I'm aware, we don't have any handlers working in Fujairah, Sir?"

Gibbs leaned on his desk, his eyes focusing on Tanner, "You are correct, we aren't conducting operations in the UAE, but…" he paused as if to find the words, "Sergeant Hunter, who you know, was on R&R in Al Fujairah."

Tanner felt the perspiration grow cold across his body.

"Before he left Tehran," Gibbs continued, "His last meeting with a CHIS, codename Salamander, had not gone well. Salamander didn't conduct himself in his normal manner according to the report. It was noted; *he seemed nervous and not responsive*, which from the file history is unusual as the relationship seemed to be on a friendly basis. Hunter reported that Salamander *lost his composure* during this particular meeting, and *emotionally snapped*, not adding much clarity as to why. Hunter was surprised by his behaviour and the meeting ended on a bad note. Salamander has since gone comms silent and not responded to any of our attempts to contact him."

Tanner was confused as he tried to work out what relevance any of this was to him, while trying to push down the sense of foreboding growing in him, "So, what does this have to do with Hunter being in Fujairah, and more so, me?"

The Boss glanced to Mr MI6 who caught his gaze before looking down at his lap. The Boss sat back in his chair. He looked at Tanner, his tone softening, "I'm sorry to say, Hunter's body was found yesterday in Fujairah. He's been murdered."

Tanner felt like a sledgehammer had struck him in the chest, “What?! How?!” Tanner struggled; he couldn't fathom what he’d just heard. “I don't understand?”

Edward Boden remained quiet and still, almost frozen in time as the Boss returned to a more official tone, “Tanner, I appreciate you were good friends. So far no one in the Unit, or his family, have been notified, and until the proper procedure has taken place, you are to keep this under wraps.”

“But how... what happened to him?” Tanner stumbled still in shock.

“We don't exactly know all the details, but from the local police report, it is clear he was murdered. He was found in a dusty car park, next to some refuse bins in Al Faseel, a local area not frequented by tourists. He’d had his throat cut.”

Tanner could hear the disgust in the Boss's voice as if the words left a bitter taste in his mouth.

The anger came flooding back before Tanner had time to check himself, “Who the fuck did this?!” he was on his feet and could feel his body heating up again.

The Boss stood, unimpressed with the outburst in front of their MI6 guest, “Colour Sergeant Tanner, you will compose yourself, there is more at stake than your personal feelings.”

Tanner sat down and took a breath. As a handler he knew he should always be in control of his emotions.

However, this was different. He and Hunter had grown up together; they were from the same estate. They’d had a great time growing up, until eventually, they’d both decided to join the army. They went through training together, and eventually, both applied for and came through selection successfully.

Hunter was a big lad, always carried a bit of timber no

matter how fit he was; 'Battle fat' he called it. Although they were like brothers, the nature of the job meant they drifted a little over time, due to work deploying them in different locations, and rotations. But nothing ever got under his skin, and if matters ever got close to doing so, one of Hunter's rules was to simply say something sarcastic and have a cigarette.

Hunter recently got engaged before he deployed. His fiancée Zoe had become quite close to Tanner's ex-wife, and it was not long before she was expecting their first child. Hunter had confided in him that his head was all over the place about the baby. His heart sank, as in that moment Tanner's thoughts entirely focussed on his own children.

He was snapped back into reality as the Boss returned to official business, "There is more to this picture, which is where things have become complicated. Mr Boden," Gibbs invited the MI6 guest to break from his silence.

"Please, call me Ed,"' he announced shifting in his chair. His voice and posture were that of private education, Tanner guessed old Etonian or Harrovian.

The different Military Intelligence agencies used the term 'Free flow of Information' as transparency between them was supposed to reduce the guesswork, promoting the ability to react to information quickly. Unfortunately, some intelligence agencies were as 'free flowing' as they chose it to be, to the point wherein the dam of information was often shut off.

"I'll try and keep this as succinct as possible," Ed began, "As Lieutenant Colonel Gibbs touched on earlier, a British submarine, HMS Aegaeon, is currently conducting an intelligence gathering covert patrol in the Persian Gulf primarily focussing on Iran. Early morning three days ago, she picked up some Telecon chatter between two encrypted mobile phones," Ed leaned forward, hands clasped together, "The fundamentals of the conversation indicated a western target arriving in Al Fujairah and then continued to relay that there was no change to the date and location of the target." Ed saw Tanner was about to speak so held a hand up to prevent him from doing so, "Not a lot to go on I know. It took a further twenty-four hours for Aegaeon to move out of the area, to safely transmit the information back to Northwood. At the same time, GCHQ was also picking up increased chatter, between several phone numbers associated with a relatively new, at the time low-level, self-proclaimed, extreme ITS group calling themselves the Disciples of the Afterlife."

The ITS, Islamic Terror Syndicate, was the generic title for all operating extreme groups like Al Qaeda, Hamas, Islamic Jihad, and Mujahidin, the list was endless with new factions continuously popping up around the globe.

"The Disciples of the Afterlife, or DOTA, as we are calling them, have been on our radar over the past six months with not much to report on. Only in the last month or so we've seen increased activity. From a combination of GCHQ reports, one of our operators on the ground, and working with other NATO intelligence agencies, we can start building a picture."

Tanner thought about how much the intelligence community is obsessed with generating acronyms for everything… now they have a new one, DOTA.

"Have any of our agents reported on this group?" Tanner interjected looking at the Boss.

"Not as of yet, but as Mr Boden tells me, they are growing in popularity at an alarming rate."

'So much for that intelligence sharing,' Tanner thought.

"Yes, they are actively recruiting," Ed continued, "And expanding fast, but what has been unusual, is how they have kept it low key for so long."

Tanner sighed, somewhat confused, "I'm still not sure how this has led to Hunter's murder?"

Ed signalled for him to hold the questions, "Well, it's here that it starts to get interesting."

Tanner felt the return of his anger rising, 'Interesting?' All he wanted to know is what bastard he needed to kill for Hunter, an eye for an eye!

"The activity GCHQ is monitoring from mobile phone spikes has shown the group is geographically widely spread across the Middle Eastern countries, and now, recently started to show contacts as far up as the southern areas of Russia."

"Russia? When did Russia start involving themselves with extreme Middle Eastern views?" Tanner tried to process the maze of information, the loss of his friend making it difficult to focus through his emotions.

"We have one of our people on the ground there," Ed continued, "As I'm sure you are aware, Intelligence suggests Russian soldiers fighting in the war against Ukraine, have been pushed back by Ukrainian forces to the border east of Mariupol, where they have taken up camp on the Russian side of the border. They have remained there for several weeks now. Reports from one of our operators on the ground are that they feel abandoned by their government, are receiving no supplies or support, and are still unpaid. They've turned the blame for their predicament towards the people of Ukraine, holding them accountable for their failure and dishonour inflicted by the defeat in Mariupol. Break-off groups of soldiers, with nowhere to turn, have been radicalised to become Disciples of DOTA, by a Russian officer, a Major Aaron Olegovich Sokolova." Once again, Ed signalled for patience from Tanner, "We are running background checks on him, it can be difficult, Russians use a *Patronymic* system, using their father's first names within their own names, so you can end up chasing your tail. Also, we are trying to establish what the relationship is between Sokolova and DOTA."

Ed paused, seeing the room fall into a moment of contemplation. The silence was soon broken however, as the Boss took over the brief, "We believe Salamander may be involved. He'd previously reported of a new group, which he did not name, but said, quote, 'they scared him,' and rumours were, they want to demonstrate 'an extreme act which will change the world' unquote."

"Nothing we haven't heard before," stated Tanner.

"Agreed, but Salamander had been tasked by Hunter to learn more about this group and befriend members to see if he could get on the inside. We shouldn't discount, that this group could be DOTA. Unfortunately, Salamander was unresponsive to this tasking, and even with guidance on how to achieve the task, he did not want to get involved. He even turned down a significant financial bonus, which I'm sure we can agree, is not the normal profile for a CHIS. Hunter's persistence led to some heated arguments in the following meetings. Hunter had also increased the meeting frequency, to every three days, to try and keep him onside, and drive the potential DOTA tasking and training. Then Salamander went AWOL, didn't turn up for his next meeting, and didn't act on any recall procedures. We sent in a reconnaissance team to monitor Salamander's address, and over a period of time neither he, his wife nor his daughter were sighted. Then out of the blue, Salamander responds to a recall and contacts Hunter. They met days before he was due to go on leave to Al Fujairah. Hunter arranged the emergency meeting with him, and as I said earlier, that got complicated, with Salamander ranting hatred towards Hunter. Salamander is now once again, missing."

Tanner took a moment, "So, what you are saying is, you believe that Salamander followed Hunter and killed him? But for what reason?" Tanner tried to remain calm. He still could not fathom using the term *killed* in reference to his friend. He also could not help but question why Hunter would even be out there, as it was clear Hunter's mental state might not have been as sharp as it should be.

"What we're saying is, we are unsure who murdered him but believe with the information being gathered, we cannot rule out the possibility Hunter was the Western target. Nor can we rule out Salamander or DOTA's involvement in this." The Boss replied.

"There seem to be several links between these elements," Ed followed up, "Weak links I'll admit, but we have since invested a large number of resources to find the answers."

Tanner felt numb, uncertain what to believe.

The Boss adjusted himself in his chair, "Tanner, as you can see this puts us in a serious situation. There is a need to find information, to fill the missing gaps. Firstly, who is accountable for Hunter's murder, and what could be a potential threat to our national security, find out what the fuck is going on with the Russians, and the Disciples of the Afterlife."

Everything Tanner had just heard didn't sit right, he knew something was missing, in fact, everything seemed to be missing. In the back of his mind he pondered, could Hunter's murder have been a drunken dispute gone wrong? He did like a beer after all. But the sinister way he had been killed felt more like a message. But from who, Salamander, DOTA?

Tanner was brought back from his contemplation as the Boss informed, “So, you are being rapidly deployed ahead of schedule to the Tehran unit. You will need to touch base with the other handlers, and start re-tasking their CHIS's, to focus on finding out about this new group and any links to Salamander, Hunter, and the Russians. You'll need to get your work and home admin sorted ASAP. You fly tomorrow evening from Brize Norton.”

Tanner wanted to respond but understood there was little point, the decision for him to go had been made, and made way above his pay grade.

Chapter Eleven

Tanner returned to his room in the NCO's accommodation block. He'd moved back on the base after he split from his wife two years ago. She'd eventually got fed up with the unpredictable nature of his job. One minute he would be home for a few months, next it would all flip on its head and he would be deploying rapidly, just as he was about to now.

Being in a relationship was hard, it was difficult for any partner to truly understand the kind of person you needed to become to do the job. Tanner could never talk about his day or what he got up to, with everything shrouded in secrecy, a factor that would take its toll on any partner after a while. Often, when returning from a tour, he just wanted to be by himself to get everything in his head squared away before switching to the alternate role as father and husband.

Eventually, it got too much. Apparently, Tanner had a wall around him and would never let her in.

Even after the divorce Tanner remained living on base.

He had everything he needed there.

His ex-wife got the house, so he couldn't afford to move out any time soon. He did miss his kids though.

He looked over at the picture of them on his desk. The older two boys were still trying to find their way in life, both working but unsure of their futures. Tanner had tried getting them to join the military, and they showed initial interest, but he thought they only did that to please him. The younger two were still at school, his daughter was bright but growing up too fast, and the youngest was fishing mad, if his school topics were on how to catch a carp, he would have aced every exam.

They still loved fooling around together and Tanner treasured how bright and beautiful they all were.

He knew he would have to call them that night and let them know about the change in plans.

Even though he would always miss them when away, he would still be buzzing before deployment. It was an irresistible excitement of doing a dangerous job; and Tanner needed that edge to live. He wished he could talk to them about it to help them understand, but they never would, and no job in Civvie Street would ever feed his needs.

Then a realization came charging at him head on, he knew speaking to his ex-wife later he wouldn't be able to divulge the truth to why he was leaving so suddenly. She would quickly put two and two together once the Unit had delivered the news to Zoe. Yet another reason for her to be annoyed with him, disjointing their already broken relationship.

Tanner settled into his cosy room. He'd managed to squeeze his life's belongings into the built-in cupboards. His bed was a small double, opposite a desk that his television sat on. The room had his military wear hung on hooks and hangers, his footwear lined up near the bathroom door. The view from the window overlooked the sports fields. It was good enough for him.

He showered and lay on his bed staring at the ceiling, his thoughts like a recipe in a blender - with a bit of Hunter, a large measure of today's information, a pinch of deployment, and the main ingredient, talking to his children. He reached for his phone to make the call. It was the hardest part of the job, telling those you love you wouldn't be around for a while.

Chapter Twelve

During the telephone call the day previous, Jafar Abdul Malik had beamed as he'd stated, "Allah Hafez," before ending the call, "May God protect you."

The news he'd received from his good friend the Elder in charge of the Fujairah cell was a glorious victory, that in his eyes, would further the message he intended to spread to the West. The founder of the Disciples of the Afterlife sat crossed legged on the floor of his two-storey house on the outskirts of Tehran. A smile stretched across his leather worn skin, increasing the wrinkles that occupied his aged face.

He laughed softly.

This was the start of the war for the disciples, another move made in his strategic game of terror against the western world. Eliminating this British Army infidel wasn't part of his original plan, but it was a good opportunity to send a message, not only to the West but to his disciples - never to betray the cause, and to never turn their back on Allah.

Jafar's thoughts played back to when he had first met the strange new man that had seen recent events unfold.

When he arrived at a meeting after one of Jafar's speeches; he'd showed interest in joining and attending future gatherings. Jafar was always wary of new faces, especially those that seemed overly keen, as this one had.

After Jafar had delivered his preaching, the man started asking questions, which wasn't out of the ordinary, but this new face asked too many questions and came across as nervous, as if he had an agenda. At first, Jafar thought he might be police or Iranian intelligence, but he already had disciples embedded in these organisations and they would have told him if someone was covertly investigating their group, and as far as Jafar was aware, they had still managed to keep their growing numbers under the radar.

As a precaution, Jafar had decided to task two trusted disciples to follow and watch this new face. He had a sixth sense when things didn't feel right, it was how he had survived this long, through all the tyranny in the Middle East and especially the Iraqi war. This stranger made the hairs stand on the back of his neck. He had watched the way he moved around the room, questioning the other disciples, too eager, too direct; he looked uncomfortable, out of place.

Chapter Thirteen

They had followed Faisal Hosseini home that evening to the less affluent area of Afsariyeh, in the Tehran Province on the edge of District 15. He lived in a one-bedroom apartment in a poorly maintained building with his wife and daughter. The area was known to Jafar, it was a high crime area, and the occupants didn't have much worth for living. It was highly populated, with families living on top of each other trying to survive - a perfect hunting ground for new disciples.

Over the next few days, Jafar's men watched the stranger from the shadows, easy to do in such an area. They blended in as they too were from similar backgrounds, outcasts, delinquents, and low-level criminals. They would report back to Jafar regularly, or if anything of interest occurred.

The first day, Faisal left his home shortly after the Muezzin had finished calling Adhan, Call to Prayer, that sang out across the city from the speakers mounted high on the tall minarets of the mosques. It was a hypnotic, soothing sound of beautiful low tones that echoed throughout the quiet streets, the sun sending a warm glow across the city as it rose.

The disciples following Faisal watched as he left his building, and walked around into the side alley of the dilapidated block he called home. Opening a locked storage space, he pulled out a two-wheeled street vendor cart. He pushed his cart across several blocks, to what would later be, the busy corner of Ashuri and Panzdah Metri-ye-Dovvom.

Here he started to set up his small business.

Faisal was a street food vendor, selling Laboo and Bâghâli.

His stalkers watched as he stacked the beets ready to be

peeled and boiled so the Laboo could be served steaming hot. Next, he set about organising the fava beans, Golpar and angelica seeds for the Bâghâli.

The beloved street food would often see customers huddled together to share a bowl and a chat, and the watching disciples noted how over the course of the day Faisal's business was a great meeting hub for locals. Later that evening he returned home, where he remained until the morning.

When Jafar was briefed on the day's non-events he mused over his suspicions, and wondered if he was perhaps getting more paranoid as he got older. He decided to have his watchers continue their surveillance for one more day, after which, he'd decide on whether to stand them down.

The next day, the watchers settled in across the street in preparation for another dull day in the life of a street vendor.

As the spectators drank their tea, the day seemed to be following an identical pattern to the one previous, when just after midday, Faisal did something different.

The stalkers readied themselves.

An older teenage boy had approached the stand and greeted Faisal. They clearly knew each other and shared a brief conversation before the vendor looked at his watch and started to walk away from the corner – the boy now taking over the vendor cart. The watchers followed Faisal as he walked a zig-zagged route through the streets of Afsariyeh, away from his home and business. After a quick update to Jafar, they maintained visual contact through the busy streets.

The disciples tracked Faisal as he walked. Occasionally he would stop and scan the world around him, before moving on again. Eventually, he turned into a long, not-so-busy street.

The trackers slowed their pace to increase the distance between them. They hadn't paid much attention to the cars passing them, but when a vehicle pulled over ahead of Faisal, they noted how he picked up his pace.

He looked around nervously as he approached the car, then climbed into the passenger side, the driver moving out into the road, driving away from them.

The car was an Iranian made white Saipa Saina, nothing out of the ordinary as nearly every other car was of a similar make and colour being one of the most popular cars in Iran.

The stalkers desperately searched the streets to flag down a taxi. They spotted two green taxicabs, but they were of no use as by law green cabs were for women only – but then a mustard yellow Peugeot taxi appeared from behind a lorry. The driver responded to their hails, and as they jumped in the watchers commanded the driver to move quickly and follow their instruction. The driver was midway through complaining at their attitude when he was silenced with a knife held to his side. This saw the driver obey their commands and soon, they were within a few cars of the white Saipa.

Navigating their way through the streets, they headed towards the outskirts of Afsariyeh, before approaching a large junction which took them north on the Basij Expressway.

The speed increased and the stalkers could see the two dark silhouettes through the tinted rear window, turning towards each other, engaged in conversation.

They kept a car between them to avoid being spotted, Jafar would not be happy if they lost the stranger.

It wasn't long before they turned down the exit slip road, navigating through a congested area before returning onto a faster, open Expressway. The taxi driver was given threatening encouragement, to not lose the vehicle.

On the Emam Ali Expressway, the speed increased.

With less traffic on this road, they had the taxi drop back.

Still observing the small dark silhouettes in the car ahead, the stalkers' suspicions grew when Faisal's shadow went from just a head to a whole form that filled the entirety of the rear window, before disappearing inside the vehicle.

Now, only the driver's head could be seen.

The watchers looked at each other in bewilderment, perhaps there was more to this Faisal than beets and beans.

The taxi blended well into the traffic and ten minutes later, they were coming off the expressway and tackling the busy streets of the city centre.

Progress through the streets was slow, and still only the driver was visible in the vehicle ahead of them.

Crossing a roundabout, they continued west onto Mojahedin Eslam, passing one of the city's hospitals.

They briefly discussed calling Jafar, but decided against it, he would have too many questions, which for the moment, they were unable to answer.

The car ahead drove clinically, never speeding, always using the correct indications and rules of the road.

Coming out of the busy city centre, they were on a stretch of road with one side-offering only a high brick wall topped with metal spikes. The formidable boundary continued the entire length of the street. The car ahead turned left onto Nofel Loshato, and as they followed, the tall boundary wrapped around the corner and continued down the road.

Fewer vehicles remained on this stretch and as the Saipa's

red brake lights illuminated – the pursuers had their captive taxi driver slow down.

On the left, there was a break in the wall with a dark blue fortress style gate allowing the car to pass through.

Cruising past, the gate closed and behind it the white Sapia Saina disappeared from view – directly into the Embassy grounds for Great Britain.

Chapter Fourteen

They came later that night as he slept. Faisal was woken by a noise outside his apartment in the hallway. He rolled over, his wife still sound asleep next to him, his daughter, now six years old, snuggled into her. She often crept in at night to be with her mother, it was warmer after the sun went down.

The view from the open window showed it was dark outside, the still silence suggesting it was the early hours of morning. He closed his eyes to resume his sleep when the noise returned – a metallic tapping accompanied by a scraping noise. He sat up more alert this time and slipped slowly out of bed so as not to wake his wife and daughter.

His wife stirred briefly, as if sensing his body heat missing from her side, but she did not wake.

His home was small with only three rooms, the one bedroom which they all shared, a bathroom, and another larger room which was the family area and kitchen.

He moved towards the bedroom door and slowly turned the handle - it squeaked seeing him pause looking back at the two bundles still asleep in the bed.

He took a breath and cautiously opened the door.

It had barely been opened an inch, when Faisal was impacted with such ferocity, it knocked him clean from his feet and sent him reeling to the floor. He clambered towards the bed; his wife and daughter, startled from their slumber by the commotion, were now kneeling on the mattress clutching one another other, screaming.

It was still dark in the room; he could make out the shadowy shapes, several men advancing in at speed.

They were on him before he had time to reach his loved ones. He felt the tight grip of numerous hands pinning him down before a bag was pulled over his head delivering him into blackness. The last thing he heard were the cries of his family before he felt a brutal blow to the head, after which his world became silent.

*

Faisal woke in a groggy state, with a thumping headache and intense throbbing at the back of his skull. He didn't know how long he had been unconscious. The bag still covering his head had stuck to his matted hair where the blood had dried. His hands were bound tightly behind him, and he struggled to breathe through the tape that had sealed his mouth shut.

He was laid face down on a hard surface; he could hear the noise of a worn diesel engine and feel the bumps in the road vibrating into his body suggesting he was in the back of a truck. The events and screams of his wife and daughter came flooding back. He started to lash out, kicking his legs as he tried to roll over, but his efforts were met with a hard boot kicking him in his stomach, the air in his body forced out and struggling to return.

"Khayin!" a voice shouted somewhere near him – *Traitor*.

Then another blow to the same part of his head. Thc pain was immense and he lay there wheezing through the tape.

The warm trickle resumed at the back of his head. Overcome with dizziness and shock, Faisal-passed out again.

Chapter Fifteen

The next time Faisal woke, he heard nothing but silence in the room. His head was still covered, thumping as if it had been crushed in a vice. He was now seated, secured to a chair by his wrists and ankles, his head lulling low to the full extent his neck would allow. He tried to move, but the constriction of the binds prevented him. He moved his head around, loosening his stiff neck in the hope he might see something through the material of the hood, but there was nothing.

He heard faint footsteps, gradually growing louder, and then they stopped. There was a clunking noise like a large key in a lock, followed by the creak of a door opening. The footsteps continued into the room, not rhythmic, but out of sync, there was more than one who'd just entered the space. Faisal started breathing heavily, the tape still stifling his efforts. His face was coated in sweat from fear more than heat. The footfalls had stopped, and the silence returned.

He tried to call out through his taped lips but just a murmur escaped. No one responded.

It felt like an eternity until something happened.

The hood over his head was whipped off in one clean movement, pulling at the hair stuck to it by clotted blood. He winced, not just from the sudden pain, but the intense light that filled his pupils; he squinted trying to adjust to the brightness, making his eyeballs ache. When the blurriness subsided and his focus regained, he recognised the man standing in front of him. Faisal was scared, and angry, trying to shout, but couldn't move his lips seeing only incomprehensible noise escape. Twisting in his chair, he stared at the figure in front of him.

His only thought was of was his family. Had they been hurt? He needed answers.

Jafar held up his hand, 'SShhh,' he mocked. He smiled, a gentle laugh leaving his throat, "I have some questions for you, and I expect you to answer them and co-operate."

Faisal could feel the presence of someone standing behind him in the darkness, but he could not turn enough to see. He couldn't see the door, but the room had mud-rendered walls and a dusty floor. There were no windows visible, and the air felt cool and damp. Above him were joists equally spaced out and cladded above with rows of wooded boards – it felt like a basement, but who's basement, and where?

Jafar walked to the side and picked up a wicker chair.

It was then that Faisal noticed a small table, the contents laid on top, glistening in the light. Panic set in as Faisal recognised the tools that lay there, various knives, pliers, a hammer, and surgical instruments. They were unclean, from a previous victim's unwilling participation.

Tears instantly ran down his face and he began to sob.

Jafar placed the chair and sat in front of him still smiling, "Calm down," his voice was low, "As I said, I will be asking you some questions, but not just yet." He paused, "I'm sure you know why you are here, there is no rush to hear your side of the story. First, you must pay the consequences of betrayal. After that, we will talk again."

Faisal wanted the tape to be ripped from his mouth so he could talk, but it never came.

"I know you will be wondering about your wife, and your very young beautiful daughter, they are safe, for now."

Jafar stood up to leave but stopped to lay a hand on Faisal's shoulder. He squeezed gently, then leaned in and whispered, "See you in a few days, Salamander."

He then strode off closing the door behind him.

As Faisal's eyes widened in final realisation, the shadowy figure he sensed behind him introduced itself over the dusty floor, as from his rear, a noose was placed around his neck.

The rope tightened, pulling him upwards, lifting him and the chair clear off the floor. He swung and was slowly strangled on the rope, suspended from a beam as he tried desperately to breathe, his eyes bulging, his face reddening then slowly fading to blue, his body fitting.

He spun around suspended in the air, his torture master now stood in front of him, holding the other end of the rope wearing a cold, expressionless gaze. The torturer stared at him before finally letting go of the rope, seeing him crash to the floor, gasping for air through his nostrils.

It had begun.

*

The next few days were a blurred melting pot of pain, relief, rest, and then more pain. Salamander's mind was an emotional roller coaster of anger, sadness, and blame.

Blaming himself for working with Hunter and putting his family in danger, then switching the blame to Hunter for putting him in this predicament, pressuring him to find out more information about this group, an act that had now led to him being tortured. He felt sick with worry for his wife and daughter. This was Hunter's fault, and the hatred grew and festered inside. Salamander wanted to speak, he begged to talk, but the torturer wasn't interested in hearing him, the tape across his mouth having remained throughout. Salamander was to suffer for being a traitor until they were ready.

Minutes rolled into hours, hours into days.

He tried to keep track of how long he had been there, but the lack of sleep and painful games played upon him, made it impossible to know. The windowless room ensured it was never apparent if it was night or day. Sometimes he didn't know if he was dreaming the nightmare or living it, his body weak through the shock and continuous perspiration. He was given enough food and water to keep him alive and conscious, just enough to feel each one of the painful inflictions.

Chapter Sixteen

This time, Salamander was woken in a different way - not by a boot or a fist - The gaffa tape was ripped from his mouth and it felt as if his lips had been removed along with it.

At first, it felt as if his brain had forgotten how to work the motion of his jaw, which just hung down. He felt a hand raise his bowed head and the cold water against his lips, filling his mouth. Salamander started to gulp down as much as he could, not sure when his next drink would be.

His eyes opened and the cup was removed.

Jafar was sat in the same chair, in the same place as he was before this hell had started, still smiling. "Welcome back," he said as if Salamander was the one that had left.

"Where is my family?" Salamander spoke weakly, as if his jaw was learning to work again.

"In case you were wondering," Jafar continued, "You have been here for five days now."

"Where is my family?"

"So, I think you are ready to talk, more importantly, I am ready to listen."

"Where is my fucking family!?" Salamander screamed, spit flying from his mouth.

Jafar leaned back and started to laugh.

Tears of desperation followed, "I just want to see them."

Jafar indicated with a motion of his hand seeing the torturer approach holding a set of snips. Salamander panicked and started to scream, "No! No! No!" his voice faded away…

He was a broken man.

The man approached, but to Salamander's relief, the only

thing the snips were used for on this occasion was to cut away the zip ties from his wrists and ankles, freeing him from the chair. He started to calm down, rubbing his joints that had been bound. He felt he hadn't the strength to stand so remained where he was, 'Is this a trick?' he thought. He stared at Jafar, "My family, please?" his voice was slowly returning.

"Your family is still safe. They are staying with a friend of mine, and they will remain there until I have finished with you. Their fate now lies in your hands," Jafar paused to reflect, "I believe Allah has sent you to me as a gift, a gift to help deliver my message." he stared.

Salamander didn't want to play games - he didn't want any more pain than he had already experienced. He just wanted his family back unharmed and would do whatever it took to see this through. He was a weak man, he wasn't ashamed to admit it, weak in taking the offer of money from Hunter, weak because he was about to tell them anything they wanted - weak for not being able to protect his family. "I'll tell you everything." he spoke softly, acknowledging his defeat. He owed Hunter nothing; it was Hunter that put him here.

"Your wife and daughter will be pleased to hear that, but I must be frank with you - you have many tasks to complete in order to get them back, alive." Jafar's tone on the last word resonated through Salamander; he knew this man would kill them without a second thought.

Over the next few hours, Salamander detailed how he was approached by Hunter, what kind of work he did, as well as what he was asked to do. Jafar asked questions throughout but let him do most of the talking. Jafar was particularly interested in what information he had passed to Hunter about DOTA and about Hunter himself.

Jafar explained he wanted him to meet Hunter again. Salamander informed Jafar that Hunter would be leaving Tehran soon to take a break for few weeks. He was told to call Hunter that day and ordered to arrange a meeting urgently. Jafar wanted to know when Hunter was leaving and where he was going - he intended to make the British infidel a part of his plan to put DOTA on the map.

Salamander made the call and the meeting with Hunter was arranged.

As Jafar conjured a potential plan, he thought about how God had sent him these gifts to strengthen his cause...

He left the room to pray in solitude.

Chapter Seventeen

That morning, Tanner got up earlier than usual and went for a run to try and clear his head. It didn't help much; he still couldn't work out what the missing pieces of the puzzle were, what linked Hunter's death, Faisal Hosseini aka Salamander, and how DOTA and Russia fell into the mix.

He returned to his room none the wiser.

At the mess hall, he had a hearty breakfast, unsure when he would get a chance to eat next. He had packed most of his kit the night previous, but still had a few items to square away.

Tanner walked towards the Boss's office, passing the rest of his team on the field still undergoing pre-deployment training without him. He waved and wondered if they had heard about Hunter yet. If they hadn't, he was sure the 'rumour drums' would soon be banging around the camp, especially with his rapid deployment. He had kept himself in his room the night before to avoid any unwanted questions.

The updated brief with the Boss that morning had not turned up anything new from the day before. Gibbs had been informed he would receive updates as and when anything new was uncovered from either their Unit or MI6.

Tanner did not need to pack any weapons or equipment, all that he needed would be waiting for him at the armoury at the Unit's compound within the British Embassy in Tehran.

Tanner managed a quick lunch on base before he collected the arranged car and headed to Brize Norton, where he would board a Royal Air Force C-130 to RAF Akrotiri, Cyprus. Once in Akrotiri, it would be another hired car into North Cyprus, arriving at Nicosia International Airport to catch a direct commercial flight to Tehran.

The C-130 engines were soon humming in their unforgettable tone, as it taxied to the runway.

Tanner settled into the well-worn seat in the back of the aircraft, earplugs inserted to make the noise more tolerable. The flight would give him time to think, and he hoped an opportunity to try and get some rest.

*

After his last meeting with Hunter, Salamander was picked up by two of Jafar's disciples. One drove, as the other sat in the back with him. After a few minutes, a black canvas bag was placed over his head, and a hand forced him down until he was out of view. Once secure in Jafar's compound, his hood was removed, the high walls preventing any visible landmarks that could help identify where he was.

He was taken to Jafar and willingly passed on all the information he had gained from Hunter, confirming his R&R dates and destination. He didn't like the way Hunter arrogantly told him his plans, it felt like he was rubbing it in that Salamander would never have such opportunities.

Salamander was unaware, that while being picked up by Hunter, he was watched by members of DOTA. They had recorded the whole event and now knew what their target looked like. After fulfilling his part of the bargain with Jafar, he hoped he would be reunited with his family, but Jafar had a different agenda. Salamander was once again locked in the basement of horrors. They had his family; he would have told them anything from the start. Every time he heard a noise, or someone came to unlock the door, he had a flashback to the last time he was in this basement of hell.

No harm had come to him, and he repeatedly asked after his wife and daughter, only to have his requests ignored.

He pondered on what was to happen next. He had not seen Jafar but prayed his family was safe and unharmed.

After several days, one of the guards informed him of Hunter's murder - how his throat had been sliced open.

The guard laughed gleefully at the telling of the infidel's demise and started to chant 'DOTA.'

Salamander felt no guilt for Hunter's death, if anything his hatred only grew the longer he was separated from his wife and little girl.

Days passed, and he spent his time inside the basement trying not to think about the worst - while praying for the best.

Chapter Eighteen

The wheels of Pegasus Airlines flight PC1923 touched down in Tehran’s Imam Khomeini International Airport at 0410hrs local time.

Tanner's anticipation started to knot up inside him.

In his mind he was planning, already asking himself questions before the seat belt sign had even been extinguished. Will there be a car waiting for him? Will the handling team prep for his arrival? Have they already re-tasked the CHIS’s? Tanner had tried to rest on the flights, but his brain was working overtime, and he needed to get to work to find the answers - too much time had already been wasted.

The sensations he was feeling were nothing new. Whenever he deployed the adrenaline would slowly seep in and increase the closer he got to reaching the operational area.

Due to the early hour in the morning, he had quickly transited through the airport processes to find himself walking outside and meeting the waiting car. The drive was no longer than 30 minutes, and Tanner was soon pulling up to the dark blue security gates, credentials checked, and moved into Embassy grounds.

The Unit was a discreet, secure compound within the embassy grounds. No insignia, just an unassuming set of buildings hidden from view, allowing them to conduct their covert business and live out of sight of other embassy employees and visitors. The compound was almost self-sufficient with the deployed *operators* only ever needing to leave their fenced area for meals in the communal dining hall and to conduct their operations. Dressed in civilian attire, their aim was to look like any other embassy employee, and not draw attention to themselves. Very few people within the embassy walls knew what the Unit did, and that was on a 'need to know' basis.

Tanner was dropped outside the compound gate. He watched the car drive away before he rang the entry buzzer, the camera above pointing directly at him.

The gate buzzed allowing him entry.

No sooner was he through the gate; he was greeted by one of his oppos, Colour Sergeant Thomas 'Tug' Evans. The entirety of the cadre numbers was small, everyone knew each other, and at some point, had worked alongside one another.

Tanner had worked with Tug during the Herrick 17 campaign in Afghanistan, conducting covert operations out of Sangin. His background was Royal Marines before passing selection and joining the Unit. Tug was a London East-end boy and had the swagger and chat to go with it. He was shorter than most in the unit, but he was stocky and a handful, and was one to have around when the shit went down - calm under fire, and one to always find the funny side in every situation to lighten the mood.

They greeted each other with smiles, back slaps, and a few reminiscent stories. Tug had won the night shift and was the only one awake, he showed Tanner to his room to let him settle in until the other operators were up.

Tanner dumped his bags, not bothering to unpack; he headed straight for the *Hub* - the admin area where the handlers conducted their planning, research, and painstaking intelligence report writing. It was a large open planned windowless room, with five desks - one for each handler and a spare - each with its own secure *top secret* computer terminal. There were only four handlers and an Ops officer operating out of Tehran, now only three after the murder of Hunter. There was a communal area within the room, consisting of a couple of standard MOD blue clothed chairs and sofas around a coffee table, an area used for planning and exploring ideas away from the desks. Tanner had spent many hours sitting in such areas in different theatres.

The walls were covered with various area maps of Tehran and the wider Middle East, adorned with coloured pins, each colour representing either a place or person of interest. Detailed routes and portraits of targets framed the maps, each connected to a pin by a piece of string. All around the hub, any spare wall space had been utilised with information, which to a civilian eye would look like a disorganized free-for-all but had a strategic function that made sense to those in the know.

Tanner walked around until he identified which was Hunter's desk. The name Salamander was on the wall next to it and the heart wrenching giveaway was a picture of Hunter with a pregnant Zoe. The realisation of finding his killer was no longer a state of business, it had become personal. He sat at the desk, nudging the mouse bringing the computer screen to life. Tanner entered his ID and password, allowing him access to the highly classified server. All unit computers worldwide were connected to a bank of server units, hidden somewhere in a deep bunker in the UK. This allowed operators to access all necessary information no matter where they were globally.

As Tanner opened the Tehran Unit files, the office door opened, and Operations Officer Captain Conor Stones walked in. Stones was a tall slender guy from Scotland, a typically styled officer, intelligent with the ability to always find the right words to say to the right people. He was the buffer between the hierarchy in the embassy and the work the team did on the ground, making the decisions on what ops to move forward with and inherently responsible for the risk.

"Tanner, I heard you had arrived, how was your flight?" he walked across the room and held out his hand.

Tanner stood and shook his hand, "Good to see you again, Stones, it's been a while. Flight was okay, how are you?"

"I'm ok, as you can imagine the death of Hunter has hit everyone hard," he paused, "I'm sorry for what has happened, I know you two were close."

"Yes, we were," Tanner sighed, "I still haven't quite got my head around what has happened yet."

"Don't worry, we will find answers, as soon as everyone is up, we'll get a briefing together to see if we can piece together a plan to move forward on."

"I just want to get started," Tanner replied, "I'm going to start reading some of the intelligence reports, see if I can get up to speed."

"Tanner," Stones said in a concerned tone, "We will find who is responsible."

Tanner nodded, before Stones turned and left.

Chapter Nineteen

After an early breakfast, the rest of the team came into the Hub together, and despite the circumstances, it was clear they were pleased to see Tanner. All three were dressed in civilian clothing, which helped them work more inconspicuously. Each carried a Glock 19, normally holstered to the side or front, but hidden from view. A Glock 17 was standard army issue, but for the nature of their covert work the 19 was preferred, it carried two fewer 9mm rounds than the 17 but the Glock 19 had a half-inch smaller frame making it easier to conceal.

It was a good team. He had worked with both Tug and Corporal Mark 'Matty' Matthews before, a Sapper from the Royal Engineers. In his younger days Matty was a bit of a handful after a few beers, hence only making the dizzy heights of a Corporal. He had joined the Unit for a fresh start. Like Tug, Tanner had worked with Matty during Herrick 19, operating in Helmand Province, Afghanistan.

The last of the three was RAF Flight Sergeant Dawn Palmer; it was Tanner's first time meeting her in a professional capacity. Palmer was a slender 5ft 5in, and although she wasn't a Handler, she was tough as nails and participated in the Unit pre-deployment training, including the squash court, in which she gave as good as she got. Palmer was seconded to the Unit and acted as the Hub's *collator*, bringing all the intelligence fed from the UK, and what was gathered on the ground locally, before linking it all together.

After greetings and condolences for Hunter, they all convened around the coffee table for a debrief.

Once Stones arrived, Tanner took the floor and began.

"I've been back briefed by the Boss at camp, with what information they had at the time on Hunter's murder, and his CHIS Salamander. In that meeting was a representative from the Firm, who contributed elements of high-level intelligence, potentially making this situation a lot more sensitive, and more complicated than first expected."

The Firm was a term the military used for people who worked for MI6, if they worked for MI5 they were known as *Box* after their old PO Box 500 address.

Tanner briefed them on information he received, and how Salamander could be connected to Hunter's death and DOTA. He updated on the intel gathered by HMS Aegaeon, and the intelligence sourced by an MI6 agent - he then told them of the link between DOTA and the Russian Officer, Major Aaron Olegovich Sokolova, currently on the Ukrainian border fighting in the conflict. "I know there is a lot still unanswered but, any questions?" Tanner leaned back in his chair.

There was a brief pause as everyone processed what they had just heard.

Palmer was the first to break the silence, "I'm struggling to connect the Russian influence and the relationship with DOTA?" her collator brain was immediately in overdrive.

"That remains a big piece of the puzzle that needs to be worked out." Stones interjected.

"We're expecting intel updates from the Firm as and when it comes in," Tanner informed, "We need to sit tight and see what we can work out ourselves in the background. Palmer, I hear you like a challenge, see what you can pull together."

Palmer nodded and started scribbling on her pad.

"I think we need to go back to the start and work on trying

to find Salamander," Tanner said, "If there is one source linking all these elements together, he could be the key."

"From this end," Tug interjected, "We had started to receive low level information reference DOTA, hence Salamander being tasked to find out more. We all read the reports and spoke to Hunter after his last meeting. By the sound of it, Salamander was scared, he seemed to have lost the plot and gone AWOL."

"We've tasked the other CHIS's to not only try and infiltrate the DOTA network," Matty added, "But also gave them Salamander's name as a person of interest, which we know is against protocol, but we have little choice as we've had no response from all contact methods. It seems he has disappeared, again."

Tanner sighed, "It seems a bit convenient, Salamander going AWOL after Hunter's death."

Stones laid down the hard truth, with an edge of authority, "The issue we have is not all our CHIS's have access to complete the tasking without highlighting themselves, we only have two with that capability, Caecilian, and Lizard." The CHIS's running out of Iran had all been named after amphibians and reptiles. "And I have to make strategic decisions on the risk level of our sources. The last thing the Unit can afford is to lose them from overzealous tasking, which could place them in danger."

The last comment angered Tanner, "One of our handlers has been killed, and you're worried about the danger to low life scum who would kill their own mother to get a payday?"

The comment pierced the room.

"I'll have you watch your tone," Stones countered, "We

may operate a relaxed rank system, but I will remind you I am your senior officer, and I have a legal obligation to the lives of the people we use as sources, scum or not. Have I made myself clear?"

The room fell into an uncomfortable silence as everyone awaited Tanner's response.

"Sorry, Sir." Tanner was still clearly angry.

"And don't call me, Sir." Stones commanded.

Tanner got things moving again, keen to break the awkward atmosphere he'd just created, "The plan as I see it… Tug, Matty, get onto your sources and continue to chase up DOTA and Salamander, we maintain contact day or night at even the slightest shred of information. Palmer, work your magic and see if you can work out any link with the Russian. I will continue through Hunter's files to see if anything has been missed and try to contact Salamander. Everyone happy?"

The group agreed and moved off to start work.

Stones remained seated, "I'll lean on MI6 and the Boss for further intelligence, ensuring we get it as a matter of urgency."

"Thanks, I'm sorry I lost my cool."

Stones nodded and placed a hand on Tanner's shoulder, "We all miss Hunter, and we all want the same outcome here. You need to put personal feelings behind you on this one."

"Do we still have a surveillance team operating in Tehran?"

"We do," Stones enquired, "Why, what are you thinking?"

"A drive past Salamander's residence if that's ok?"

"Get the plan together and brief me, I'll put them on standby." Stones agreed.

Chapter Twenty

Salamander was awoken by the door of his makeshift cell being unlocked. Hidden from daylight, the room had its usual chill, not only because it was dug into the earth but due to the phycological impact his previous incarceration had instilled.

The usual guard brought in his breakfast. He never spoke, just delivered a tray with flatbread, feta cheese and sweet tea, though it seemed this morning he was to be treated to a side of jam too.

As the guard departed, he did not close the door after him. This was unusual, was it intentional, or had he just forgotten? Was this his chance to escape and find his wife and daughter? His mind was running wild with opportunist thoughts. He got up and stepped closer to the door, then stopped. What if he came face to face with the guard in the corridor? He knew he wouldn't stand a chance, he was big, almost twice the width of him and at least a foot taller, the fight would soon be over and not in his favour. He looked around the room for a possible weapon but the only thing he could see was the plastic knife laid on the tray, only good for spreading jam.

'Run…' his mind was yelling… 'RUN!'

Before his body had chance to react, Jafar appeared in the doorway wearing a smile. Salamander wondered if the look on his face betrayed his temptation to take flight. He felt inexplicably guilty and had to break what seemed an uncomfortable silence, "My family?"

Jafar held up his hands, "Relax my friend; they are being taken good care of."

"You promised I would see them. That we would be back

together and go home after I did what you asked." Salamander contested curtly.

"Shut the fuck up, traitor, I promised nothing!" Jafar's demeanour switched in an instant, stepping into his face as he yelled. The guard's silhouette appeared, filling the doorway.

Jafar's voice lowered into a chilling tone, "You will do exactly what I say, when I say it. Be thankful I haven't killed you like I have your infidel friend!"

"He's not my friend," Salamander hissed, "I despise him, I'm glad he's dead."

Jafar offered a slow sinister chuckle, "You're angry. Good, that's good. You need to use that anger to carry out your next task and help us fight against the western disease. You want to see your family again - You do what Allah commands you."

Salamander fought to fight back the emotion; he knew he had to keep the hope alive if he was to be reunited with the two people he loved most in this world, "Please… Please let me see my family, I'll do what you want." At that moment he felt his family was in even greater danger than before.

Salamander slumped onto the edge of his bed.

Jafar pulled up a chair and sat facing him, "I need you to deliver something for me, it's of utmost importance and failure will not be tolerated."

Salamander sat with his face in his hands.

Jafar's next words drove deep into his heart, "If you fail, your beautiful wife and pretty young daughter will suffer the same fate as your infidel friend - after I've let my men have some fun with them."

*

Later that day, Salamander was allowed a brief reunion with his family before he would be sent away to carry out Jafar's orders. Jafar knew seeing his wife and daughter would be an incentive in Salamander succeeding, offering him a thread of hope.

Hope, the killer of men.

As soon as he walked into the room they ran to him.

In tears they formed a circle and squeezed each other tightly, not wanting to ever let go. They calmed one another, the tears soon replaced with smiles. He could see they were both well and his wife assured him they were being looked after. This gave him a sense there could be some truth in Jafar's words. They sat, talked, laughed, and cried some more. Faisal was shocked to learn they had been in the same compound all this time, only metres from one another. He explained he had no choice but to do a task for Jafar and was unsure how long it would take, but not to worry about him.

He promised he would return, and they would go back to their lives again. He decided not to tell his wife about the relationship he had with Hunter, or how they ended up in this sinkhole of dread. In the back of his mind, something lingered there, he tried to shut it away and enjoy the moment, he did not want to think the worst.

The guard came for him after an hour.

Faisal said his goodbyes and they had a prayer, followed by more tears, and then he left.

In another hidden part of the compound Salamander was handed a mobile phone and told only to use the logged number in an emergency or for brief updates. He would receive further orders as time went on. Under no circumstances was he to use names or locations when talking or texting.

Keys to a white Peugeot Persia 406 were passed to him together with two lots of cash in different currencies, one roll in Iranian Rial, the other, Turkish Lira - the vehicle was to make the delivery and Jafar handed him an address with detailed directions, the last line read, Istanbul.

He was to cross the border into Turkey.

He'd never even been out of Tehran let alone Iran.

The look on Jafar's face burned into him. Salamander looked around at Jafar's disciples, their faces hardened, ready to kill. There was a wooden box on the table. No bigger than a pallet of fruit. It was solid on all sides, the wooden lid resting on the top. Jafar moved the lid aside. Inside packed tight with hay and old newspaper were two glass-like bottles, each capped with a metallic seal. Each cylinder was filled with a liquid, stained in a gentian violet colour.

Jafar explained if the glass was to break, he would fail to save himself and his family. The cargo was very fragile, the sight of it scared Salamander enough to make him shudder.

Salamander's questions about the cargo were bluntly dismissed, but he understood whatever it was it was clearly bad news. His head was spiralling out of control, but he had to get a grip on himself, his family were depending on him.

After a nod from Jafar, one of the disciples added extra packaging over the top of the glass cylinders and secured the lid by gently tapping tacks around the edges. The box was placed into the boot of the car, which had been modified with a hidden compartment where a spare wheel would usually be seated. Once hidden, they filled the boot with bags of clothes, making it awkward to see or search. If Salamander was stopped, he was to use the cover story of traveling to visit family - a cover story Salamander thought cruelly ironic as that was what Hunter had trained him to use if he was ever questioned. Look how well that worked out.

Salamander was given a forged passport, a document he had never owned or applied for in his life.

Before he left, they held a group prayer led by Jafar, followed by chants of excitement for DOTA by the other disciples. Jafar's final words aimed a message of warning to Salamander, of what would happen if he were to fail.

As he drove out of the compound, Salamander's mind was a whirl of doubt and questions - what was in the boot of the car - would he ever see his family again - and then, a sudden realisation of where he was.

Chapter Twenty-One

Tanner had spent the morning in the Hub with the other handlers. He started by sending a covert recall to Salamander via text to his mobile phone. Tanner wasn't too hopeful about getting a response. He had briefly read a couple of Hunter's reports but focussed his time on putting the operation together, to check Salamander's residence.

Palmer had passed him all imagery of the location, both aerial and ground level, of surrounding streets, entrances, and exits into Salamander's apartment block. These had been collected on the last reconnaissance mission, also blueprints of the internal building layout.

The plan was to observe from a distance and see if anything looked out of the ordinary. He had planned his detailed routes to and from the area, taking into account anti-surveillance, protocol, and routes if the *op* had to take any emergency actions. This included enlarged photos of areas and buildings they could use if they needed to fortify, hold, and wait out for extraction if the shit hit the fan. Tanner had been to see Stones, who would in turn authorised the, *Go ahead.*

Tanner briefed his Orders of Operations covering all eventualities. His audience was small consisting of Stones, and two surveillance guys James and Danny. They were attached to the Unit from Special Reconnaissance Regiment - SRR. Much like Tanners Unit, personnel could put themselves forward for selection from any branch of the British Military. SRR specialised in a range of classified activities related to covert surveillance and reconnaissance.

The SRR lads very much kept to themselves. James was

not your typical Essex boy like Tug. He was of average height and build, had blondish hair, and was the quieter of the two, happy to let Danny do the talking.

Danny was the louder one, an excitable Brummie who stood over six feet, well built with a shaved ginger head, he was not the easiest to hide in a crowd, but once he was wrapped in local attire, he could blend in well enough.

After the orders had been completed and questions put to rest, Tanner went to the internal compound armoury to collect his weapons and ammunition. He placed his Glock 19 with a fully charged magazine into his front holster that was discreetly clipped to his belt, concealed down the inside front of his trousers. His main weapon of choice was the 5.56mm C8 Carbine assault rifle, locked and loaded with a 30-round magazine. It had a multi-position telescoping buttstock and was fitted with a laser sight and an underslung torch - based on the C8 Diemaco, it could deliver a heavy, high-accuracy message to any target, and was a good all-rounder for both range and Close Quarter Battle - CQB.

The rifle was placed in a sports bag, the easiest way to move it around without drawing unwanted attention.

Over his right shoulder, attached to a makeshift sling of flexible cord and tucked under his armpit, he carried the Heckler & Koch MP5K, the K meaning *Kurz* which was German for 'short', ideal for concealment on the body. The weapon housed a thirty round 9mm magazine, the fire selection switch always engaged to fully automatic. It was not an accurate weapon and would only ever be used to unleash hell. When fired, the sound of the rounds leaving the chamber at such a high rate was enough to make anyone hit the deck or run for cover - just enough time to allow an operative to either get the hell out of there or find cover for a firing point utilising a chosen main weapon. He wore a covert body armoured vest. More discreet than its solid Kevlar plated cousin that was worn in the field during overt operations, it also minimised any restriction of movement and visibility.

Over the armour was an assault vest, allowing him to carry spare magazines for the Glock, and C8. The vest had allocated pockets which he filled with L83 smoke grenades, flash bangs, and a couple of L109A1 grenades. Loose fitting clothes covered and concealed him from the local populace.

Tanner secretly loved this part of the job. To the outside world he was just another face, but underneath he was armed to the teeth, and no one was the wiser. It gave him a buzz.

He remembered when he first started to covertly carry weapons in the UK. It felt uncomfortable, it felt obvious. Concealing with the use of loose clothing, it still felt that all eyes were on him, that everyone could see the lumps and bumps of weaponry protruding from his body. It didn't take long to get used to it and start to feel more comfortable.

Now it had the opposite effect, he felt naked when not carrying weapons, almost like he had forgotten something.

The SRR guys were also tooled up and had left the Unit's compound and embassy with Tanner via a discreet gate, which very few knew existed.

Once out in the streets, Danny drove the white Saipa Saina car and James navigated from the passenger seat. Tanner sat in the back observing people and vehicles that might want to tail them. It took them forty-five minutes to navigate Tanner's planned route across the city to Afsariyeh, on the edge of District 15. They used a combination of major and minor roads to maintain an indirect route. They kept comms with Palmer who mapped their progress ready to deliver updated intelligence as it came in, such as impromptu police roadblocks that could see a team exposed and searched. The Iranian Government would not take kindly to any clandestine British military operations being conducted on their home soil.

They cruised down Salamander's street passing the front of his apartment block. It was a ten-storey, double-breasted building. The front entrance was in the middle with no locks or security measures to prevent a breach.

Salamander's home was located on the fifth floor facing the street. At first glance, the building was run down, and nothing looked out of place in and around the street area.

They circled the block and approached the building again. Danny pulled over to allow them a view from about four hundred yards. The plan was to hold up for a while, before moving on to avoid any unwanted attention.

Ten minutes had passed, when Tanner recognised the lone male figure walking with vigour, looking around before entering the main entrance.

Chapter Twenty-Two

On leaving Jafar's compound, Salamander had established he was in Hekmat, District 1 in the outskirts of North Tehran. He recognised the green mountain backdrop and remembered bringing his daughter through this area only last year to visit Jamshidieh Park, one of the oldest and most beautiful parks in northern Tehran. She loved the outdoors and adventure, so they had visited the Stone Garden at the base of the mountains to enjoy the open green space away from all the city pollution.

His heart wrenched at the memory.

After arguing with himself on the merits of it, Salamander decided he would make a quick visit to his apartment to gather some personal effects.

He had been sat in the car further down the road with Jafar's compound gate in sight of his rearview mirror. No person or vehicle had left while he had been sitting there.

He was on his own now.

His decision made, he put the car into gear and pulled away slowly, heading towards the southeast of the city.

He would be there within the hour.

He didn't want to be seen by anyone he knew, driving up in a car he could not financially afford would spark questions. He pulled over and parked one street over behind his apartment building and sat for a while contemplating his judgment.

'What if they learned he'd returned here, would it endanger his family?' He also concerned himself with the package he was carrying in the boot, 'Would it and the car be safe?'

Salamander stepped out of the vehicle, locking the doors and double checking them by walking around pulling on each door handle and the boot latch.

He entered a side alley that led to the street running parallel to where he had parked. The air in the narrow alley was consumed with stale odours and wisps of sewage that rose from every drain. Bin bags were piled up along one side, waiting to be removed by the city's waste collection that rarely graced this neighbourhood. The tall buildings on either side of the narrow passage cast a dark shadow blocking out the sun.

As he approached the opening to the main street, he halted and moved back against the wall between the bags of rubbish. The rancid smell of decay hit his nostrils, causing him to breathe through his mouth.

He questioned himself again; he had a feeling deep in his stomach he couldn't explain. He took a deep breath and started to walk. Entering the open street he picked up his pace and kept his head low. As he left the shadows the sun hit him, he made the turn left around the edge of his building, it was only a few yards to the entrance, and within seconds he was pulling on the large wooden door to gain entry.

He moved quickly across the corridor to the stairway, taking the steps three at a time to the fifth floor. He passed an old lady on the fourth floor moving slowly down the stairs, neither recognised the other.

Once in the dimly lit fifth floor hallway, he jogged to his doorway and turned the handle - it was locked.

A panic quickly filled him, he felt exposed, standing outside his door looking up and down the hall, for what, he did not know. Seconds passed and his sense came back to him, he reached up to feel along the top of the door frame for the spare key. The feel of thin metal on his fingertips sent a flood of relief coursing through his body. He slowly placed the key in the lock and as quietly as he could, turned and pushed the door open. He waited a moment to listen for any sounds from the inside. Nothing. He opened the door fully and stepped inside closing it behind him and leaning against it. He suddenly realised how exhausted he was. Slumped into a sitting position against the door, he was home, but it didn't feel like home without the two people he loved most.

Salamander slowly walked around his small lifeless apartment, looking at each room littered with memories.

His eyes came across what he had come for.

Sitting on the shelved unit in the living room was a framed photograph of the three of them together, back when times were good… happy times, the incentive he needed.

He took the photo out of the frame and held it in his hands. He looked down and was overcome with sadness. He folded the picture and tucked it in his pocket. He had brought this dangerous predicament upon his family, and he was going to finish the job to save them, even if it meant his death.

He walked into the bedroom to collect some clothes. Looking down at the bed, flashbacks hit him like a train, bringing memories of the night they were taken.

Anger welled inside him, his fists clenched, teeth gritted, and he wanted revenge on Jafar.

Suddenly, Salamander flipped back to the present as he heard the gentle creak of the front door handle turning.

Chapter Twenty-Three

"Hotel One, Romeo come in."

"Go ahead Romeo," Palmer responded.

"Hotel One, Romeo, I have confirmed sighting of Salamander on location. Permission to go Foxtrot and engage?" Tanner could feel the adrenaline rising at his coded request to go out on foot. After a moment his earpiece hissed, "Wait out for Bravo update, Romeo."

The three of them sat in silence as they awaited permission from the Boss, call sign Bravo, in this case Stones at the embassy compound. Inside the car they all maintained a fixed stare on the entrance door. The seconds ticked slowly by, each one feeling like a minute. Tanner was taunting himself; the answer to Hunter's death is behind that heavy, dark wood door, and he wanted it so desperately.

Tanner spoke to Danny and James.

"Right, if we get the go ahead, I'll head straight in, I memorised the blueprints of the building so I know where I need to be. James, if you step out and cover the entrance from this side of the street. Danny, you go mobile and circle the block. Be ready for a quick evac, hopefully with one extra person on board. Any Questions?"

No questions came, only an immediate, "Roger!" to show their acknowledgment and understanding.

"I'll drive around the block to the back of the building," Danny announced in his Brummie accent, "Then loop back down, that should give you enough time to get in and out."

Tanner agreed.

Their alertness heightened as the radio earpieces came back

to life, “Romeo. Hotel One, maintain overwatch and wait out.” Palmer reported.

“Fucking Stones!” Tanner punched the car door, “Fuck!”

Having heard the same message, Danny and James remained silent.

Tanner was furious, convinced that all Stones was thinking about was his future promotion - he didn’t care about Hunter’s death, he just wanted to have a smooth tour with no incidents on his record. ‘Fucking Rupert!’ Tanner thought, *Rupert* being the nickname for officers in the Armed Forces.

Then in a moment of madness, Tanner asked, “You two remember the plan?”

They didn't have time to respond as Tanner was quickly out of the vehicle and walking across the road.

“Call it in Danny, we're going to have to go along with this.” James said exiting the car. He moved to keep overwatch in the street, placing a mobile phone to his ear as if on a call.

Danny pulled away from the curb and started relaying comms back to the base unit. “Hotel One, Lima. Romeo has gone foxtrot. Tango is foxtrot now giving overwatch. Lima is mobile, will satellite location.” There was a brief silence before Hotel One asked to repeat the last transmission.

Danny repeated, knowing that everyone back at the Unit would be going ape shit, especially Stones.

Tanner had reached the door and walked through with a confidence that suggested he belonged there. He was going over the build schematics in his head, locating the stairway; he passed an old lady at the foot of the stairs seemingly catching her breath. He swiftly proceeded upwards to the fifth floor.

Entering the hallway, he engaged his comms, updating the

listening audience. He turned right and moved slowly until he was standing outside door 517.

Tanner took a moment and looked both ways to check there were no eyes on him before he un-holstered his Glock. Holding it close to his chest, his firing hand pointing the weapon in the direction of travel.

With his left hand, he reached for the door handle and slowly started the turn. It creaked a little.

He pushed at the door, elated it was unlocked, the voice in his head stating, 'I know you are in here.'

*

On hearing the front door open, Salamander quietly moved across to his bed, reached underneath, and grabbed an iron bar. He had kept a bar there since he'd started to work with Hunter.

When held captive, he'd wondered many times on why he hadn't reached for it that fateful night but took some solace in the fact if he had they might all be dead.

On this occasion, he didn't hesitate to take it in hand.

He stood, and waited behind the bedroom door, bar raised ready to strike. He was trying to keep his breathing under control, everything was so quiet, it made silence feel deafeningly loud, and he could feel his pulse thumping like a drum. He gripped the bar tighter.

Tanner moved into the small corridor and on towards the living room. He moved silently, drawing on his experience and training to clear such spaces. The first room was a small open planned living area and kitchen; his eyes searched the obvious places for a would-be attacker before moving around the perimeter in a clockwise, sided-stepping movement, ensuring all blind spots had been accounted for.

"Room one clear." he whispered.

Everyone on the radio network would be keeping chat to a minimum. Back at the Unit, he knew Palmer and Stones would have all Tanner's plans, including the apartment layout, on the ops board in front of them, following his progress.

Once Tanner was happy the room was clear, he moved toward the two remaining closed doors.

Salamander remained perfectly still. It was quiet, but occasionally he heard movement over the floor beyond by someone who was taking great care not to be heard. The rhythmic beating of his heart pumped frightened blood around his body, the sound filling his ears. His palms were sweaty, and the bar began to feel heavy in his hands.

A footstep sounded closer than before.

Tanner reached the two doors; both were identical in panelled white wood. From memory, he knew the right-hand one was the bathroom - room two, as it was indicated on the plan. He paused before turning the handle.

Being a tiny box room; he knew it would be better for a rapid entry to gain the element of surprise. He entered with haste. It took seconds to clear, and it stank of shit. He backed out and closed the door, pinching his nostrils to wipe the smell away. "Room two clear." the net remained silent.

He moved towards the final door, room number three. Tanner took a moment to listen for any movement on the other side of the door - nothing. He started to doubt himself; did he see Salamander on the street? He pushed his doubts away, knowing that man's face was ingrained in his memory. He adjusted his grip on the Glock and moved forward, reaching out and turning the handle. He pushed the door open exposing the room, adrenaline coursing through him as if standing next to a large bass speaker that vibrated through him. He extended his pistol forward and stepped into the bedroom.

The door swung open towards Salamander, he pressed himself against the wall trying to be as flat as a hung picture. The door bounced back away from him a little.

He held his breath; afraid he might be heard breathing, perspiration running down his face. He was scared.

Who was this in his apartment?

He had to get out, get back to the car and complete Jafar's request or... He didn't want to think about it.

His head pulsating, he saw the barrel of a pistol slowly coming into view, passing the door's edge, and pointing into the room. This was the moment, possibly his only chance to escape. As the barrel crept forward, the hands came into view holding the grip. 'Now!' his mind shouted and this time his body listened.

Salamander brought down the bar as hard as he could, causing a loud metallic crack as it connected with the top side of the pistol. Hearing a loud male yelp, he then shoulder barged his side of the door with all his might, forcing it into the intruder. There was a loud thud, as the man fell to the floor. With speed, Salamander moved around the door, still holding the iron bar, he saw the pistol loose on the floor. He jumped over the body in the doorway and made to run out of the apartment. He suddenly felt a strong, tight clasp round his ankle like he had been shackled, and he too fell to the floor into the living room. He kicked out at his assailant freeing himself and scuttling backward on all fours. The next word froze him on the spot... it was spoken in English.

"Stop!" Tanner yelled.

He had retrieved his Glock and pointed it at Salamander. Tanner sat upright, fighting the pain where his fingers had been crunched by the metal bar causing him to drop the weapon. He was pissed off; this tall skinny fucker had got the better of him, disarming him and knocking him to the floor. He felt a twinge in his knee where he'd fell, a possible twist he thought, an old injury, they always come back to haunt you. But he had the upper hand now, sat upright on the floor, aiming at his target.

A mixture of shock and fear was painted across Salamander's face.

"I'm a friend of Hunter's." Tanner said calmly.

He looked back at Tanner in disbelief. Salamander felt safer knowing it wasn't a member of DOTA, but knew, he could not be involved with this man either.

Tanner lowered his weapon, trying to subdue the situation, knowing that dealing with a source was never just about physical force; it was a psychological relationship, to control them to your way of thinking, to achieve the purpose. "I need to talk with you. I can take you somewhere safe." Tanner said in a persuasive tone.

Salamander started to shake his head, indicating that was

not going to happen, “My family is in danger because of you, I need to get to Istanbul.”

Tanner tried again, “Let me help you, and your family.”

“No!” Salamander's voice grew firmer, “I have to go.” With that, he sprung to his feet, and sprinted to the door, out into the corridor.

Tanner raised his weapon again and shouted after him, knowing he couldn't take the shot. It would be against the Rules of Engagement, and Stones’ risk factor.

More importantly, this man had the answers he needed.

A CHIS is no good dead.

He got up to follow and limped at pace, feeling his left knee give way slightly.

By the time he got to the corridor, Salamander was nowhere to be seen.

Tanner went to send a comms report but realised his earpiece had fallen out when the door hit him. He re-holstered his weapon and went back to retrieve the earphone.

Chapter Twenty-Four

James was uncomfortable with the long radio silence. Tanner should have cleared the final room by now. He was also aware of how bad the covert body comms system was, having experienced loss of comms many times before.

He'd been standing on the opposite side of the road, acting as if engrossed within a call on his mobile in a shop doorway while discreetly watching the entrance and the street.

Then, in a flash, a man flew out the door and whipped down the alley to the side of the building, before sprinting away. In the car earlier, James had not got a look at the man Tanner had seen going in, so he couldn't confirm with certainty the person fleeing was the target. The chances of someone running out of the same building were remote at best. 'Besides,' James thought, 'No-one ran like that in Iran.'

Putting the phone in his pocket he trotted across the road trying not to draw attention to himself. Standing in the mouth of the alleyway he contemplated his next move. Tanner was nowhere to be seen, and zero comms had been sent. Does he give chase to the man running down the alley? No. They were already split on the ground with poor communications, and Tanner's situation was unknown.

As he watched the runner grow further away from him, he pressed his comms button, "Tango, Lima over."

"Lima," came Danny's voice at the other end.

"Zulu running down the alley to the side of the building should exit street to the rear. Tango going to assist Romeo." Zulu was the callsign for a person of interest.

"Tango over, mobile on street now."

As James entered the lobby doorway, his comms started crackling in his ear.

"All callsigns, Salamander on the run, intercept if possible, unarmed. Romeo clear."

James not only heard it in his ear, but he could also hear the voice calling it coming down the stairway, he started to climb the stairs when Tanner came round the corner.

Danny was moving slowly up the street in light traffic. He'd already passed the alleyway. In his rearview mirror, he saw the Zulu appear as if he had been spat out of the passage.

He was about two hundred yards behind him.

"All callsigns Tango, eyes on Zulu. Foxtrot moving south."

He was moving in the opposite direction to Danny.

Danny made a move to turn the vehicle around, the radio now alive with chatter. He could make out that Tanner and James were making their way down the same alley, so he should see them soon. Danny's attempt to turn around was hindered by a taxi coming the other way.

He could see Salamander getting into a white vehicle. Realising he'd been unable to turn and follow, Danny watched as the car pulled out, knowing all he could do was take note of the model and license plate number. By the time Danny was able to turn and head in the same direction, Salamander was already down the road, turning right at the next crossroads and out of sight.

He called it in, "Zulu now mobile in X-ray, white, ID Iran 76 G 189." As he approached the alley, it spat out another two flustered figures, both of whom he recognised.

He pulled over and picked them up.

Chapter Twenty-Five

Salamander couldn't believe he had made it back to the car; he fumbled for his keys pressing the fob erratically, trying to unlock the door. It took him several attempts to insert the key into the ignition; a bag of nerves, he eventually started the vehicle. In his panic to drive away, he nearly hit a motorcyclist as he pulled out. The rider blasted his horn and shouted something inaudible, waving his arm as he rode by. Salamander was soon speeding through the suburban district streets, taking unnecessary risks, overtaking vehicles, and pushing through gaps of pedestrians as they tried to cross the road. Gradually, he eased off the accelerator, and took deep breaths to compose himself. He felt his hands aching where he'd been gripping the steering wheel too tightly.

'Relax,' he told to himself.

He reached down and turned the air conditioning to full.

He felt like he was burning up and needed to feel a cold breeze on his skin. He checked his mirrors continuously, looking for anyone trying to follow him, but there were too many cars, and he could barely think straight. His focus now was to get onto the main arterial roads and head out of the city. Excluding rest breaks, he'd figured it would take two days of actual driving to reach Istanbul.

The thought of trying to get through the border with a fake passport was his next concern, it could all end very quickly if he were stopped and arrested there. He would have failed.

He said a quiet prayer for his family.

Soon, he merged onto Route 2, the Sheikh Fazlollah Nuri Expressway. He made himself comfortable; he would be on this road for the next 394 miles. He tuned the radio to Radio Farda; he liked listening to this station.

Keeping his speed constant so as not to draw any attention, he watched as Tehran faded from his rear-view mirror.

Jafar watched the woman and her child playing across the courtyard. He had urges when he looked at her, she was young and attractive, the type that would never enjoy his company, but he didn't care. If he wanted something he would take it. But not yet, he would wait.

His thoughts drifted back to his courier and the delivery of the package. If successful, it would put DOTA on the map as a new wave of terror against the western world.

A grin drew across his weathered face.

His only worry was the safety of the contents in the box.

The Botulinum toxin.

Chapter Twenty-Six

"What the fuck do you think you're playing at Colour Sergeant Tanner?" Stones demanded standing up and leaning on his desk - both fists clenched.

Stones had used Tanner's rank; he knew he was in the shit now. Standing to attention on the opposite side of the desk, Tanner attempted to respond, but the barrage continued.

"I told you to maintain over watch. No, I ordered you to maintain over watch, and you completely disobeyed that order and went on your own personal crusade."

Tanner wondered how many others in the Unit were listening in. He went to speak and was cut off again. 'Perhaps I'll just stay quiet.' he thought.

"As soon as you left that vehicle you put other team members at risk - they had no choice but to cover you. You're not thinking straight, you're a danger to yourself and you are endangering others. What's worse is, he got the better of you."

The last words stung Tanner wounding his pride.

"I'm struggling to think why I shouldn't hit you with an RTU right now - the explaining I now have to do up the chain, because one of my handlers is out of control!"

The threat of an RTU, *Return to Unit*, was a serious one. He looked at Tanner shaking his head, a huff of air inflating his cheeks, "Do you want to be dishonourably discharged?"

Eventually his tone and posture eased, "I'm starting to think this is too close to home for you, Tanner."

"Sir, if I may?"

Stones waved a hand signalling him to continue.

"Firstly, I apologise. What I did was reckless and stupid,

and yes, my personal feelings took over. I assure you I will put them aside. This will not happen again. I know I've put you in a predicament with the hierarchy, and for that, I am sorry too."

Stones knew he was sincere. The thought of being RTU'd or kicked into Civvie Street was enough to put the fear of God into any soldier. "You need to get your head out of your arse and bury those feelings if you want to remain on this team."

"Sir."

"Don't call me Sir." Stones snapped back. He gestured to Tanner to take a seat. "I've got heat on me after your stunt today, and I need to smooth it over. As far as everyone in this compound is concerned there was a comms failure, and you didn't receive the message to wait. Have I made myself clear?"

"Crystal Clear."

"The only reason, I'm allowing you to stay and continue with this is the fact you made contact with Salamander. Word has it MI6 believe they might have found some links and are checking their sources before passing anything over. Palmer has also been digging, and we have intelligence from Tug's source, Lizard. We will have a debrief shortly after this."

"And Salamander?" Tanner asked, "Referencing his family being in danger and having to go to Istanbul? There seems to be a bigger picture forming we are not seeing."

"You're right, this does seem to be growing arms and legs. Hopefully, Palmer has uncovered some hidden gems."

*

The Unit's windowless briefing room had a conference table that seated twenty with a large 50-inch flatscreen mounted at one end. The three Handlers scattered themselves on each side of the table as Palmer made ready to present her findings via her laptop.

Stones walked in with an unknown suited man. The man was in his mid-fifties, tall, with a full head of greying hair. He did not speak but smiled at those looking at him. He took a chair away, seating himself at the back.

Stones positioned himself at the head of the table.

Palmer took this as her cue to start, "Good afternoon, everyone." She clicked the mouse transferring her slides onto the large screen, "I'll start with the recent update, reference the intelligence gained from the last operation at Salamander's residence. We know the vehicle of interest is a White Peugeot Persia 406 saloon, Iranian registration 76 G 189. We have checked the system and this vehicle has not been registered with anyone, not unusual here in Iran. We also believe from Tanner's contact report, Salamander is driving to Istanbul." She paused to check her screen, "Istanbul is a 1500-mile journey, taking a day and a half without stopping. The most direct route would see Salamander crossing at the Gürbulak–Bazargan border near Dogubayazit in Turkey."

"How can we guarantee Salamander is driving to Istanbul?" Matty asked, "Or even using that car to get there?"

"Two good questions. We've checked the Iranian Government system with the help of the embassy, and Salamander does not hold a passport, so flying is an option we have ruled out. As for the vehicle, I believe he is using the same car, and I will brief you on the reasons why, shortly. That aside we've requested drone coverage to look at all main routes out of Tehran and toward the border to see if we can spot the vehicle. But as you know, white is the most popular colour choice for vehicles in this region."

Stones' officer voice rolled across the table with an air of authority, "The drone request has been approved, but as it is last minute, will only be available between current tasking. Palmer has worked out an estimated window of opportunity if Salamander were to cross the border, and that is when the drone will have eyes on." He looked at the ghost sitting at the back of the room who nodded in agreement.

"Thank you," Palmer said, "I have more to brief, but for now, I'll pass you over to Tug."

"Okay, as you know we have re-tasked our sources to find any information on the ITS group, Disciples of the Afterlife, or DOTA as it's being referred to," Tug informed in his east-end twang, "This was the same tasking that Salamander was leading, and we can only take a guess, that his contact with DOTA led to his current behaviour." Tug paused, "Now, earlier this morning I had an emergency Telcon from my source Lizard. He is a trusted source, and his information over the past few years has always been collaborated and come up trumps. He informed me that, DOTA, isn't as well kept a secret as we may have first believed. He has come across many men who are or know of someone who has joined or is joining them. They, for obvious reasons call themselves Disciples, and the best bit of crack he delivered is that the leader goes by the name of Jafar Abdul Malik or Jafar Cakes to his mates." Tug let out his infectious laugh which saw the others join.

"Settle down." Stones said, restoring order. "Good work Tug any more to add?"

"No that's it, I've given Jafar's name for Palmer to work her magic."

Tanner jumped in, "Tug, did Lizard report anything regarding Russia?"

"No. He'd only been tasked over the last forty-eight hours; the focus was anything to do with DOTA. Of course, after this morning's call, I've extended his tasking on DOTA and when I meet up with him, I'll add the Russian element and see where it goes." Tug closed his notebook and sat back.

Tanner smiled, so we have a name. Jafar Abdul Malik.

As Palmer readied to retake centre stage, the mystery man at the back stood up. He placed a hand on Stone's shoulder and leaned to whisper close into his ear.

The words were inaudible and saw all gathered straining to try and lip read them - He then left the room.

Stones looked up, "Please continue." It was clear he wasn't going to enlighten anyone as to who the mystery man was.

Palmer eyed all within the room, "So, here comes the juicy part… I'm hoping this will pull a lot of the puzzle together," there was a sparkle of excitement to her tone, "I have spoken to our American friends, and they can confirm that Jafar Abdul Malik, is a known POI, and has been on their watch list since the Iraq War back in 2003. The good news is they have a file on him, and they have sent it over."

"Did they send us everything they had?" Tanner asked.

"As we are all aware, they will only send us what they want us to know, but it's a pretty big file and currently answers our immediate questions." Palmer continued, "I will brief his background shortly. First, I want to go back to Matty's earlier question about the car, and do we believe Salamander will use it to get to Istanbul." Palmer went on, "As I said, Jafar is on the Yank's watch list, so they have been regularly taking satellite pictures of his compound area daily for observation. And yes, before you ask, we now have his residential location too. Speaking to the case owner, they have seen a rise in visitors to the compound over the past few months, which is another reason they have been watching a little closer."

Palmer aimed her laser point at the screen, "Here you can see eight satellite images, one for each of the last eight days. The first image shows no vehicle in the compound, then, seven days ago, a car appears under a shoddy tarpaulin roof." She steadied her light on each white rectangle, representing the shape of a car on each slide. "This vehicle remained inside the compound for a further five days. In this image, taken at 1206 hours today, you can see the vehicle is no longer there. The same day you have seen Salamander in a white car. Running these images through a recognition programme and using open-source pictures of the make and model of the vehicle Danny reported - mass analysis tells us it's a ninety seven percent match. So, in answer to your question Matty, yes, it's highly probable he is driving that vehicle to Istanbul."

"All we need now is drone confirmation of Salamander driving it over the border." Matty said looking pleased.

"So, what we are assuming thus far," Tanner began putting the pieces together, "Is Salamander, was potentially holed up in Jafar's compound until today. And now he is driving to Istanbul in the same car we are seeing in these images?"

"A good assumption I'd say." Tug stated.

"Can we also make an assumption that Salamander's family is in Jafar's compound? And after hearing how desperate he sounded earlier, they are there against their will?"

Tanner's brain filed through the different pieces trying to put it all together.

Stones offered, "So we are saying Salamander isn't going to Istanbul by choice, but likely by force or blackmail?"

"I think there are some valid theories there," Palmer interjected, "But let me go over Jafar's background and hopefully, this should add a little more meat to the bones."

Tanner was busy scribbling down notes, he had one big question he hoped to see answered in the next part of the brief.

Palmer pushed her glasses up from the bridge of her nose, "I'll skip a lot of the irrelevant stuff, but the report is available on your system if you want to delve any deeper. Jafar Abdul Malik, born Abishai Malik, 24 November 1950 at Dr. Sapir Charity Hospital in Tehran, a Jewish hospital now closed. Parents were Jewish, mother died giving birth to Jafar, seeing him raised by his father, who was the local schoolteacher. Jafar was brought up Jewish, but it is believed, he started to move across to Islam during his university days. He did well at school, he is an educated man, and studied at Cambridge University back in the late 1960s early 70's. Achieved a First with distinction in chemistry and physics and went on to do a *master's* in *chemical compounds*. Having completed Uni and converting to Islam, he returned to Iran changing his name to Jafar Abdul Malik, where he was recruited by their government to work within the weapon research programs."

"I'm starting to not like the sound of this." Matty said, his comment mirroring the thoughts of everyone else in the room.

"From there, Jafar seems to drop off the radar until 2003, when he pops up in Iraq during Operation Iraqi Freedom. Again, minimum information during this period, but source reporting and intelligence says he was working as a biochemist in an undisclosed location somewhere near Baghdad." She checked her notes, "He is believed to have been working on Saddam's chemical weapon programme, both build and design. As we know neither NATO or the UN have any true understanding of exactly what was developed and how much of it during that period. When the coalition started to win the war, he scurried back to Iran. Since then, he has kept a low profile, until now." She saw Tanner move in his seat ready to speak. Palmer put her hand up adding with a little sarcasm, "Wait for it." Tanner remained quiet seeing the others smile.

"Jafar's known associates from Iraq... there are a few on the list but the two that came up of interest are, Amooz Karimi, aka the Elder, an engineer born in Iran who now resides in Fujairah," Tanner's ears pricked up, "And Oleg Leonardovich Sokolova, born in Moscow. Not much more than a name at the moment, but that I believe is the Russian link." Palmer sat down, pleased at the impact her words had made on the group.

There was a short period of contemplation.

"Excellent work Palmer," Stones acknowledged, "I think we can all agree that pulls some big pieces together. The brief is available on the system for all to go through in their own time and raise any questions. I'm sure there will be some updated tasking for our Sources. MI6 is pushing the Russian background checks to see if there is any relation with Major Aaron Olegovich Sokolova. The two names probably answer the question, but we need to be sure." He checked his notes, "Let's push everything to see if we can get collaboration on this intelligence. We have a team flying out tonight to set up in Fujairah, their focus will be the Elder, Amooz Karimi, and the link with Jafar and DOTA - and of course, Hunter's death."

Tanner's brain was working overdrive, 'A link to Jafar and Salamander - Jafar is the known leader of a terror group - Hunter's link to Salamander - Jafar now with a link to Fujairah and therefore a potential link to Hunter's death. And now we have a link between Jafar and Russia!'

Tanner had to put the question to the room, "So, why Istanbul?"

Chapter Twenty-Seven

Abishai Malik did not enjoy his early years at Cambridge University. From the beginning, he was made to feel like an outcast due to his Middle Eastern ethnicity. When they found out he was of Iranian descent; he was often scorned on Islamic values and the opposing votes against liberalization laws concerning women. There were many protest groups during the 1960s; everyone had something to scream about. Although he was a Jew with a Jewish name they only saw his Persian skin. Even his fellow Jews shunned him.

Abishai slowly became invisible at the University, minimising any social activities. He worked hard at his studies bringing further disdain from his peers when he excelled.

After receiving a First with a distinction in chemistry and physics, he was at a loss as to what the future would hold.

As time passed, he was approached by two fellow Iranian students he'd never seen before, most likely because he spent most of his time studying in his room.

They introduced him to others, and for the first time since coming to the UK he began to feel a semblance of acceptance.

The summer after he'd finished his degree, he felt he had friends, and often confided in them as to the uncertainty of his future. During this period, one of his fellow Iranians introduced him to an older gentleman, visiting from Iran.

They met in a coffee shop well away from the usual campus areas. He was smartly dressed and openly introduced himself as a member of the Iranian Government. After their meeting, which involved Abishai mostly talking about himself, the gentleman said he would be in touch. A few days later the opportunity presented itself for Abishai to stay and study for a master's in chemical compounds, and it was to be fully funded by the Iranian Government. He would also get an allowance to cover his living expenses. The only clause in the agreement was that on completion, he returned to Iran to work with them.

Abishai didn't need to think long and hard about his decision, he'd intended to return to Iran at some point, now he would have a job waiting for him. A few months prior, the thought of staying longer in Cambridge would have filled Abishai with dread, however with his new friends and Iranian brothers he was no longer alone. For the first time in years, he was enjoying life and he'd accepted the offer.

It was during this period he was introduced to Islam. He'd found solace with his new friends and witnessed how several of them had keenly followed this path. Abishai started to read the Quran and learn the ways of Allah, and the commitment to life, to become an Islamic follower.
He felt this was very much a calling and converted into the brotherhood, becoming a devout Muslim.

Jafar Abdul Malik was born.

After completing his master's, Jafar returned to Iran and started work in the government's weapons research programme. He quickly found he had a natural flare in this arena, and started to take a keen interest in politics, while remaining a passionate Muslim.

Years passed, and his work became more classified. The number of colleagues he worked with dwindled to but a few. In his time there, he'd seen western invaders wage war on neighbouring countries, in what they believed was a just cause. In 2003, when the world turned against Saddam Hussein, another Iraq war had started. With his government's secret support and contacts, he'd travelled to Baghdad.

He was met by more officials, this time Iraqi, and was quickly transported out of Baghdad, which at that time was under regular bombardment by NATO forces.

Moved to a desert location hidden under wind swept dunes, Jafar lived and worked many levels below ground. As a biochemist, he experimented with different chemicals and toxins to make lethal weapons. His work was often frustrated by failure but equally rewarded with success. He had many colleagues that lived and worked as he did in the depths beneath the sand, but the two men he'd worked closely with developed into lifelong friendship... and come the end of their time in dunes, a mutual belief in the word of Allah.

Amooz Karimi - the Elder, was a Muslim and fellow Iranian. Like Jafar, he was an intelligent man, and they shared many common interests, especially in the field of engineering, which worked nicely alongside his skills in chemistry and the development of weapons.

The other was an unlikely relationship.

Oleg Leonardovich Sokolova, was Russian born with an equally bitter taste for the western world, despite the fact his wife was English. Oleg had met her at Oxford. Later she'd moved with him to Moscow where soon after she had given birth to twins. He was a physicist, who'd been working with the Iraqi government's science division. This was an umbrella cover for some undisclosed research methods, a joint venture between Russia and Iraq. Oleg had regular communication with the Federal Security Service, FSB, the new incarnation of the KGB, after it was dissolved in 1991.

The focus of the three men was to develop a modernised weapon variant of the R-400 bomb. There had been attempted use of older variants against American troops back in 1990 during the first Gulf War, Operation Desert Shield.

Unfortunately, the bombs had failed.

Some of these older models had been stored in the deeper levels of their bunker providing hundreds of litres of left over Botulinum toxin - and the three men had formed the perfect team to achieve the goal set before them.

During the time they had worked together, Saddam was overthrown and captured by the close of 2003.

His high-ranking officials in the regime kept the project moving forward, defiant in the eyes of defeat.

By the time Saddam was executed in 2006, fewer orders were being received and people visiting and working in the bunker had started to diminish. They knew it was time to go their separate ways before the facility was uncovered, and they would be held accountable for their involvement.

In late January 2007, Jafar packed his belongings that included several canisters of a Botulinum toxin variant he had been working on. One gram of this particular toxin held the capability to see a million people killed if inhaled.

Before crossing into Iran, the three friends parted ways, but vowed to stay in touch.

Jafar returned to his lab-work, but his years away had changed his outlook. The people he worked with were younger and more of a western persuasion, which made him seethe.

He decided to leave his role, and like his early days slipped away into the background, only this time with a new ambition.

The Disciples of the Afterlife were quietly formed.

Chapter Twenty-Eight

Salamander arrived near the Gürbulak-Bazargan border later that night. After stopping at a local shop to get some food and water he parked the white Peugeot in a secluded corner of a truck stop. He was exhausted.

The emotion of seeing his family - the realisation of the task he had to complete - the long drive - not to mention the tussle with the Englishman in his apartment - all had drained him of energy as events finally caught up with him.

He reflected. Why did the Englishman want him?

Do they think he was responsible for Hunter being killed?

He thought back to the moment the man's gun was pointing at him, he'd thought that was the end, his life over, the mission failed, and his family killed. He shuddered and let out a long yawn. He could barely stay awake.

He hadn't touched his food but gulped down the water. He assumed the border crossing would be quiet so late into the night, and as such, he'd make himself an easier target, more likely to be searched. Tomorrow morning the border should be busier. That would be the time to cross. Climbing over onto the backseat, he pulled a tasselled blanket over himself.

No sooner had he shut his eyes, he was asleep.

Salamander was woken by a truck passing his car as it pulled out of the truck stop. He didn't know how long he had been asleep or what the time was, but the sun was high, and already heating the inside of the car.

It felt like the inside of a greenhouse.

He stretched some of the stiffness out of his body.

He could smell himself, so he opened the rear car door to let the fresh air in and some of him out.

He stretched again, fully this time with no obstructions.

The sky was a bright light blue with not a cloud in the sky. His mouth was parched, his throat dry and he struggled to swallow. He looked at the dash clock, 10:16.

The traffic on the main road had increased into a steady flow. Before he would leave, he'd use the truck stop amenities, freshen up and refuel his body with food and water.

At 11:01 Salamander pulled out of the truck park, turning north onto Route 32 towards the border. He headed into the contraflow lanes toward the checkpoint. He knew once he had filed into them there would be no turning back.

He had friends that had crossed the border before, and it took them hours to get through the laboured, corrupt system. He thought back over their words and on what he should expect. Despite every sense in his body tingling with apprehension and fear, he had to remain calm.

He could not afford to be stopped and searched.

Entering the border area, he approached the first blue and white poled barrier. Armed border control carrying AK-47s stood everywhere - his body was so tense he thought he was about to cramp up. Salamander was waved toward a carpark flagged by large boulders each alternately coloured in blue then white, forming a barrier that surrounded the park.

No way out now.

He followed the multitude; left his car and walked to the small Customs office where he joined a queue. Gripping his fake passport, he tried to take his mind elsewhere, while trying to control his breathing.

After thirty minutes, he was called forward to complete a *barg e voroodi* - entrance paper. The uniformed man at the desk only asked two questions, where was he going, and why? 'If he knew the truth about the last question,' Salamander thought. The officer did not require his passport.

After a few signatures and some enthusiastic ink stamping, he was handed the form and instructed to move to the next part of the process.

Again, following others, he left the customs office and moved to the next building. The office of the Oil Company. When exiting from Iran to Turkey travellers are charged for any fuel held in the vehicle's tank. Salamander could see the going rate was 7200 Rial per litre. Another corrupt setup lining the pockets of someone higher up.

They call this process PETROL.

In the petrol office, he was asked how much fuel he had in his tank. The confusion of the melee all around him had almost put the package in the boot to the back of his mind.

He struggled to remember what the needle said on his fuel gauge, so not wanting to draw attention to himself he overcompensated and told them he had half a tank. They did not check, and Salamander was given an invoice which he paid using the money he'd been given.

Once he had the petrol invoice, he was directed to an entrance of another building, this was the Departure Terminal. Salamander tried desperately to mask his tremble as he handed over his passport, his stamped entrance paper and paid fuel invoice together with the registration plate scrawled on it. The recipient of the paperwork was a uniformed officer with a holstered sidearm. Armed with the registration of Salamander's car, he ambled out towards the vehicle to conduct a check.

Salamander looked at the office door and wanted to run. What would happen if they found the box? What was in the box? He didn't even know himself. This could all turn against him at a frightening pace. 'They won't find it,' he told himself, 'They won't find it.'

From the waiting area, he watched the armed officer approach his vehicle; he was in no rush to carry out his duties. The officer's idle approach was almost unbearable and without realising, Salamander placed his right palm over his heart as if to check it was still beating.

Using the fob, the officer unlocked the car and causally walked around inspecting the exterior. The 'fate maker' then opened the driver's door and sat in the seat.

A whispered prayer left Salamander's lips, recited and repeated, in the hope that God would listen.

The officer was out of the seat as quickly as he'd sat in it. Jumping out, he waved his hand in front of his face, venting his nostrils to see the smell that had just hit him subside.

Salamander could not help but smile at the sight. It had occurred to him the smell of his body odour had soured the inside of the car, along with the cheese baguette he'd bought but had not eaten, which had been slowly cooking in the sun's heat all morning.

Salamander sniffed to check his scent, his smile quickly fading as the officer circled to the rear of the car. The vehicle faced the waiting room window. From where Salamander sat, he could not see the inner of the boot as the lid was swung up.

The officer ducked down and disappeared behind it.

Time stood still, he heard no sound, he was aware of no-one else in the room. Like a blinkered horse his eyes only absorbed one narrow arc of sight, that of the white Peugeot Persia 406 looking back at him. Headlights for eyes, it was as if it came alive in front of him, the grill had started to grin.

He was snapped out of his trance when he saw the boot slammed shut. His heart made an attempt to escape his ribcage, beating harder and harder, in time with every step the officer made towards the office. Pulling open the door, he strode quickly towards Salamander who braced himself for protest. The officer reached him, and without breaking stride, handed the documents with a single command, “Go.”

Salamander felt like he wobbled back to the car, his legs struggling to carry him under the intense inner torture he’d just endured. Collapsing in the driver’s seat not noticing the stench of himself with a hint of cheese, he drove the car out towards the barrier where he had started. The approach this time was welcomed, the bar rising, allowing him to pass underneath.

He drove onto a piece of road that felt like no man's land, the Iranian border sign behind him - the arched Turkish sign with national flags flapping in front of him.

The single line of traffic approaching Turkey started to slow. Ahead there were more border control officers - similar uniforms, only this time the beret had gone from desert kayka to royal blue. He could see they were randomly waving vehicles into a drive-through x-ray machine. The panic returned. Would there be a clear opportunity to just floor it?

Four cars away.

‘If they wave me in, I'll just floor it, and hope there are no barriers.’

Three cars away.

‘They have weapons; surely they won’t be able to engage me quickly enough.’

Two cars.

‘Fuck! Fuck! Fuck!’ He watched a car ahead being waved towards the machine.

One car.

He pulled out the picture of his wife and daughter.

His car.

The Turkish guard raised his arm.

Salamander was waved through beneath the red Turkish border sign. As he entered Turkey he looked to the sky, certain he was being looked down upon by God himself.

*

It was less likely the God Salamander imagined as looking down on him - but a MQ-9 Reaper UAV military drone, navigated from Creech Air Force base in Nevada, by UK/US Joint Forces pilots. Watching from twenty-five thousand feet, its colour/monochrome optical camera had not taken its focus off the vehicle for the last three hours. Its high optical zoom had been searching out car shapes, which were then fed through data recognition software. Any resembling a Peugeot 406 would be highlighted and allow the camera to zoom in enough to be able to read the license plate.

The drone had been on task monitoring the traffic on Route 32 with only a handful of hits, and none of those matching the registration ID. It was only after widening their search away from the main arterial road leading to the border that they saw a white vehicle, which had highlighted itself by being the only car in a truck stop park. The recognition software pinged it as a shape match, and the drone circled to achieve the correct viewpoint. From a range of two miles, the advanced lens zoomed in and read the number plate of the vehicle.

Sitting in a small operations room in Nevada, the drone pilot and co-pilot read back and confirmed with each other the registration… this was the target vehicle.

The next few hours were uneventful. They watched the Zulu eventually move to the border where the car sat being processed - throughout, the Reaper camera rotated under the belly of the drone, never taking the crosshairs off the target.

The last recorded footage was of the vehicle moving off, slowly navigating its way through the border crossing into Turkey. The pilots just had time enough to witness the target pulling over and stopping in Gurbulak, the first Turkish town once Iran was left behind. It was time for the Reaper to return to its undisclosed NATO base for refuel and its next tasking.

It banked high in the sky and disappeared.

*

It had taken three hours of mental and physical torment to cross the border. After entering Turkey, Salamander drove into Gurbulak and pulled over. He let out a huge sigh of relief and even started laughing to himself. He felt he was going mad.

He looked down in his lap at the picture. His wife and daughter looked up at him. He fixed the picture to the dash; he needed to see them as a constant reminder to succeed.

Salamander pulled out the mobile phone and switched it on. Soon he had four bars and the usual sales texts from the provider, Turk Telekom. He thumbed a simple message, 'Across the border,' to the only number in the directory and hit send. He put the phone back in his pocket and turned onto the expressway E80, ready to begin his journey to Istanbul.

*

He was mid-prayer when his mobile phone vibrated.

Jafar paused then continued muttering the words of the 'Salat', the obligatory act of five daily prayers. It vibrated again as he came to the end of his ritual, reminding him of the unread message. He stood and rolled up his *sajadat alsala* prayer mat then walked the room to loosen his legs from their previous kneeling position. His bones were getting old, but he was a devout Muslim, and would continue his prayers through the pain. He picked up his phone and opened the text message.

A callous grin filled his face as he read, 'Across the border.' He had not admitted to anyone how much he feared the border crossing element of his scheme. It could see his careful plans undone with one twist of fate. The toxin had remained undiscovered however and was now continuing its journey.

There was still a long way to go, with potential threats that could scupper his plan, and in that moment, he felt he might well unroll his mat and begin praying again. He had two people whom he needed to inform of the package's progress.

Opening his contacts, he sent a simple message to the person listed as 'Major' and repeated the same message to another. He knew that Major would respond in good time.

The *other* would simply read and delete it...

He never expected a response.

Chapter Twenty-Nine

Major Aaron Olegovich Sokolova, flipped open his phone and received the message, 'Package is in Turkey.' Reading the message warmed him, which was a welcome sensation as he sat in his tent on the outskirts of Latonovo in Rostov, Russia.

He knew his sibling would have received the same message and would be equally pleased. They were close, but geographically at this moment in time, were so far apart.

The Major looked at the message again.

He'd only met the man once but had complete trust in him and in their joint beliefs. His father had talked of Jafar constantly over the years, and Aaron had begun to understand his father's views and calling.

Major Sokolova's father, Oleg Leonardovich Sokolova, had met Jafar when working in Iraq when the Major was still a young boy. Oleg was a scientist for the Soviet, then Russian government with close connections to the FSB.

Oleg had met Aaron's mother while she was studying foreign politics at Oxford University. She was a typical English rose and they'd quickly fallen in love. After graduation, they'd moved to Moscow to be married and soon after, the twins arrived. Aaron remembered a loving, happy childhood growing up with his family.

He was only eleven years old when his father went to work in Iraq. Oleg didn't have a choice, as if he were to refuse, he would end up in prison. Aaron had watched his mother cry for weeks when his father left, as Aaron himself went through months of silent mourning, as indeed had his twin, Max.

They had missed their father.

Years went by when one day his mother brought home and introduced them to a Ukrainian man who was to be lodging with them; it was confusing as to why. It wasn't long before he and Max could hear discreet footsteps at night, then muffled noises of adultery from their mother's room.

After a while, the discretion became less and less until their relationship was completely out in the open.

His mother explained that their father would not return and was no longer welcome. The twins hated this Ukrainian and saw him as the reason they would never see their father again.

The Ukrainian had taken an instant dislike to Aaron and beat him for the smallest of reasons. His mother tried to intervene, and on one occasion received a good lashing from his belt for her troubles. From then on, she turned a blind eye and allowed her son's beatings to continue unchallenged.

The older he became, the harder they became.

Aaron's hate for all Ukrainians festered and grew with each strike. Over the years their father never stopped contact, writing letters to them and via phone calls whenever he could. He was never aware of the abuse, and he was never told, after all, it was the fault of their mother.

Oleg would also visit whenever he was able and Aaron's love for his father had grown ever stronger.

He felt the opposite for his mother. Aaron's misery was her fault; she had broken the vows of marriage preventing their father from returning and seeing their happy life continue.

Before Aaron decided to leave home to start his own life their father had arrived unannounced in Moscow to talk and spend time with his children.

He spoke of his life and of all that had changed over the

years. Aaron remembered how he and Max had both been transfixed, listening without interruption.

Their father touched on the work he'd been doing in Iraq, and more importantly on the man he had met there, Jafar.

He described how before he could leave Iraq to return home, their mother had revealed she had met someone else, and that their marriage was no more, and not to return. He explained how it had almost broken him, how he'd loved their mother with all his heart - but how it was the thought of losing his children to another man that near destroyed his soul.

He told them how he lost focus on his work and his faith in the Russian Orthodox Church, and how he'd contemplated taking his own life.

His friend Jafar had been by his side throughout, supporting him and steering him toward hope. He explained how Jafar was the reason he was sitting before them that day. Jafar had given him a purpose, a reason to live, and rebuild his life. He told them how he had become a Muslim and started to practice the teachings of Allah. They were both taken aback by this admittance, knowing it was not an acceptable practice in Russia, but Aaron loved him so much he didn't care.

Their father continued to talk about when he left Iraq.

At the time, he had already been passing information to the FSB who, he explained, approached him as he reached Istanbul on his journey back to the motherland. They knew about his circumstances and his conversion of faith and informed him that Russia was no longer the place for him.

Instead, they offered an opportunity to work as an FSB operative living in Istanbul. Understanding he did not have a choice he agreed, but only on the proviso he could on occasion return to Russia to see his children.

Aaron Sokolova left home shortly after their father's visit and joined the Russian Army. He quickly found he was made for the lifestyle, enjoying the discipline and the honour of wearing the uniform. Yet his father's words never left him. Their contact became more frequent and inspired by his father, Aaron later followed in his footsteps when secretly he converted to his father Oleg's faith.

Their father passed away just over a year ago and Major Aaron Sokolova had travelled to Istanbul for the *Janazah,* Muslim burial, where he had met Jafar for the first time.

The Major had expressed to Jafar his anger, and that he would avenge his father's death against all Ukrainians.

Jafar sympathised, and they talked more.

Up until now, the Major had kept his religious beliefs hidden, he would never have been promoted to the rank of Major if the truth had been known, and more likely, could have ended up in a barred hell hole. But now he had been abandoned by his superiors and it was time to show them all who he really was, and what he was truly capable of.

Chapter Thirty

A few weeks previously, Major Sokolova and his men, were fighting in the streets of Mariupol, Ukraine.

The Russian invasion had been going well, offering the Major a chance to kill Ukrainian men.

His troops had started to run low on ammunition, and the Russian Federation's lack of replenishment had seen them forced back into Russian territory.

He had voiced his anguish to Jafar, not only losing against the men he hated most but the abandonment of him and his troops by his own country.

Jafar had told the Major of his plan and offered him a role in it, which he did not hesitate in accepting.

The Major and his small group of hardened soldiers were camped outside Latonovo near lake Sarmatskaya. He had formed a base camp with what men he had left, a few disloyal cowards having fled when they crossed back over the Russian border. Those who'd remained he could trust, they were comrades, an elite brotherhood of fighters, willing to carry out their commander's orders without hesitation.

Over the months of bonding and closeness with his men, he had slowly seen their vengeful focus lined with his own… *Death to all of Ukraine.*

They had been abandoned by their Commanders and Chiefs in Moscow and while Putin was losing his game of political chess, they now had the freedom to fight for their cause... In their eyes Moscow had lost the right to give orders the moment they stopped paying and feeding them.

The Major had been giving inspirational speeches daily

about becoming followers of DOTA, and to grab an opportunity that would give them the revenge they craved. Having unquestionable respect, they would happily follow him into any battlefield whether that meant fighting for DOTA or anyone else who would enable them. In truth, most of them didn't care who or what they fought for and certainly couldn't care less about any religious aspect; they just wanted war.

From his tent in Rostov, the Major wondered where his twin would be now. He and Max had met in secret the week previous to discuss the finer details of the planned attack they had composed with Jafar.

Max should by now be waiting for the delivery in Istanbul and should have received the same good news message from Jafar. Leaving his tent, he decided to make the announcement to his troops. The weapon was on its way.

Chapter Thirty-One

Palmer sat with Tanner at Hunter's old desk watching the live feed of the Reaper drone currently on task. When they started, Tanner wasn't hopeful, thinking the possibility of finding the vehicle was a million to one. But sure enough, when the image on the screen zoomed in to show the number plate, Tanner couldn't believe his eyes. He had called out to the others, and they gathered around the screen for a moment to watch what little was happening before forcing themselves away and returning to their workloads.

As they watched the car cross into Turkey, they hoped this offered confirmation that Salamander was indeed heading to Istanbul. The question remained... Why?

A couple of hours after the drone movie had finished, the Hub door opened, and Stones stepped in, asking Tanner and Palmer to his office.

Stones' workspace was the opposite end of the décor spectrum when compared to that of the Boss back in the UK. There was no lavish old school furniture, no comforts or personal touches. Then again, when you are only on tour for 6 months before returning home, why bother? The furniture was standard Ministry of Defence bulk buy. The same style furnished every office and meeting room the MoD owned around the globe.

Tanner and Palmer sat opposite Stones who tapped at the keyboard on his desk entering his user ID and password before the screen unveiled its secrets.

Palmer sat back, notepad at the ready.

"So, we have had an updated intelligence report from MI6,

and I have also received a separate secure email from Edward Boden." Stones began.

"Oh, you mean Ed?"

Tanner's sarcastic over-familiarisation received an upward glance from Stones before he continued, "The intelligence suggests Major Aaron Olegovich Sokolova, is the son of Jafar Malik's associate, Oleg Leonardovich Sokolova. Oleg died just over a year ago at his home in Istanbul. When he left Iraq, he became an operative for the FSB and spent the rest of his life working out of Turkey. At some point, he converted to Islam and his relationship with Jafar Malik continued. Married once. Children, twins, Major Sokolova as we now know, and the other sibling according to records died at birth."

Palmer was busy scribbling when Tanner spoke, "So they have confirmed the Russian link, and tied in a relationship with Jafar and DOTA?"

"Indeed," Stones replied, "There is more. GCHQ has been monitoring mobile phone activity in the three key areas of interest for us. Tehran, Istanbul, and southern Russia near the Ukraine border. An MI6 agent has confirmed this is where the Major is located. They also picked up Jafar Malik's mobile, sending text messages earlier today. The location he sent them from confirms that he is currently in his known compound in Tehran. The collection of data shows the messages were received, one in Latonovo, Russia, where Major Sokolova is reported to be, the other is in central Istanbul."

"That strengthens the link," Palmer surmised, "That something is happening between Jafar and the Major."

"'There can only be two reasons Salamander has gone to Istanbul," Tanner suggested, "To deliver, or to collect something? The fact that message was sent from Jafar after Salamander crossed the border is too much of a coincidence."

"Are we saying Salamander is delivering something to someone and this has the potential to end up in the hands of the Major in Russia?" Stones questioned.

"Possible," Tanner replied thoughtfully, "But what?"

Palmer looked up from her pad, "So, we have a chemist in Tehran, Jafar. A physicist in Istanbul, Oleg, who is now dead and was FSB. Both had worked together on the development of weapons, both follow the same faith, and possibly Oleg was part of the extremist group DOTA, which Jafar leads."

"And according to Ed," Tanner interjected, "Jafar's link with the Russian was an opportunity to make a big statement for DOTA, and that Oleg's son, Major Sokolova and his men were seriously disgruntled and looking for payback."

"Are we all thinking the same thing right now?" Stones looked to each of them, "Not only could this package be a weapon, but that Salamander is delivering it on behalf of Jafar, and there appears to be a very credible possibility this could be a biological weapon!"

Palmer put her pen down and looked at Tanner, then back to Stones, the three of them considering the potential nightmare just uncovered.

*

Tanner and Palmer returned to the rest of the team to update them on the potential theory, that a biological weapon was likely heading to an unknown personality in Russia.

Stones got on the hotline to Whitehall and Ed Boden,

briefing the collective conclusion with the intel to back it up.

It was clear from the responses the powers that be supported the theory.

Stones called Tanner back into his office.

"I've briefed London on everything, and they agree we have a strong reason to be concerned. London will back our decision that a biological weapon could well be in play."

Tanner sat in silence to Stone's grave update.

"Tanner, you've been tasked to get yourself to Istanbul as quickly as possible. Track down Salamander, intercept the weapon before it can reach its final destination. We need to know what's happening in Istanbul. You are booked on a flight early tomorrow morning, so get your kit together."

"Where do I even start when I get there?"

"Mr Boden said his agent arrived in Istanbul a few days ago and will meet you at the airport when you arrive. They will supply you with any weapons you'll need."

Tanner questioned, "I thought that agent was in Russia?"

"The last report sent from the MI6 agent was that Major Sokolova is still in Latonovo. The Major and his men seem to be sitting around, waiting for further orders from Moscow. So, the agent has been relocated to Turkey to follow this next lead. The agent will update you when you get there."

Tanner was frustrated, a bioweapon on the loose and only half arsed intel to work with from the Firm.

"London cannot conduct an air strike. If this is biological a strike could potentially release whatever they are planning on using and cause mass fatalities. It would be looked upon as an act of war. You're on your own this time. Find Salamander Tanner. The clock is ticking."

Chapter Thirty-Two

Salamander approached the outskirts of Istanbul early in the morning, before the rush hour traffic.

He was travelling on the E80 coastal expressway. It was a glorious day as he looked out over the Gulf of Izmit.

Crystal blue waters stretched for miles, the sun glistening off the lazy swell. The sea air blew into his face through the open window and even though he was exhausted and scared he felt a surreal moment of calm wash over him.

He had read about this beautiful city and shown his daughter pictures from a book a few years ago. He would like to bring her here one day. He looked at her face smiling back at him from the photo on the dash.

Istanbul was scattered with mosques, colourful mosaics, and dramatic architecture. It was also the home to the Hagia Sophia, that once featured as one of the modern wonders of the world. He turned northeast towards the city centre, but not before admiring the Osmangazi Bridge. He'd never seen a suspension bridge, and its magnitude as it spanned the Gulf of İzmit was quite a sight. He bypassed the area of Gebze to the south of Istanbul and was soon passing the turn-offs for Sabiha Gokcen Airport. He looked for a rest stop to replenish before contacting Jafar and waiting for his next orders. He finally pulled over after passing the airport and edging closer to the city. Parking the car, he got out and leaned against the bonnet, admiring the beautiful silhouette of Istanbul's skyline outlined in monumental minarets with skyscrapers and plazas.

He took several gulps of water and pulled out his mobile phone. He sent the simple text, 'In Istanbul,' then waited.

Chapter Thirty-Three

Tanner's morning flight to Istanbul landed at 0705 hours.

With no baggage to collect from the hold he moved swiftly through passport control and customs.

Stepping out from the cool air-conditioned building, the early morning sun met his skin with a pleasant warmth.

He stood outside in the pickup area, not knowing who was meeting him. He imagined some stuffy man in a suit with a degree in Russian politics, a typical Firm recruit.

Tanner was thinking about what Stones had said, 'You're on your own.' Watching each car pass through the pickup zone, Tanner faced the oncoming traffic, making himself visible to anyone looking specifically to collect him, while utilising the concrete pillar behind him to remain out of the public eye.

An unassuming white Renault Clio came toward him with tinted windows and new registration. Pulling abruptly up to the curb, the electric window slid down and an attractive woman looked at him. "Tanner?"

He nodded.

"Get in." she said, with a Russian accent.

He slung his rucksack on the back seat then climbed in.

No sooner had he closed the door, she engaged first gear and sped off without even glancing his way, her eyes remaining fixed on the road. "I'm Nina, I work for Ed."

"Frank Tanner, nice to meet you." Tanner felt himself staring, not quite the stuffy suit he was expecting. Nina was intriguingly attractive, with long dark hair tied in a high ponytail, exposing her features. She had a brush of paleness to her skin - he thought she must stem from the eastern bloc, but as she was MI6, with some British heritage. She looked at him, her blue eyes piercing, “Cat got your tongue?”

He’d been caught. “No,” he said with a smile, “You're, just not what I was expecting.”

“Let me guess, a man in a suit?” her accent was more Russian than he would have expected.

He smiled looking out the window, “So does Nina have a last name?”

“Just Nina.”

“Whereabouts in the UK are you from, I wasn't expecting a Russian accent?”

“Why? Do you want to send me a postcard from Istanbul?”

“Just making conversation. How long have you worked for the Firm?"

“You ask a lot of questions Mr Tanner.”

“Please, let's drop the formalities.” He was still smiling. Her expression was yet to change, no smile, no emotion, just a hardened edge to it. Tanner pressed, “Where are we going?”

“I have rented a small apartment in the centre. It's nothing special but we can keep a low profile, and it's a good location to move around the city. We can back brief each other when we get there, I have some equipment for you too.”

“Thanks.” His smile remained.

“And for your information Tanner. My Russian accent is kind of a necessity where I work.”

They drove in silence from then on, until they reached the apartment.

Chapter Thirty-Four

Salamander didn't have to wait long to receive a reply from Jafar… 'Max will contact you.' He was thinking of asking how his wife and daughter were, but he thought better of it.

The last thing he wanted was to make Jafar angry.

He didn't know how long he'd be waiting, so he bought some food and returned to the car. He sprawled on the back seat with the windows open to allow the breeze in and his odour out. As he tried to rest, he couldn't help but wonder about the violet-coloured liquid Jafar had shown him, now held in a box in the boot. Temptation got the better of him to take another look at it, and he took himself to the rear of the vehicle and began removing the bags of clothes. He lifted the carpet exposing the hidden compartment. He'd parked out of view under the shade of some trees, but still he looked all around him until happy there were no prying eyes. He took the screwdriver that had been left in the boot to remove the compartment cover until he could see the sealed crate.

He stared at it nervously. Would they know if it had been tampered with? He only wanted to look. Would his curiosity further endanger his family? He sat on the edge of the boot churning over the temptation.

It was then his mobile phone came back to life, startling him. He removed it and opened the message.

'Meet me at the following address. I'll be waiting. Max.'

The tone felt cold - he didn't like it.

He turned and looked down at the crate again, then replaced the cover and pulled the clothes back across the boot… thinking better of it.

Chapter Thirty-Five

The city flashed through Tanner's senses as they drove.

Located on both sides of the Bosphorus, Istanbul was the congested strait between the Black and the Marmara Sea, bridging Asia and Europe both physically and culturally.

They arrived at the apartment on the eastern side of the Ümraniye district. Nina managed to park a few car lengths down from the entrance lobby. It was a narrow street, with a steady bustle of people and traders working, with a few cafes and small businesses dotted on either side of the road.

Tanner understood her choice of location, enough going on that people wouldn't be interested in you, but quiet enough to get in and out quickly.

The building was five storeys high with each floor housing four small apartments. The outside walls were rendered in a sandy yellow which looked brighter than it should in the sun. All the windows had been updated and the entrance door was a large block of mahogany.

They pushed the heavy door to go inside. The lobby was clean, the floor decorated in traditional Turkish mosaic tiles of woven red and blue patterns. No one else was around.

Tanner knew Nina had similar training to him, she would never have rented on the ground floor. Too much opportunity for unwanted visitors to come through the windows. They climbed the two flights of stone stairs and moved towards the front, left-hand side apartment, which looked over the street.

She opened the door and walked in front of him.

Her initial reaction was to go to the front window and watch the street both ways. Looking for anyone or thing that might be out of the ordinary.

It was a small but tidy apartment, with an open plan kitchen-lounge area, bathroom, and two bedrooms, a single and a double. He could already see where she had been sleeping, so the single room was for him. He took his rucksack off and dropped it in an armchair.

"Our cover story... We are a couple on a romantic getaway. The story stops when we enter this apartment. Yours is that room." She indicated the single bed.

Emotionally she was very cold, clinical almost. Tanner smiled at her and sat down, "So, are you going to update me on what you know so far?"

"Probably the same as you. Ed has briefed me on your side and you mine."

Tanner could tell this was going to be hard work, "I feel we might have got off on the wrong foot. I was of the understanding we are here to help each other - and try to find my source Salamander, agreed?"

She remained quiet for a moment, "Agreed," she said. Sitting on the sofa opposite, she crossed her legs. She looked good and Tanner's mind began to wander - she was athletic, strong but not overly muscular. She wore a black leather jacket over a white blouse, transparent enough for him to see a sports bra underneath. Tight black denim-style trousers and white trainers. Casual but ready to react if a situation arose.

"So, what can you tell me about this Salamander?"

Tanner spent the next fifteen minutes updating her on all he knew.

"And do you know who he is meeting, or where?" Her Russian drawl was almost soothing.

"No. That's the hard part. We know he is travelling here, and when he left the Iranian border - he should be arriving anytime now, if he isn't here already."

"I am waiting for a GCHQ update. Hopeful we can get a ping to give us a rough area to start with." She informed.

"Can you tell me more about this Russian Major?"

Nina's phone vibrated, and she quickly responded.

"Updates?" Tanner questioned.

"No. I have sources here in Istanbul, I have them working out and about. They are looking for the car registration of your source. Hopefully, we will have a bit of luck, and it will be spotted." Her tone remained curt.

Tanner knew not to ask about other agencies' sources. They would never be revealed, as he would protect his own.

"The Major?" he questioned again.

Nina back briefed Tanner, informing him she had been running out of Latonovo. She told him it was common knowledge the Major and his men were camped on the outskirts, but nothing seemed to point in their direction, certainly not to be receiving a biological weapon or making such a statement.

Tanner hadn't learned much more than he had already, but she seemed to soften a little as they talked, the harsh edge gradually leaving her voice.

She was a professional and he respected that.

"So, what's the plan?" Tanner asked.

"I must meet a few of my sources. You're free to do what you need to do. I'll be a few hours. Shall we meet back here around 1500hrs? In the meantime, if I get anything new, I can call you."

“Sounds good, I'm going to have a look around and try and work some leads.”

They exchanged numbers and she handed him a key to the door. As she headed out, she turned in the short hallway, “There is a case under your bed, I choose a few weapons for you. I hope you like them.” For the first time she showed a slight smile, then she was gone.

Chapter Thirty-Six

Max had been waiting thirty minutes in a secure single room dwelling in Gülsuyu, a neighbourhood in Maltepe district, a slum part of Istanbul. The streets were a maze of washing-lined alleyways and desolate houses, occupied by the wrong sorts of people. Max felt comfortable in these types of areas, easy to disappear once you understood the networks.

Law and order were kept in check by the residents themselves with crime the largest employer. Reputation is survival on such streets, and even though Max's European features stood out in this Asian side of the city it was of no consequence. Max was known by the pockets of Russian mafia operating the area to be armed - with FSB connections, and as such was left well alone. Max was a ghost.

Max went over the next stages of the plan - to get the complete package to Major Aaron Sokolova, Max's twin brother. Whilst waiting for Salamander, memories kept repeating of their father, and the promise Jafar was helping them unleash upon the Ukrainian people.

A rare smile spread across Max's face.

Max's only concern was the intelligence received in the last twenty-four hours of a British military intelligence operator coming to Istanbul, looking to find Salamander and potentially disrupting their plan. The boss had called with the information, he didn't say much, but he did send a picture, always good to know who to look for. Aaron had been informed - he trusted Max to deal with it. An eye was to be kept on this situation.

Lethal force would only be used as a last resort.

The British were already reeling at the murder of one of

their Intelligence operatives, to add to another to the list would bring far too much unwanted attention.

Max looked at the time then to the blanket on the table that hid the mechanical part of their weapon.

He should be here soon with the final pieces, courtesy of Jafar on behalf of DOTA. Max wasn't a disciple… but was certainly a follower of Aaron.

*

As Salamander drove into the Maltepe district it felt strangely similar to where he had grown up. He'd purchased a street map earlier when receiving the text message from Max and found where he needed to be.

He cautiously drove down a cobbled street, scattered with litter, looking for the identifications scrawled on the fronts of buildings in flaked paint or faded chalk, until he found the numerical value that matched the one he'd been sent.

There were a few other cars on the street, so he didn't look too out of place. The only difference was his Iranian registration plate which had received a few glances from some unsavoury looking groups of men huddled in doorways.

He was anxious and he didn't know what to expect.

He looked at his photo and pulled it off the dash and into his pocket, "I'll soon be back with you both," he muttered as if they could hear him.

He exited the vehicle, trying to look as casual as he could. He retrieved the wooded box from the boot.

An old woman in a headscarf waylaid him from the opposite side of the street, sticking out her hand and muttering something about a fee. She sat in front of a reinforced door, with a vicious looking guard dog that initially barked then sat by her obediently. She was a Muslim, for whom dogs are *haram*, forbidden. From what he'd seen, Gülsuyu seemed like a dangerous neighbourhood, and it appeared she was at ease in breaking a few rules.

Salamander made his way up the external stone steps between two grey block buildings, to the first floor.

Heading along an open walkway to the rear of the building, he read the door numbers. There were metal railings to his right preventing a fall to the corrugated metal roof below.

Doors and windows looked in disrepair.

Looking across the slum town rooftops, his view was of the cluttered living these people endured.

He had it better in Tehran.

Reaching his destination, he noted the curtains were drawn. He paused, 'What awaits me on the other side of this door?'

He jumped suddenly, as a 'whacking' noise came from behind him. He turned quickly to see a lady, hitting the dust out of a carpet over a clothesline a couple of rooftops over.

He turned to face the door.

It opened without him knocking.

Chapter Thirty-Seven

Max watched via a small monitor as the nervous character walked along the balcony towards the door. The discreet camera had been installed to watch for any approach - it was the final apartment at the end of the walkway, so there could be only one reason for anyone to travel this far.

He was carrying a wooden crate and Max felt a flutter of excitement. Right hand on the grip of the pistol tucked into the rear waistline, Max opened the door before the man had even had chance to knock.

There was more for this man to do, orders from Jafar that the Iranian was yet unaware of. Jafar was a ruthless man, but it was a necessity to achieve his goals for DOTA.

"Come in." Max was blunt, "Stand there."

Salamander stepped across the threshold and did as he was told. The door closed behind him, followed by the clunks of several locks. His contact proceeded to pat him down checking for weapons or wires.

"Put the box on the table, and sit over there," Max indicated to a chair at the far side of the room.

Salamander recognised the accent as Russian; it was direct, calm and calculated, this one also had an air of *don't fuck with me* to it that sent a chill down his spine. He did as he was told and watched as the package was inspected.

Max pulled out a combat knife and gently pried open the tacks that held the outer lid in place, before setting to work on the screws of the inner packaging. With the pieces set aside, the two glass containers filled with Botulinum toxin were revealed, like the opening of Pandora's Box.

Salamander watched as Max moved further along the table to remove a blanket revealing two metallic coloured boxes with a slight sheen. The boxes were riveted along the edges and corners, and small black nozzles protruded from the centre of each side. 'What the hell am I involved in?'

The lids of the two metallic boxes were detached. Max carefully removed each glass container of toxin and placed them, one at a time, in each of the boxes. Reaching inside, Max secured them in place with a stainless-steel strap.

Stepping back, Max gazed at the lethal creation and smiled.

Max looked at Salamander, "Would you like to see a part of what will soon become history?" waving him over. Salamander stood nervously, and walked across to the table, not breaking eye contact with the grinning menace standing before him. He looked down into the metal boxes. Within them, a tubular frame was welded to the inside edge, the glass-cylinders containing the violet liquid, held in place by a retaining strap. At the neck of the cylinder, a silver cap held the dangerous liquid at bay. In front of the cap a pointed instrument was located and primed, waiting to pierce it - its mechanism hidden within the black box to one end. Housed on the topside of the inner black box, was a digital read-out, currently not powered, with a nine-digit keypad located beneath it. Wrapped in a thick blue film, was a battery pack, with wires peeking out from the edges. Entwined amongst the inners was a network of pipes that connected to each of the black nozzles. It looked professional, and deadly, like something seen in a movie. He was certainly involved in something that was way beyond his rationale.

Salamander remained silent and took a step back.

"Do you know what you are looking at?" Max asked. Salamander's silence spoke volumes. "It's a statement, a message, a game changer. It is a biological weapon, filled with Botulinum toxin."

"I don't want to know." Salamander shook his head while staring at the deadly creation.

"Well, you have played an integral part in completing these bombs, so sit back in the chair, and listen carefully."

Salamander did not argue, he returned to his seat feeling numb, his body heavy with the reality of the current situation.

Over the next few minutes, Max spoke about the fatal effects of the toxin, and the part Salamander had just played in weaponizing it... But he didn't listen, he was in another place far away from this one.

Max explained how Botulinum toxins were one of the most lethal substances known, and when released into the atmosphere via an aerosol or bioweapon, the toxin will quickly contaminate food and water supplies - and that following inhalation of the toxin, symptoms would become visible in the first three days, with a long painful death to follow.

Max described how Botulinum toxins would block nerve functions and lead to respiratory and muscular paralysis. How others exposed to the substance could die from infections or problems caused by being paralyzed for weeks or months. Max said this was their revenge on the Ukrainians that stole their father from them and ruined their lives - as well as DOTA's message to the western infidels.

Max didn't seem to care whether Salamander was listening or not adding finally, "Pretty fucking nasty way to die." The dark chuckle that followed broke through Salamander's daze.

He looked into Max's eyes, cold and vengeful.

He could see death in them.

"I need to go, I've done what I had to, I'm going to return to my family." Salamander stood up to leave but was quickly halted by the gun drawn and pressed at his forehead.

"I encourage you to sit back down." the voice was calm and deadly, the hammer thumbed back, the pistol cocked.

He felt increased pressure from the barrel pushing him backward and thought he was going to soil himself standing right there.

Chapter Thirty-Eight

Tanner opened the toughened grey peli-case.

Inside the moulded egg-box-like foam was a selection of weapons. First, he took out the Sig Sauer P229 9mm compact pistol. It came with an additional four magazines together with various belt holsters for the weapon. As the handgun of choice prior to the Glock 19, it was a weapon Tanner was familiar with. Next was a Russian SR-3 Vikhr whirlwind. A gas operated, compact assault rifle, used by the FSB and private bodyguards across the eastern bloc - it was capable of firing in semi-auto and full-auto modes, with a twenty-round magazine capacity. Its simple iron sights with settings for one or two hundred metres and fold over buttstock, meant the weapon could easily be hidden on one's person.

Tanner was impressed with the selection. It couldn't have been easy to get the weapons at such short notice.

While she was out, he tried to figure out how the weapon they were hunting was going to be smuggled out of Istanbul. He'd laid a complete street map of the city across the table and set to work looking at options. If he had to get a biological weapon from here to Russia, how would he do it?

Neither of the airports would be viable options. Security would pick the weapon up too easily, the risk simply too great.

Both the train and driving options would not be workable. It would take too long, and the train is too public to transport such a weapon. It then struck him, the truth of it staring Tanner in the face... across the Black Sea into Russia.

The Black Sea was so vast, it could easily allow a smuggler to disappear until reaching a chosen destination. It would be the safest most discreet way.

He studied the map further, identifying what options there were to leave Istanbul by sea. There were plenty of marinas with yachts and motor cruises, mostly on the European side. Would that be too public he thought? Would a boat like that attract attention arriving in Russia? No ferries headed in that direction, and passing through customs would be a high risk.

"What would I do?" The words floated from his lips as he tapped his finger against them. Tanner pulled out his secure phone, scrolled through his contacts and pressed call on the one he hoped would have the answer.

It rang once before it was picked up.

"Hello, Operator, how can I help?" Palmer said.

"It's me."

"Hi, how's the holiday with your new girlfriend?"

"How did you know?"

"Word gets round. I could tell you, but I'd have to kill you." Palmer laughed.

"You're just jealous I'm on vacation."

"How can I help?" She was straight back to business.

"If I wanted to cross the Black Sea discreetly from Istanbul, what options have I got?"

"I take it you have looked at marinas and ferry terminals?"

"I have, but none of them are workable."

"Checking now." Tanner could hear the rapid tapping of a computer keyboard. Within a minute she was back.

"Ok, looking at the type of sea traffic in the Black Sea, and considering similar types of ports both where you are and where I believe you are thinking of reaching... The best most discreet way would be by a Fishing Vessel. Fleets are running out of the Beykoz district. I'm sure there are some shady fishermen looking to make a quick buck."

"Thanks, I think you just nailed it. I'll be in touch." He hung up. Tanner started looking for fishing ports in Beykoz, his research landing on the commercial fishing port of Gümüşsuyu. Tanner felt confident, "This is where I would choose." He said aloud.

He holstered the pistol and grabbed his coat.

Before leaving the apartment, he circled the fishing port on the map for Nina to see.

Chapter Thirty-Nine

The dimly lit room felt like a frost had taken hold when Max delivered further orders from Jafar. The accent that recited Jafar's words added extra weight that felt like a knife being plunged and twisted into his heart. Salamander's next orders were to personally take the two biological weapons to Russia, where he would be met by another contact.

Max could see how each word tore into Salamander's flesh, seeing all hope disappear from his eyes. He broke down into uncontrollable tears, reciting, what Max could only assume, were his wife and daughter's names.

He slumped on the floor, his head in his arms that rested on the seat of the chair.

What a pathetic man.

Max had no time for weak people, it was survival of the fittest in the real world. It was clear why these types of men got used, they allowed themselves to be manipulated and threatened. No dignity. No balls.

Salamander felt the kick to his backside and the words, “Shut up!” He wiped his eyes and looked up, trying to take a grasp of his emotions. It had been made clear, his family would pay the price if he chose not to carry out the next task or tried to disrupt the plan.

This was emphasized by the weapon in Max's hand pointing at him, and the invitation to end his pathetic life right there and then. He could feel it inside of him. The last single thread of hope. He reached into his soul and held it tight, what choice did he have.

When composed, Max had given Salamander a change of

western clothes that would help him blend in during the next phase of his journey. He was given a map highlighting his route to the next location and where he was to park the car.

He was told to study the route while Max placed the weapons inside two large, dark blue sports holdalls.

Salamander was then told he would be travelling to Russia across the Black Sea, on a fishing vessel. He had never been on a boat before let alone travelled across a sea.

Max gave him the name of the vessel, and the location of the port he would find it. Salamander struggled to pronounce the Russian boat name and growing frustrated, Max gave up with the pronunciation and instead wrote it on the map for him. Max then passed over the holdalls while reminding Salamander how the lives of his wife and daughter depended on the delivery of the weapons.

It was not needed.

*

Max watched Salamander on the camera fed monitor, walking defeated, back up the walkway towards his car.

'He is the weak link in the plan,' the thought repeated in Max's mind as a text was sent to update the two other people in the loop, 'Package complete. Courier re-tasked. Leaving today.' It was time for the next stage to ensure the bags arrived onboard the boat, Max's personal addition to the plan.

Max headed out to the rear of the building, hopping over a wall, and cutting through a couple of alleyways to reach the car parked a few streets over.

Once inside, Max was soon gunning down the street to get

ahead of Salamander. Max was taking no chances and needed to make the overwatch position of a chosen rooftop - from there Max could watch and ensure the wretched man delivered himself and the bags aboard the fishing vessel.

A safety net to ensure nothing could go wrong.

Thirty minutes later Max parked on a quiet back road.

Removing a black rucksack from the boot Max made the short walk to the metal fire escape at the back of the restaurant. Max swiftly climbed the five floors of the external zig-zag staircase to reach the flat rooftop - Max had recce'd the area a few days prior - it was the highest building around, perfect for no one overlooking while offering a good vantage point that met the needs of its secondary purpose.

The rooftop was empty, except for a rusted block of white air conditioning units that hummed incessantly. The sun had been up a while now and the rooftop surface was hot.

Moving over to the east side of the roof first, Max looked over to see if the targeted area was still visible. Clear.

Opening the rucksack, Max removed the six parts of a *Valkyrie concealable-backpack precision-sniper rifle,* placing each element neatly down on the surface.

Max extended the stock out of the main body before removing the protective cap. With the barrel screwed into place, the free-floating *forend* was slid over and locked into position, and the bipod attached to the belly. Once resting on the bi-pod legs, the suppressor was wound onto the end of the barrel in order to make the shot close to silent.

Lastly, the bolt was slid into place and the ten-round magazine pushed home.

The single round bolt action rifle was ready for action.

Max loved this weapon, it was compact, accurate and no tools were needed to put it together. Looking through the Sniper Tactical 4X32 RGB fibre optic scope, already attached and zeroed, Max rested the legs onto the roof edge and scanned the area Salamander was instructed to park the car. Max surveyed for any abnormalities before resting the red dot on various unaware members of the public. Max adjusted the scope allowing for the slight breeze.

As Max waited, the heat of the sun beat mercilessly down.

Twenty minutes later, Salamander's car pulled into the street where he was instructed to park, unaware he was in the crosshairs of a killer.

*

Salamander pulled into the street as his map instructed.

He found a spot at the side of the road and parked between two other vehicles. He sat in the car for a few minutes, contemplating what was to come next. The question ate at him, 'Once aboard the boat, would he ever see home again?'

He checked his pocket for the photograph, feeling it through the material, he rested his hand upon it. He took in a deep breath as if to fill himself with air, to help him rise out of the seat. He got out, leaving the keys in the ignition, removing the two blue sports holdalls from the rear seats.

The bags felt heavy. Holding one in each arm, he could feel the awkward shapes knocking against his legs as he walked.

He had memorised the route to the fishing port.

When he reached the end of the block, he turned left to see the open square a few hundred yards away, across from which was the water's edge and several commercial boats.

*

Max watched Salamander waddle down the road in his new western clothes. He looked like he was struggling with the weight of the bags. As he turned left and out of shot, Max moved to vantage point number two on the northwest corner of the rooftop. From here the street opened onto the square. Through the scope, Max scanned the open spaces and exteriors, before resting on where the fishing vessel was moored. All good.

Max turned the focus back to the street just as Salamander strolled into the crosshairs once more.

*

The weight of the bags was starting to stretch Salamander's arms and his hands started to pulsate. He walked across the square towards the harbour. The area was saturated with little cafes and restaurants and the occasional boutique shop selling traditional Turkish goods to tourists.

He longed to be at one of those outside tables with his wife and daughter, enjoying food, smiling, and laughing.

He approached the harbour and walked down the floating gangway. The tide was high.

As Max had said, there was no security to stop him. 'Perhaps the security was also on the DOTA payroll?'

He walked further along the dock until reaching jetty number four, that extended further out into the water.

The fishing vessel would be near the end.

As he passed each boat, he checked the names until he recognised the one he was looking for, KALINOVKA.

The trawler's name was painted in white on a black background representing the shape of a plaque. The top half of the hull was painted green, its' belly white, in depiction of the vessel's name - *Kalinovka* being *Snowball Tree Village* - in Russian. Patches of rust ran from wherever a piece of metal was attached to the body. A row of white and blue fenders hung unevenly along the side, occasionally squeezed, as the weight of the boat pushed against the jetty.

To Salamander, the boat resembled a floating scrap yard, piled with chains, ropes, and nets.

The smell of fish was not a welcoming one.

The bridge stood tall in the middle of the boat with windows surrounding all sides. A dirty man in a white roll neck jumper and cigar hanging from his mouth, stood in the bridge doorway - the captain. "Max?" he asked.

Salamander nodded and was waved onboard.

The gangway was narrow and difficult to walk up with the two bags. Does the captain know what he had brought on board? The man met him as he reached the top and showed him to a small double bunk cabin towards the aft end in the bows of the vessel, next to the engine room. He was told his bags would be safe and they were departing in four hours.

Salamander was informed if he wanted any food or drink for the trip, it might be an idea to provide his own, as the chef would be whoever could be bothered at any given time. He was then given the one rule whilst onboard, once they slipped, he was to remain out of the crew's way, it was a working vessel and their livelihoods depended on it.

The captain walked him back up to the top deck and indicated back to the square where the shops would be. Salamander didn't need to be asked twice.

He got the feeling they didn't want him in the way.

In truth, Salamander didn't leave the boat for the want of food, he just didn't want to be around the horror of the chemical weapons that now dwelled in the bowels of the trawler. The boat also felt cramped and dirty, forever tainted by the smell of the sea.

He walked back into the square and headed for the street. He remembered seeing a convenience store earlier.

Halfway across the square however, Salamander froze.

Chapter Forty

After seeing Salamander board the Kalinovka before disappearing with the bags below decks, Max remained in overwatch, scanning the area and its populace through the scope. The little girl, crying where she had dropped her ice cream while the mother reprimanded her. A tourist taking a picture of his wife with the harbour at her rear. They looked overfed on the good life. Americans came to mind.

Max moved the focal point back to the fishing vessel, only to pick up Salamander now walking along the jetty away from the vessel. 'What the fuck is he doing?'

Max swallowed the anger and followed him wanting to pull the trigger but knowing the consequences.

The scope tracked him as he casually bimbled back to the square as if he had no care in the world. 'He's left the bags!'

Max made the noise of the gun going off pretending to shoot the insolent fucker.

Suddenly, Salamander disappeared out of the optical glass. Max tracked back a fraction and there he was, standing still like a mannequin as if he had seen a ghost.

Max swung the rifle in the direction he was looking, scanning the faces on the far side of the square…

It wasn't long before one of the faces stood out.

Chapter Forty-One

Tanner had flagged down a taxi from the apartment to Gümüşsuyu. He had the driver pull over a couple of streets away from the square to complete the remainder of the route on foot using his phone's map. He didn't want to announce his presence by arriving in a bright yellow car with 'TAKSi' emblazoned on its roof. He also wanted to get a feel for the place, before walking into his predicted target area.

Time to compose himself.

The streets were of medium density made up of locals and tourists. The area appeared for the most part to be pedestrianised with only limited vehicles permitted.

Cobbled roads such as these added to the old-world charm of the Asian side of Istanbul.

The buildings on either side were tall enough to keep the street in the shade making it a welcome break for those seeking shelter from the warm air and hot sun.

Tanner walked slowly down the street taking in his surroundings. He could see the long street ahead opening into the square. The street was bustling with shops, with stalls set up outside selling tourist gizzits, books and paintings. The buildings were painted alternatively in bright colours, adding to the attractive scene. Peppered between the shops were cafes and restaurants their menus bright with local dishes. Each eatery had an outside dining area, protected by a canopy of various shades and patterns. In different circumstances, Tanner thought he could enjoy a stay here.

He approached the open square.

As he crossed into it, he stood strategically taking in the

makeup of the area. More of the shops, cafes, and parasols circled the entirety of the square, allowing paying customers to choose their view. Further afield, the Bosphorus stretched out like a turquoise carpet across to the European side. Tanner scanned the faces as they presented themselves when he had a strange sensation. He felt a set of eyes burning on him.

Looking across the square it soon became apparent, as Tanner's eyes met those of the needle in a haystack.

Salamander was no longer in his traditional clothes and carrying no packages. Where was the weapon?

Salamander's look spoke volumes. He didn't need a voice, his mouth dropping in utter shock upon seeing Tanner.

'The fucker is not getting away this time!' Tanner instinctively moved to draw his Sig pistol but held off, taking in how public the location was, while officially, he shouldn't even be operating there. Tanner made a step forward seeing Salamander bolt toward the opposite side of the square where the road led up alongside the Bosphorus Strait.

Tanner gave chase.

Chapter Forty-Two

Salamander was dumbstruck - of all the places in the world, the man he'd escaped at his home in Tehran was now standing three hundred yards away, staring directly at him.

He realised he had held the stare too long; he should have put his head down and kept walking as soon as he saw him, but he'd assumed his eyes were deceiving him.

It was too late now; he had been seen. He had been found. There was no other reason for the British man to be here, but to find him. There was a pregnant pause between them. Everyone around them was suddenly moving in slow motion. Then in a flash, time caught up. Salamander watched Tanner take the first step towards him, his eyes focused only on him.

Salamander turned and ran.

Before Tanner's first step toward Salamander landed, the Iranian turned on his heels and was off sprinting.

If only he knew Tanner wanted to help him get out of the predicament he was in.

Tanner was fitter, faster, and stronger, but as he picked up pace, he was faulted by groups of tourists blocking his route to the escapee. Tanner had collided with a few people already, and on seeing Salamander's distance between them increase, he threw caution to the wind and turned himself into a human battering ram, forcing anyone in his path to the floor. Shouts and screams of disgruntled people lay in his wake as Tanner began closing the distance as they ran along the water's edge.

Max watched as the start of the chase played out through

the scope of the rifle. The zoomed in picture was no longer needed once they both cut a swathe through the sounding crowds. Max couldn't afford for Salamander to be caught.

As they both ran towards the corner of the building Max was perched upon, it was time to get involved.

Looking over the edge of the roof onto the waterside, Salamander ran past below. Tanner was in close pursuit, breaking through the crowds.

Max picked up the rifle by the carry handle and started running parallel to Salamander five storeys up. As the edge of the roof rapidly approached, Max knew there was no choice but to make the jump between the buildings. Sizing up the distance quickly Max's pace did not falter, breath held, the firm footing of the rooftop was replaced with air.

Swinging the rifle forward for extra momentum, Max leapt the gap clearing the alleyway below. The building Max landed on was one storey lower, forcing a crunching landing. Looking ahead, the remaining flat rooftops were now all the same height. Each dotted, with air condition fan boxes and vents.

Max felt the adrenaline rush after landing the jump and felt pumped for the next one. Looking over the side Max was almost level with Salamander, with Tanner slightly behind closing the gap. Max needed to get ahead of them.

The next alley below presented itself - the leap required similar to the last. Max committed to the jump, knowing thc gap would be harder to clear without the added height between take-off and landing. Max attacked it, and midway over the gap, looked below and saw Salamander turning left, up the alley being jumped. This was the advantage to get ahead.

Landing firm, Max changed direction and started running

diagonally across the building, hoping Salamander's next turn would be to the right, away from the square.

Tanner could feel the gap closing, he pumped his arms to increase his speed, his breathing rhythmic. As the buildings whipped passed him to his left and the water to his right, he could see his target looking over his shoulder, exhausted.

This increased his vigour to catch him.

Tanner was surprised at how quickly Salamander moved; he couldn't imagine him doing much training, but when you are running for your life, you find new strengths.

As Tanner passed a narrow alley to his left, he could see Salamander disappear from view down the next one.

'Don't lose him now,' he told himself.

With the next alleyway vaulted, Max was now at the halfway point over the building. Salamander should still be running up the narrow alleyway perpendicular.

After one more launch, Max had landed on the fourth and final building at the opposite parallel from the starting overwatch corner. The next jump would lead only to death.

In a swift movement, the rifle bi-pod legs were clicked out, and Max looked back down the street and watched Salamander fall out of the shadows, into the middle of the cobbled road. Max slid into position and breathed as Salamander ran directly into the path of the waiting Valkyrie sniper rifle.

Tanner flew into the confined space between the buildings levering himself off the wall. The bright sunshine gave way to cool shade, and his eyes took a moment to adjust. One hundred yards ahead the body movement told Tanner his target's energy was fading, but Salamander would soon be at the alley's end and into the next street.

Tanner drew his pistol and took up a firing stance, 'Stop!' he yelled, firing a warning round into the air above him. The noise of the shot reverberated around the confines of the narrow space, causing his ears to ring.

Salamander kept running and reached the next street. Tanner watched him dive to his right and disappear again.

With the gamble failed, Tanner gave chase again to make up the seconds lost.

With controlled breathing and a slowing heartbeat Max's vision remained steady through the scope, four floors up on the rooftop. As the two figures hurtling up the street came closer, Max could see Salamander was ready to give up, his body a mess, his face reflecting his condition.

Max was speaking the words as if Salamander could hear them, "Keep going, keep going." Moving the crosshairs, from the front runner to the man quickly bringing up the rear.

Tanner had the look of someone who could go another ten miles and as such, was gaining fast. All Salamander needed to do was turn when he reached the street corner.

Max remained hidden up high.

Salamander made the corner and turned...

There was only one chance to end this chase and allow Salamander to escape to the boat.

Tanner came storming toward the corner ready to dart left.

Max moved the cross hairs of the site, Tanner's head bobbing in the sight as he ran. Max had one shot. Too early, it wouldn't have the desired effect. Too late, and there would be a dead body and a shit storm coming.

Ten metres from approaching the corner, Max let out a slow breath. Max moved the site forward to the corner of the wall at head height to Tanner, then squeezed the trigger. *Psssttt* - the suppressor minimised the sound as the round left the barrel.

Tanner had seen the change in direction of Salamander and could see he was ready to quit. The distance was closing rapidly, he would have him on the next street. Tanner was one metre from rounding the corner, when a dull thud hit the sandstone of the building next to him, splinting at head height throwing out fragments of stone and a puff of dust.

In one motion, Tanner stopped as if he had run into an invisible wall, twisting away, raising his arms to protect himself and adopting the kneeling position.

Fuck, someone was shooting at him.

He backtracked, moving towards a doorway set in the wall hoping it would provide enough cover. Tanner scanned the street doors and windows for a possible muzzle. The few people around never heard the shot, so the only reactions of those looking at him was to keep their distance clearly believing him to be he a madman. His heart started to pound, and for the first time since the chase started, he broke into a sweat. He drew his weapon and held it discreetly out of sight by his side. He dared to look timidly out of his cover towards where the round struck. He looked around at all the possible arcs for a shooter, but there were too many.

Psssttt - Max let another round go, near the wall where

Tanner was trying to find safety in cover. The round struck closer in a spurt of dust and fragments, causing Tanner to back into the gap even further. Again, nobody else was the wiser, the split second of a thud and dust being over before people could register anything happening.

'That should keep him rooted there for a while.'

Breaking the rifle down into pieces, Max hid them in vents on various rooftops and was on the move. Whilst walking toward the far side of the roof towards the waterfront, two quick calls needed to be made. As it rang Max headed down the internal staircase for the ground floor.

Salamander was ready to give up. He turned breathless and broken with his hands on his knees. He looked to face his chaser, but to his surprise, he wasn't there. He ducked into another street to disappear himself. As he moved, he took big breaths to replenish the life that had been sapped out of him.

The mobile phone rang in his pocket.

Answering it, the cold Russian voice was on the other end. The words were fierce and pierced him as they were spat out. Both his and his family's lives were in immediate danger. His body pricked with a chill as he looked aimlessly around.

Max told him to loop back to the boat that would now leave as soon as he stepped aboard. He was told his chaser had been dealt with, and eyes were now on him, if he didn't make it back in the next five minutes he too would be dealt with.

With nothing left in the tank all Salamander could muster was a staggering jog back to the Kalinovka fishing boat.

He achieved the five-minute window.

Chapter Forty-Three

Nina walked into the square and looked around. Not seeing Tanner anywhere, she chose a parasol table and ordered a coffee. She sat observing, watching the square and the harbour.

When the coffee had been placed in front of her, there was still no sign of Tanner. She plucked out her phone and dialled.

It rang a few times before it was answered, he sounded angry. Nina explained she'd arrived in the square and where to find her. He hung up saying he would be there shortly.

Nina continued people watching through her dark Gucci sunglasses, enjoying the sun's rays warming her face.

Tanner approached her table. She looked relaxed, the polar opposite of Tanner at that moment.

He sat in the chair opposite, looking flustered.

"You, ok?" Nina questioned, moving her sunglasses down the bridge of her nose to peer over the top toward him.

"I take it you saw the map back in the apartment then?"

Nina acknowledged waiting for him to keep talking.

The waiter appeared and Tanner ordered a whisky on the rocks causing Nina to remove her shades and lean forward, before questioning him again on his wellbeing.

The whisky arrived, and Tanner took a large gulp, then began to tell her what had happened. He had been standing in that doorway for twenty minutes until she had called him. Only then had he stepped out hoping all would be clear, and the shooter, gone. The hard fact of losing Salamander for a second time hurt his pride the most.

She seemed shocked and concerned, trying to comprehend that a potential sniper was now in play. Her only theory,

Salamander must be tracked by either DOTA or the Russians, to ensure delivery of the weapon.

Tanner agreed, “So, what's the plan now?” he asked.

Her phone buzzed, she flipped it and quickly read it before returning it to her pocket. “Well,” she said, “My sources have spotted Salamander's car a couple of streets from here, I think we should check that out first. Was he carrying any packages when you saw him?”

“I wish… the chase would have ended a lot differently.”

“Not if he was being protected by a shooter.” she corrected.

“I think if they wanted me dead, they could have taken that shot. I think they just wanted to scare me, keep me from getting to him.”

“Sounds plausible, it would be hard for them to move about if you were found dead in the street. They would have had this place shut down pretty damn quickly.”

Tanner nodded, bitter from the chase, “We still have the weapon on the loose.” Tanner's words cut him like glass.

“It could be in the car?” She tried to sound hopeful.

“More likely on one of those fishing vessels.” Tanner nodded in the direction of the harbour.

“Let's check Salamander's car first,” Nina reaffirmed, “The package could still be there if you disturbed him from moving it and he hasn't had time to retrieve it yet, could be clues too.”

Tanner finished his drink in one final gulp.

Nina covered the bill and they headed to where the vehicle had been spotted.

Chapter Forty-Four

The White Peugeot was parked a couple of streets over… Nina led the way. They had stopped a distance away to gauge if any others were also watching the car, or if anyone looked suspicious around the area. The last thing Tanner wanted was to be a moving target again.

His hand rested on his weapon through the lightweight jacket, a slight reassurance it was ready for action.

The side-street was quieter than the main street.

They approached from the far side of the road.

Nobody was paying any interest in them or the vehicle.

They moved across and walked around the car.

Nothing appeared out of the ordinary.

Tanner's biggest fear was if the vehicle was boobie trapped. He'd seen too many people lose limbs and lives to car bombs. Nina noticed the keys were still in the ignition, and looking through to the opposite door saw that the doors were unlocked.

Starting at the rear, Tanner gingerly tried the door handles.

He held his breath as they each popped open with a clunk.

Nina stayed on the sidewalk, casually observing the street, looking for any familiar faces approaching.

Tanner opened the driver's door and eased inside to look around. The stale stench of body odour hit him immediately, seeing him revert to breathing through his mouth to airtight his nostrils. He looked at the keys with a frown - lesson one in car bomb school, never turn the ignition.

In the door side pocket, he found a map. Pulling it out he opened it up. Orientating himself, he could see a route marked on it. One end of the route was where he was sitting, the other end led to another part of Istanbul that was not known to him.

He waved Nina over.

“Looks like Salamander left us a clue,” he said, “This map has a route on it, and the fishing harbour is circled too.” Tanner indicated with his finger as Nina looked at it.

“Not too bright this man of yours, is he?”

“I've worked out this is where we are, but where is this area?” his finger ran to where the route started.

Nina examined the map, “Gülsuyu a neighbourhood in Maltepe. A district we would not be welcome in, and likely wouldn't end up leaving.” she said with a serious tone.

“We are armed and trained,” he batted back, “I'm sure we could handle ourselves.”

“Look, I know you're pissed off at losing Salamander, but going in there is not going to achieve anything. And even if we got to the other end, the slum is built on top of each other, we wouldn't even know where to begin.”

“But it's worth a try?” he heard the desperation in his voice.

“Tanner you’re not listening to me. Get your head back in the game. The police don't even enter that area, they let the gangs run it. You have the PKK, Turkish mafia, drug trafficking, and the Russian Red mafia, all will outgun and out-manoeuvre you before you could have a chance to react.”

He acknowledged Nina’s insight.

Searching the map further, he noticed a name penned towards the top. “What does this mean?”

“Snowball tree or something like that.” She translated.

“I have a feeling that could be the name of whatever Salamander needed to meet in the circled harbour area.”

“Should we check the boot before jumping to

conclusions?"

Tanner nodded, then escorted her to the other side of the street before pressing her into a doorway.

Her annoyance showed in her soft protest.

With the key fob in hand, he pushed the boot release button seeing the boot open with no loud explosion. He turned to her, "No sense in us both going boom!" he said with a smile, before walking back to the car.

Inspecting the contents of the boot didn't account for much. Underneath the bags of old clothes was a loose plate that revealed an empty hidden compartment.

It was large enough to hide a potential bomb.

They both tracked back to the fishing harbour and split up to search. The security guard tried to stop them, but Nina lashed out a whip of Russian words, and the guard soon got back in his guard box.

Nina suggested she take the first five jetties that stretched out into the Strait, and Tanner take the last five.

It took them a good half-hour to check all the boats. The name Kalinovka that was written on the map, was nowhere to be seen. Tanner turned some questions over in his head. Was Kalinovka a boat name or something else? Had it left already?

They both decided to return to the apartment and re-assess.

On the way back, Tanner put a call into Palmer giving her the name on the map.

Chapter Forty-Five

Major Sokolova had been receiving regular communications from Max. He was pleased to hear that the Botulinum bombs would have left Istanbul and should be entering the mouth of the Black Sea towards Kerch.

The vessel should arrive in a little over forty-eight hours.

He had already selected two of his trusted soldiers to go to Kerch and meet the Kalinovka, then bring the bombs and their custodian to a secluded area away from the rest of the men.

He wanted to make sure all was as it should be before the weapons set to rein terror on the people of Ukraine, would be presented to his soldiers.

One of the messages he'd received said Max had run into a complication and would follow-up, but that Max was still aiming to meet at the pre-determined location as arranged.

The men were starting to get restless and hungry, some, drinking too much locally brewed vodka and losing focus.

He would gather them and brief them on the good news.

They can drink and celebrate tonight but it's the last time before they moved across the border to the west.

In his tent, Aaron decided to roll out his prayer mat and pray, thanking Allah for choosing him to deliver this message for DOTA. He would also thank Jafar, for answering his prayers to help fulfil his revenge, on behalf of his father.

His last prayer would be for Max to join him safely.

Chapter Forty-Six

The Kalinovka engines were already running when Salamander stepped onboard gasping for air, his limbs feeling like lead. As his feet hit the deck the captain shouted out the bridge door for Salamander to get below and stay there until he said otherwise.

Standing in the cramped cabin, he could barely turn around to shut the door. The two squeezed together bunks each had a blanket and pillow on top. One bunk for him the other for his two unwelcome guests. He felt imprisoned with the two bags staring at him - the two packages that could be the cause of so many deaths, and he, the one delivering them…

Faisal, Salamander, the Grim Reaper.

Located next to the engine room, the cabin was humid, with no air con - the noise of the engines increasing through the bulkhead as the revs were brought on to make way.

The platform started moving and already Salamander wasn't liking the motion. He lay on his bunk and closed his eyes trying to shut the whole world out.

Salamander woke with a startle. He was disorientated.

His reality soon returned when he looked upon the opposing bunk, seeing the bags masking the weapons.

He brought his hands to his face rubbing his eyes back to life. He must have dozed off, hardly surprising he thought, every ounce of energy had been drawn out of him.

He thought back to the chase - how did he get away? The man was fitter and stronger than him, yet he had disappeared. He had a strong suspicion Max was involved.

There was a knock at the door and uninvited, it opened.

A big-bearded man who looked like a giant oil rag filled the doorway and instructed Salamander to the bridge.

As he made his way up two decks, the gentle sway was making him queasy. He reached the top of the last ladder, the bright daylight beaming through the bridge windows making his eyes ache until they adjusted. “How long have we been at sea?” he questioned, “I fell asleep?”

The captain let out a deep, slow laugh as he rolled the cigar in his mouth. Sitting in his chair, he held a small wooden ship’s wheel. In front of him were banks of switches all labelled with a purpose, and a radar which Salamander recognised from films, along with screens filled with lines and dots that only the captain needed to understand. Still looking ahead, the captain spoke in a Russian accent, which Salamander had decided he’d never want to hear again once this was all over. “We are not at sea; we are still on a little river.”

Salamander knew he meant the Bosphorus Strait.

“When you can no longer see land then we will be at sea.” The captain turned and faced him, “I don't know who you are, and I don't want to know why you are here, or what you are carrying. That is your business. Is that clear?”

Salamander nodded.

Removing the cigar from his teeth he added, “I have been paid well by Max to ensure you, and your cargo, has a safe passage to Kerch, and I will. But if you jeopardise this vessel, my crew, and my money, you’ll find yourself dining with the crabs. I'm sure you understand.”

Salamander stood motionless not sure what to say, if indeed he should say anything at all, after this latest threat to his life.

The pause was interrupted as the boat chugged under the Yavuz Sultan Selim Bridge. At over three hundred metres, its two concrete towers in the shape of an upside down 'V' looked to one another from an equal distance on either side of the Strait, holding its roads and railway track out of the water. Countless steel cables stretched from top to bottom of the pillars, crisscrossing the suspension bridge like a spider's web.

Salamander was fascinated by this grand piece of architecture. He had never seen anything like it.

Passing underneath, they neared the end of the Strait, which saw the captain spread both arms wide and grin, exposing what few teeth he had left, “Welcome to the Black Sea.”

Chapter Forty-Seven

They had arrived back at the apartment.

Nina busied herself making phone calls, alternating her language from Russian to English, depending on the recipient. Tanner assessed she must be talking to Ed and then sources in Russia as she kept out of the way in her room.

Tanner had called Stones and explained what had happened with Salamander and the shooter, then spent the rest of the time pacing up and down and staring at the map.

He checked his phone again, waiting for Palmer to call.

Nina came out of her room and slumped in the armchair. For the first time, Tanner could see signs of strain across her face. Probably not telling him everything she knows, he thought, the Firm always kept things to themselves, so much for collaboration. “Any updates?” Tanner asked.

She rubbed her brow, even under stress she looked alluring.

“Nothing that is of relevance to you.” she snapped, the coldness returning, “Sorry,” she said with a forced grin.

The uncomfortable moment was broken by Tanner's phone, vibrating on the glass topped coffee table. He answered it.

“Palmer here, how's the holiday?”

The joke was wearing thin.

“Quickly needing some new activity.” Tanner responded.

Nina sat watching, hanging off any snippets she could hear.

“I ran the name Kalinovka through the system and as predicted, it is the name of a fishing vessel.” Palmer said.

A wave of relief and excitement swept over Tanner.

“It is Russian flagged, IMO number is...”

“Never mind that, where is it?” he interjected.

"I was getting to that part if you wouldn't interrupt me," she sounded annoyed, "I put Kalinovka into the Marine Traffic System and it left Gümüşsuyu commercial fishing port in Beykoz six hours ago."

Tanner quickly calculated the time backward, working out how that was roughly the same time he was shot at.

"Usually, it could be tracked via its AIS," Palmer continued, "The Automatic Identification System uses onboard transponders to provide its position, identification, and other information to other vessels and coastal authorities," she added, "Unfortunately, once it entered the Black Sea, the vessel switched off the AIS, so it can no longer be tracked. But its next port of call was registered as Kerch."

"Kerch?" Tanner's geography wasn't the best.

"Peninsula of Crimea, Russia," Palmer reported, "The Kerch Strait connects the Black Sea and the Sea of Azov, while Kerch itself is a large fishing port."

Tanner put his hand over the receiver and told Nina, "We need to get to Kerch."

"Its last AIS data drop said it was steaming at ten knots on a north easterly bearing, which calculated, will reach Kerch in two days. I did some digging on the skipper. Unsavoury sort, a string of offenses, and recently a particularly large sum of money appeared in his account." Tanner knew Palmer would have that proud look on her face as she finished her report.

"Thanks Palmer, brilliant work, looks like I'm going to the Crimea."

"One more thing. Stones will be calling you after this, he has some updated intel for you."

"Thanks again." Tanner said.

Tanner back briefed Nina who listened intently.

"The only way we are going to reach them is to take the same route, by the same means. All other options have too many entities that could hold us up or delay us, and certainly would not allow us to carry weapons." Nina stated.

"How much influence have you and your boss got to get us a boat down at the harbour, ready to depart in the next hour? If we need cash, I'm sure we can pull it together."

"I'll see what I can do. I'll need to make a phone call, but it would be better if we go to the harbour so I can talk to the different captains face to face."

Nina went to make a call closing her bedroom door, prompting Tanner to follow suit, making a beeline for his room to pack and prep his weapons.

Chapter Forty-Eight

As they arrived at the harbour jetties, the same security guard recognised Nina but remained mute in his hut.
Tanner's phone started to ring and he took the call while Nina went in search of a vessel. "Tanner, it's Stones."

"Any good news?"

"Yes and No. I had an update from our man in the Firm. I'll start with the horror story. After Operation Iraqi Freedom, the United Nations Special Commission was formed. UNSCOM was an inspection syndicate, created to oversee Iraq's compliance with the destruction of chemical, biological, and missile weapons facilities. When they inspected the facility Jafar and his friends worked in they audited everything and found there was a small amount of Botulinum toxin missing."

"Excuse my lack of chemistry, but what does that mean?"

"Botulinum is a fatal toxin that if inhaled or ingested can lead to a nasty ending. I'd say, stringing all the pieces together, our weapon is biological, filled with the missing toxin."

"So, the son of Oleg Sokolova, the Major, is working with Jafar to make a statement for DOTA and his own cause?"
Tanner sighed, 'Two birds with one bomb,' he thought.

"That's what we are thinking, and Salamander is the one being made to deliver it, to save his family." Stones added.

'Fuck,' Tanner thought, "Does Nina know about this?"

"I assume if he briefed me he'd have briefed her too."

Tanner thought he'd keep this piece of intel to himself for the time being, it was clear Nina wasn't telling him everything.

"Has Palmer briefed you on what she told me earlier?"

"She has." Stones informed Tanner, "Your next steps have

been approved, but I must stress the point, no government will intervene or come to your aid. There are too many people protecting themselves from mistakes and coverups that are starting to surface. Do you understand?"

"I get it. We are on our own." Tanner ended the call then looked at his watch. They were eight hours behind the bomb.

Nina returned, and using whatever influence she and MI6 had, she'd commandeered a Russian flagged fishing vessel and its crew. Tanner was certain her persuasive personality and brick-walled approach didn't leave them much choice.

He was also sure they would be handsomely paid.

*

Home for the next two days was to be the OSTROVNOY.

Piled high with metal cages and an abundance of orange buoys, Ostrovnoy was a crabbing vessel. A steel ship of good size and speed, its blue and white livery was stained with patches of bronze discolouring, its mast stretching out of the bridge with various antennas, and navigation lights.

The sun had disappeared over the horizon as the boat made ready to depart, but the air was still warm.

As they boarded, they were greeted by the captain, Viktor Morozov, who exchanged a few words to Nina in Russian as she reached the top of the gangway.

She then headed below deck with Tanner in tow.

They left the jetty and were soon powering up the Bosphorus toward the Sultan Selim Bridge. As the Ostrovnoy passed beneath it into the darkness of the Black Sea, they were now twelve hours behind the Kalinovka and racing to Kerch.

Chapter Forty-Nine

As the Kalinovka steamed through the water Salamander stood on the port side upper deck, leaning on the gunnel, and looking out over the vast area of dark sea.

The gentle sound of the wash below felt soothing to him, and his earlier sickness had passed.

It was a clear night, and the surface was illuminated by the moon. It was nearing midnight when he had woken from a deep sleep. He wandered to the galley to get some food. There were leftovers from dinner and a goulash still warm in a pot.

He had the freedom of the boat now they were away from land. The crew had ignored him completely, it was like he did not exist. He didn't mind if it gave him time to rest and refuel.

It would be a long way back to Tehran when they freed him of this disastrous burden.

He looked up, the breeze cooling his face.

The stars were out, he wondered if his wife and daughter were looking up at the same sky as he was right now.

He remembered sitting on the outskirts of Northern Tehran near the mountains, away from the city's light pollution and noise, with his wife, Anahita. They hadn't known each other long but had soon fallen head over heels in love. He was a young street trader, new to the world of the streets, but with an entrepreneurial mind. When he first met Anahita, he was selling Châghâle Bâdum, unripe skinless baby almonds still wrapped in their green shells. The local snack had offered a quick and easy way into the street vendor scene and allowed him to start making money.

The day he saw her walk toward his stall, it was like the

people in the street had parted. Her black head scarf respectfully covered her head, with little fringes of jet-black hair falling from the edges. Her skin shone and her wide oval brown eyes looked like beautiful chestnuts.

When she smiled at him his heart had melted.

He knew he had to make this woman his wife.

He had given her a free pot of his street wares, and once granted permission from her family to court her, they soon became inseparable.

It was a starry night on the Black Sea, just like the night they'd gazed upon when he told her he was going to ask her father for her hand in marriage.

She'd cried with joy, and soon they were wed.

He increased his business to selling Laboo and Bâghâli, and soon Anahita announced they were to have a baby.

Daria was born.

He had to smile at the irony of his current location, *Daria* meaning Sea. Daria was the most precious, beautiful gift, and life was good. They were happy and wanted nothing, they made each day count and loved each other dearly.

Six blissful years had gone by. Then Hunter came along.

He pondered over Hunter and his death briefly, he didn't feel guilty, but no one should have to die the way he did.

The pang of heartache from being separated from his family was all consuming and he decided to return to his bunk. As he headed to his cabin, he took one last look at the sky, wondering if he would ever see Anahita and Daria again.

Chapter Fifty

As they stood on the deck, the clear night glistened with stars. The moon shone down like a spotlight, its reflective light shimmering off the calm dark water.

The only sound was the soft drumming of the diesel engines, faint in the sea air, the gentle stirring of the wake rolling down the sides of the vessel.

They'd had little sleep over the past days and the sway of the boat only encouraged their fatigue.

There was only one spare cabin onboard. It was confined, with a single bed, limited floor space, and small bathroom.

Tanner suggested Nina take the bed and that he would hunker down on the floor. He told her he'd give her a few minutes of privacy, before coming below.

Her alluring blue eyes held his gaze before she offered a smile, the first time Tanner had seen her tough exterior soften. She then turned and left him on the upper deck.

He felt as if some unspoken message had just passed between them. Had he imagined it? 'Damn, she is beautiful,' he thought, 'Too beautiful for me.' She had shown no warmth toward him until that moment. He looked out to sea and could not help but picture her undressing in the cabin below.

'Did I just misread the look she just gave, or is she thinking the same?' They were two of a kind after all, living a job, self-disciplined, sometimes lonely and in need.

'Focus!' he told himself, 'You don't have time for this.'

A few minutes passed before he made his way below deck. Outside the door, he paused and could feel his heart pounding.

He was instantly annoyed at letting such fantasy take

control. He knocked quietly on the cabin door.

"Coming," her Russian accent sounded softer.

The cabin door opened a fraction and on seeing Tanner, she opened it fully. He stepped inside to see her standing before him, wearing only her partially unbuttoned blouse. Her toned legs stretched from beneath the hem, which only just covered her underwear. Her hair hung loosely over her shoulder, a sea of brunette waves encompassing her face, her head tilted, revealing her slender neck.

Tanner could feel the perspiration on his skin and the sudden tightness in his trousers. The confined room brought them closer together and as Tanner moved to pass Nina, he felt her breasts brush against his chest. She breathed sharply at the touch and soon they were face to face, eyes locked together.

She could feel her blood pulsing around her body and felt the heat radiating off his.

It felt like there was a force field between them preventing any physical touch. No words were spoken, as at that moment, they both understood they wanted each other.

Tanner took off his shirt before placing his hands on her hips. She shuddered at his touch, her breaths quickening.

His strong hands slowly moved over her buttocks, pausing to feel the firm roundness, pulling her closer to him.

Nina could feel his arousal press against her.

She spoke softly, "Do you trust me?"

Tanner didn't understand what she meant but nodded.

She reached to his side and pressed the locking clip on his pistol holster, sliding his weapon out and drawing the barrel slowly across his chest, before placing the Sig Sauer on the sideboard. The cold metal barrel felt alien against his skin, but the action stirred him all the same.

She placed her palms against his chest as Tanner ran his hands over her blouse, tracing his fingers across her neck until his hands cupped her face. For a moment they were lost in each other's eyes. He brushed the hair from her face, each touch like electrical sparks coursing through their bodies.

She ran her hands over his abs, before resting her fingers on the waistband of his trousers.

Their lips lingered close for a moment and then they kissed.

The kiss was firm and full, the pent-up frustration forcing their mouths closer together. Tanner felt desire explode throughout his body and he gently pulled the back of her hair seeing her gasp. Their feverish kisses slowed to a more tantalizing pace, savouring the moments to come.

He trailed his lips down her neck as her hands reached the entrance to his trousers to swiftly uncouple the buttons.

She reached inside and squeezed.

He tensed, then stepped into her, guiding her back until she felt the wood of the bed against her thighs.

She moved her hands to the sides of his trousers and pushed them down with his assistance.

Standing naked he moved his hands to her shirt and ripped it open, tearing the buttons from their thread. He admired her body and traced his fingers over various scars no doubt collected due to the nature of her work.

He moved his mouth to tease her already hardened nipples, the salty taste of perspiration increasing his lust.

She pressed his head into her bosom - reaching down to take him in her hand again.

He pushed her down on the bed as she pulled him onto her,

her legs parting as he nestled his hips between her.

The heat between her legs was immense, and she felt his excitement press against her.

She wanted him inside her right now.

He pulled her underwear aside - their eyes locked. No words were spoken, only the sound of their excited breaths.

She moved her hand down, guiding him into her. They both stifled an intake of air, his low moan reverberating through her as she started to move her hips to match his rhythm.

Their bodies were one and she wrapped her legs around his waist pulling him in deeper. He leaned on one arm as the other wrapped under her lower back keeping them close as they kissed. The moans of pleasure increased as did the pace of his thrusts, and it wasn't long before both were climaxing hard.

He rested on his arms above her, their hot breaths exhaling onto one another. Still, mute their expressions said all that needed to be said - they had both needed each other that night for reasons of their own.

Exhaustion from the last few day's events finally caught up with them both, and they drifted to sleep entwined in each other's arms, not caring what tomorrow would bring.

Chapter Fifty-One

Major Sokolova stood in his tent surveying the temporary camp. The rain had come overnight making everything sodden. The ground, after weeks of being churned by boots and vehicles, had become a swamp that no one wanted to venture over unless they had to - but today was a must.

He'd been putting the final parts of the plan into action.

The previous day he had sent two of his most trusted soldiers and a driver to meet the unwilling courier in Kerch with the weapons. They would be there waiting on the dockside for the fishing vessel, Kalinovka, to arrive.

The Major had struggled to sleep the night previous, playing the plan out in his head, ensuring he hadn't missed anything. The only uncertainty was the *complication* Max had to deal with. He left the tent to check the troops were on track.

Today his men were closing camp, and moving to Kuznetsi, just over the Ukrainian border.

His Second in Command, 2iC, would wait for him there.

The troops would be leaving in the next few hours.

The Major toured the camp as his men busied themselves with the task in hand. As he passed, he received nods and the occasional salute voicing the acknowledgment, “Major.”

Morale was high and the soldiers looked ready.

The fight was coming soon - he expected resistance, but was confident in their victory, especially with what they were about to receive in their arsenal. He continued his stroll admiring his men. No individual was dressed the same, each man dressed in a semblance of a Russian uniform, whatever they could find that best fit and kept them warm.

One of the three Ural-4320's, a general-purpose off-road 6×6 truck, was being loaded with the collapsed tents, along with radio equipment, ammunition, and what provisions they had left. The other two Ural trucks were for carrying men.

Since deploying from Moscow, they had received no replenishments of any kind. Food and water had to either be asked for or was donated by the surrounding Russian people. When across the border in Ukraine, the soldiers would just take what they wanted, including ammunition and sometimes women, to which the Major turned a blind eye.

Each soldier carried an AK-74M, known as the AKM assault rifle designed by Soviet firearms designer Mikhail Kalashnikov, as a replacement for the more famous AK-47.

The enemy also used Russian weapons against them, which meant ammunition was easier to come by.

Parked in front of the row of Urals was a BTR-80 armoured personnel carrier. This version was equipped with a new turret mounted DShK .50 calibre machine gun. He could see the rear doors were open, the cramped space inside filled with ammo boxes and equipment, with no room for soldiers.

The Major knew there would be very few Ukrainians anywhere near the border. Once crossed, they would travel by road directly to Mariupol. En route, he hoped he would come across pockets of Russian soldiers that would rally to join him. As for the Major, he'd be travelling to a secluded spot just outside Nikolayevo. Here he would meet the courier and have the weapons in his hands and check all was in order.

Max planned to meet him there, and together they would unleash the Botulinum bombs on the Ukrainian city.

His smile grew at the thought.

Chapter Fifty-Two

Salamander woke to an unanticipated hangover.

The evening before he had been disturbed by a banging noise coupled with an intermittent whistling of a tune.

He'd opened his cabin door and there leaning over some pipes, working on one of the diesel engines was the engineer, Mr Oil Rag.

He had taken an interest in Salamander and more so what was in the bags. At first, Salamander had said nothing and retreated into the cabin closing the door. A few hours later there was a knock, and the engineer was back, this time with a bottle of home brewed vodka and two shot glasses.

He'd said not to worry about the captain as he never came down to these depths of the trawler.

"Just remember," he'd said, "The engineer is always in charge. No engines no fishing." He'd laughed at his own remark then offered up a shot of Vodka.

Salamander had never had a drink in his life, and tried to kindly refuse, but eventually gave in to the affable giant.

The first shot stole the breath out of his body, and he dry retched at what he could only imagine petrol would taste like. He thought he had been poisoned. The oversized oil rag started laughing and declared, "Salut," downing his shot without so much as a wince. The engineer invited himself into the cabin and sat on the bunk next to the bags with Salamander opposite.

The big man poured them both another shot.

After one bottle was empty, another somehow appeared, and they'd chatted into the early hours.

It was the first time in a long time he'd felt any kind of

relaxation, with someone being nice to him. He had a nagging feeling the engineer had looked in the bags while he'd been fighting the effects of the moonshine, a suspicion confirmed as he noticed traces of oily prints near the zip-openings of each bag. He had the hazy sense Mr Oil Rag had appeared disinterested in the bags contents and hoped that nothing would ever be said about his hidden cargo.

He rubbed his forehead.

He needed some water and fresh air.

After quenching his thirst, he drank a strong coffee and went to the upper deck to take in the cooling sea air.

He took long breaths to try and clear his head.

In the distance, he could see the port of Kerch slowly reveal itself through the mist.

As the boat chugged ever closer to land, he wondered once more what was waiting for him there. The thought reignited the fears that last night's vodka had temporarily drained away.

Chapter Fifty-Three

Tanner stood at the port bridge wing, a fresh breeze tingling his senses. He wasn't a sea lover and was itching to get back on land, hence why he'd joined the Army and not the Navy.

His thoughts replayed events of the past forty-eight hours, in particular, the two evenings spent in the cabin with Nina.

On the morning after their first sexual encounter, he had woken alone with Nina nowhere to be seen. Her words, 'Do you trust me?' had rushed at him, seeing Tanner retrieve his weapon to carry out a check before loading a round into the chamber. He'd dressed and re-holstered the pistol before going to the galley to retrieve a cup of coffee.

He'd made his way to the bridge wondering if there would be any sense of unease between them. On his approach, Nina had been mid-conversation with the captain, their Russian dialogue quickly fading as Tanner arrived. Nina had then invited him onto the bridge and updated him how they'd been making good progress and were in fact six hours ahead of their predicted port arrival time. Her demeanour throughout, was as if the night before had never happened.

They'd returned to the cabin and spent their time going over every scenario they could possibly face once they'd reached the mainland. Tanner had intended to bring up Stones' MI6 update on the Botulinum but he'd decided to keep his cards close to his chest for the time being, and see how events would play out. Then, later that night, they'd once again ended up in each other's arms, resulting in a second unexpected night of passion that had been a complete shock to Tanner.

When morning arrived, Tanner had once again found himself

alone in the bed, so he'd headed to the bridge where he now observed the faint shadow of Kerch as it took greater form in the growing light.

He could hear the speed and volume of the wash as the Ostrovnoy sped through the water. After a time, he heard Nina approach to join him on the bridge wing.

"We've made more time - should be alongside in two hours." She said, in the same casual manner as the morning previous.

"That's good. We'll only be a few hours behind Salamander." His eyes never left the horizon.

After a short silence, Nina announced, "I'm going to carry out a few final checks." She then left him to his solitude once more. Tanner turned and watched her leave, trying to figure out where her head was at. He then found himself wondering how often she might visit the UK with the Firm.

Would there be a chance to meet again?

He laughed at such hopes, 'You need to keep your focus on the job!' he reminded himself once more.

He took a deep lungful of the sea air then headed down to the cabin. Nina was already maintaining her weapons and supplies as he arrived. Tanner followed suit stripping and cleaning his firearms before carrying out checks to prevent any chance of stoppages, if and when the time came.

Both Tanner and Nina were now far away within their thoughts, visiting their respective mindsets utilised to prepare them for operations. Everything would be boxed up and compartmentalised to focus on the mission.

After a time, the Ostrovnoy's engine revs decreased into a lower rhythmic tone. They were approaching Kerch.

Chapter Fifty-Four

As Kalinovka came alongside Pier 32 in Kerch harbour, the captain had ordered Salamander to remain below in his cabin until called for. He could hear the low drum of the engines come to an almost silence, and the vessel's motion cease.

There were muffled shouts from above on the decks.

He just sat, transfixed by the two blue holdalls.

He could hear footsteps approaching as someone clattered down the ladder. His door opened and the engineer stood there filling his doorway again. It was time to leave.

He collected the weapons, one in each hand and as he left the cabin, the oil rag placed a hand on his shoulder and stated sincerely, "Good Luck."

Salamander stepped out onto the upper deck awkwardly carrying the bags. The air was cooler than Istanbul and the sun peeked in and out from the scattered clouds. Seagulls swooped and dived around the various styles of moored fishing vessels, their screeching warble piercing the busy harbour.

Kerch port was a lot larger than Gümüşsuyu and was by far a more commercialised setup.

Looking across the water past the fishing fleet, he could see several cargo ships. The docks were scattered with huge yellow cranes each resembling a steel giraffe that either loaded or unloaded the many containers.

As Salamander walked towards the top of the gangway, the captain stood in the bridge doorway. He signalled a courtesy salute towards him, still sporting a cigar held between his teeth. Salamander started to descend the gangway to the dockside watching his step as he went.

When Salamander reached the dock, he was thankful to feel the return to a solid surface that no longer moved.

He looked up and saw two hardened soldiers in Russian uniforms carrying assault rifles, each stood with a stance that meant business, their chiselled faces showing no sign of a welcome. Salamander felt cemented to the spot and looked back at the bridge door which was now vacant.

The soldiers both walked towards him.

The first to reach him slung the rifle over his broad shoulder and with care, took the two bags from Salamander, understanding the contents. The second took the bicep of Salamander's slender arm in his vice like hand and offered, with his other arm, the direction in which he wanted him to walk. When he didn't comply, the grip tightened and the soldier spoke a single word, “Move,” in the deep accent he’d recently learned to despise.

Salamander was escorted up the jetty to where an olive, moss green, and tawny brown camouflaged all-terrain infantry vehicle sat waiting for him. In the cab behind the intimidating extra-large nudge bar at the front of the vehicle, he saw a third soldier, waiting behind the steering wheel. He stared through the split windscreen, his face showing no emotion.

The soldier carrying the bags stowed them in the rear of 4X4 while the one holding Salamander opened the rear door, hinged in a suicide door motion, and assisted him in climbing aboard. The tops of the tyres were waist height to Salamander, and the assistance was needed. As he clambered onto the rear bench seat, the opposite door opened and the soldier from the rear joined him. His assistant joined the driver up front.

There was no conversation as the diesel engine fired up.

As they started to leave the dockside, he could see the passenger up front make a call on his mobile.

Salamander watched their progress through the window.

After a short time, they reached a vast channel of water, and this time instead of passing under a grand bridge, he was crossing one. The Crimean Bridge stretched over the Kerch Strait and would take them from the Kerch Peninsula of Crimea to the Taman Peninsula of Krasnodar Krai in Russia.

He watched a blue and white fishing vessel below as it passed under the bridge, heading into the fishing port he had just left. It slowly drifted from view the further they drove.

Salamander felt drained once more, still unable to comprehend what had happened to him over the last week.

He had travelled from Tehran to Istanbul, crossed the Black Sea, and was now in Russia. Anyone looking from the outside and not knowing the circumstances would think it a great adventure - but the truth was a twisted nightmare.

The biological weapons in the rear came to the forefront of his mind. What was he to do? He remembered the engineer's words as he left the boat, 'Good luck.'

Chapter Fifty-Five

The eye-in-the-sky MQ-9 Reaper had been conducting reconnaissance operations over the Kerch since the earlier hours of the morning. Operated by U.S. airmen working closely with the Polish Air Force out of Miroslawiec.

The 52nd Expeditionary Operations Group's normal operations covered the current Ukraine conflict, and the area of Ukraine's Crimea peninsula and Donbas region, which had remained an active conflict area in Eastern Europe.

The orders for the tasking had come direct from the U.S. Air Force Operations Group Commander, so was a priority.

The drone pilots were conducting a large circular holding pattern, until they received further intelligence. This intel came when the Kalinovka fishing vessel, re-established its AIS as it approached Kerch port, giving the Reaper an exact GPS position to lock its high-powered camera crosshairs onto.

Watching the live feedback in a hanger from Miroslawiec, was the operations commander.

The green and white hulled Kalinovka, slowly moved towards the port area. The recce conducted earlier had already highlighted a camouflaged Russian Gaz Tigr waiting on the dock, which gave them a good indication as to where the boat could be mooring.

Once alongside, they watched from high above as two soldiers in mish-mashed uniforms deployed from the vehicle.

They observed the scene as an uncomfortable looking Iranian entered the fray. He was quickly taken control of and the bags taken out of his custody. Only the commander watching knew the contents of the holdalls, hence his rare presence in the operations room.

With the bags in the rear of the vehicle, the soldiers and the coerced man mounted up, and the Gaz Tigr pulled away.

The fixated crosshairs kept them in sight as they passed over the Crimean Bridge and onto the mainland.

The commander made a phone call further up the chain, out of earshot of the rest of the room. The information was short. The weapons had arrived, they would continue to track the vehicle and the contents.

The Reaper's 950 horsepower turboprop hummed as it carved its way at forty thousand feet, following the prey.

Chapter Fifty-Six

Tanner grew more impatient as he stood on the upper deck surveying the dockside for any clues from afar.

The speed had become torturously slow, and he was already prepped, wanting to hurl himself over the gunnel before the berthing ropes had even been passed across.

His weapons were all at hand, the Sig Sauer P229 holstered on his belt and the SR-3 Vikhr compact assault rifle tucked tightly under his right armpit, everything covered by his jacket. The backpack he carried contained his extra magazines. Nina chose the MP-443 Grach pistol, an unusual choice from the standard MI6 Glock. Tanner supposed working in Russia the weapon carried would say a lot about who you are. She also carried the MPK5 slung in a similar position to his rifle.

Nina was on the bridge talking with the captain.

It helped in this profession to forge relationships, as you never know when you might need to call on certain individuals again. He looked up as they passed under a large bridge wondering what traffic came and went from the Peninsula.

Tanner's operational mind returned his focus to the only lead they had. To head to Latonova the last know location of Major Sokolova. They were still behind in the chase.

Once the boat was alongside neither hesitated to hit the dockside. Kerch port was a large industrial site, and they needed to find transport to get out as quickly as possible.

Nina suggested splitting up to save time. She wanted to go and look for the Kalinovka and check for any information or if Salamander was still there. Tanner was to search for a suitable vehicle to get them to Latonova.

He watched Nina disappear down the dock, before he turned and headed out in search of a car.

En route, his mobile phone picked up reception, and he sent a text message to Stones informing him they had arrived.

Tanner soon found what he was looking for. A carpark away from the port area with no obvious onlookers. About forty to fifty cars were parked there, most likely designated for dockyard employees. Tanner walked amongst the rows of vehicles with confidence, as if he should be there. He knew what he was looking for, an old generation car that still operated on a mechanical ignition rather than the modern-day computer. He needed something rugged as it was unknown what kind of terrain they would be up against.

After a few minutes, he found a Lada Niva off-roader. It was about twenty years old and had a classic look about it... Pale green in colour with a dent here and there - sporting steel wheels it looked basic, but most importantly, it was stealable.

He had a quick pan round to check no eyes were on him, then tested the door handles in the hope it might be open.

No such luck. He removed his pistol and struck the rear side window, the glass disintegrating onto the rear seat.

Reaching inside Tanner unlocked the driver's door.

Before jumping in, he used the sole of his combat boot to smash the plastic cover off from under the steering column.

He got in the Lada and found the wiring harness connector. He pulled aside the battery, ignition, and starter wire bundle. Tanner identified the brown ignition wire and the yellow starter wire. Pulling them free and stripping the ends with his teeth, he twisted them together. Using the stripped battery wire, tapping the open wires together to generate a spark, starting the engine. He gave it a few revs to prevent it from stalling. The Lada was alive.

Tanner's phone rang. He checked to make sure no-one had witnessed his actions then answered, “Tanner.”

“Stones here, do you have a moment for a quick update?”

“Shoot.” Tanner was keen for anything that could help.

“While you’ve been at sea, we’ve had eyes on from above, waiting for your man to show. He has been picked up, by the Major's men we believe. They are travelling in a *cammo'd* Gaz Tigr, three up and armed. Our man now with two packages.”

“Two packages?”

“Yes, two packages,” Stones confirmed, “Twice the complication.” He was cautious with his words while talking on the phone, in this part of the world.

“Ok, where are they heading?”

“We are monitoring their route and will update as changes come in. For now, head in the direction you initially planned.”

“Understood, we have transport and will be moving shortly.”

“One more thing Tanner,” Stones added, “They left the dock almost three hours ago.” He then ended the call.

Three hours ahead. Tanner tried to calculate the distance, but it was irrelevant, they had to close the time gap.

He exited the carpark and drove back to the dockside.

Nina was already waiting for him.

“Nice wheels,” she said as she jumped in.

Tanner smiled and gunned it, following the signs for the port exit under Nina’s swift navigation and translations.

Once on the open road and crossing the bridge, Nina briefed him how nothing of note was discovered during her visit to the Kalinovka. Tanner updated her on Stones' call and what vehicle they were looking for, more importantly, how there were now two weapon packages to deal with.

Nina started tapping away at her phone informing Tanner she was contacting her sources in the region, trying to retrieve any information that could help.

Latonova was approximately a six-hour drive.

The chase was on once again.

Chapter Fifty-Seven

Major Sokolova ended his call that had informed him the courier and biological weapons had been met and collected and were now making their way to the arranged rendezvous.

He had yet to receive a call from Max.

Sitting in his Gaz Tigr, he felt a silent sense of elation at the news. Beyond the vehicle, the men around him dismantled and packed his tent ready to deploy.

Another step closer, another part of the plan ticked off.

He closed his eyes and envisaged the carnage he was set to release. The pleasure engulfed his mind as he imagined himself standing in Mariupol, the bodies of countless dead Ukrainians surrounding him. He took a deep breath.

He was ready, willing to be a martyr for his father and DOTA's cause. He had one more request to fulfil for his friend Jafar - to dispose of Salamander as and when it felt necessary. An easy ask after everything Jafar had done for him and Max.

The Major met and had a quick brief with his 2iC.

Once all orders were confirmed the convoy departed west for the Ukraine border.

In Kuznetsi they would wait for the Major to join them.

A few hours later he stood against the bonnet of his Tigr and watched the vehicles roll down the road. As the trucks passed him carrying the troops, they hung out the back offering enthusiastic shouts of victory to come.

He smiled back and returned a jaunty salute.

The Major climbed into his vehicle, ready to start the journey to his meeting point outside Nikolayevo. The exact coordinates were only briefed to those who needed to be there.

Starting the engine, he headed in a southward direction.

His mobile phone buzzed, acknowledging the receipt of a text message.

He looked down at the screen… It was Max.

Chapter Fifty-Eight

Tanner and Nina were off the bridge over the Kerch Straits and onto the main road heading East towards Krasnodar. They determined the chosen direction would not only be the fastest route to their destination but was also a quick enough road to rapidly clock up some distance between them and where Tanner had stolen the Lada. Tanner was confident they could catch up, after all, they were chasing an armoured vehicle.

The Tigr could match motorway speed, but the Lada could be pushed that little extra, though they'd have to be vigilant to do so without hitting any police speed traps along the way.

The conversation between them was minimal - both Tanner and Nina had drifted into themselves, self-assessing and rolling scenarios over and around in their heads… the *what ifs*.

After a few hours, they reached the western outskirts of Krasnodar. They chose the ring road looping to the north of the city to avoid the inner-city traffic, and soon joined the expressway E115 heading northeast.

The only problem with stealing a car is there's no guarantee of a full tank of fuel - and soon they had to pull over to fill up. It was a good opportunity to grab some much-needed food and water. Tanner also bought a roadmap.

They were soon back on the E115 that would take them directly to Rostov-On-Don, which they hoped to make within a few hours. The roads were not busy, and the traffic flowed at a good pace. Tanner felt like he was driving blind, despite the fact he had a good idea of where to head. It could all lead to nothing if they didn't receive an update from the Reaper.

Salamander and the bombs could be anywhere by now.

Tanner had to trust there was no change to them heading to Latonova, that there was no need to change the plan.

He looked across at Nina, she remained quiet staring out of the window and watching the scenery pass by.

Tanner thought he'd use the time to try and break down some of her walls, "So, how did you end up in MI6?"

For a moment, she remained silent and still, her gaze remaining unchanged as she continued to look out the window. Her reply seemed a long time coming, "You ask a lot of questions, Tanner. You may notice I don't ask any of you."

Her alluring Russian accent still aroused his ears.

"Ask away, I have nothing to hide."

"Maybe I'm just not interested." she turned to him and smiled, her frozen complexion, threatening to thaw.

He smiled back, "I'm just curious that's all. Trying to make conversation. We are both in similar lines of work, just wondered if we also came from similar backgrounds?"

Again, she remained silent for a time, until with an exaggerated sigh she appeared to thaw a little more. "My mother was from England; my father was Russian. Of course, I became fluent in both languages, but I grew up in Russia."

"What was that like? Living in Russia?"

"I have both good and bad memories. Of course, it was harder than being brought up in the UK, you certainly develop a thick skin."

"And the Firm?" Tanner pushed a little further.

Nina paused to reflect, "I returned to the UK to study Russian Political studies at Oxford University. I must have caught someone's attention and was approached. *Nu vot i nachalos* - And so it began."

"Siblings?"

"No. Your turn," She diverted back to Tanner.

"Not as colourful as yours. Both parents were born and raised in a place just outside of London as was I - the middle of three children. School was fun but for all the wrong reasons. By the time I left, I'd had a few indiscretions with the law. One of the Bobbies took me aside. He showed me the path I was on and where it was going to end up, and I didn't like the look of it. So, I joined the Army with a mate of mine."

"What is a Bobbie?"

Tanner laughed, "It's slang for a policeman."

"Is your friend still serving?" she asked.

It was Tanner's turn to pause for thought, "He's the reason I'm here. He was murdered, while working with Salamander. I was sent to find out why."

"And it escalated from there." Nina surmised seeing the silence resume. After a time, they reached Rostov-On-Don.

Sticking to the plan, they were to skim around the outskirts to the west and continue to Taganrog then on to Latonova.

Driving on the ring road, Tanner's phone rang. He held it to his ear and listened to another update from Stones.

After an acknowledgment of understanding, he hung up and back briefed Nina. Stones had reported that the drone had watched the X-ray continue west on the E58 past Taganrog instead of heading north towards Latonova. He also reported that the Major's camp was no longer in the Latonova area and was last seen heading towards the border.

Nina took out the map and searched for the road.

He predicted they'd likely be just an hour behind - but they were still completely in the dark as to where they were going.

Once on the E58 they too continued west.

Regular updates from the Reaper, took them past Lakedemnovka and crossing an estuary bridge over the mouth of the Sea of Azov towards Natal'Yevka.

Since leaving the ring road behind, the roads were rural minors, and the traffic had become light and infrequent.

As they crossed the estuary, Tanner received one last update from Stones. The X-ray had taken the only righthand turn off the E58 they were currently driving on. The bad news, they were now on their own. The Reaper had to peel off to return to Poland for refuelling. Tanner relayed this to Nina.

"Just you and me then." she commented. They were close.

Soon, the righthand turn was in view.

The light had started to fade, dusk was coming, but they still had at least another hour or so of light.

The road they turned on looked long and desolate.

Tanner pulled over to look at the map with Nina.

"I'm familiar with this area. I have worked sources near here." Nina studied the map.

"Thoughts? Where could they be going?"

Nina ran her finger up the page, "Here," Her finger rested on a woodland dirt track close to a small village called Nikolayevo. "If I wanted to conduct business out of sight, this would be a good place."

"What have we to lose." Tanner announced. He tried to text the location to Stones, but his phone had entered a black spot.

He opened the windows so they could listen to their surroundings then continued northbound up the road.

The adrenaline tap had started to open.

Chapter Fifty-Nine

The camouflaged Gaz Tigr slowly moved along the dirt road, surrounded by the combination of larch, pine, and fir trees, standing tall above them on either side. It drove into a clearing and parked in front of a twin version of the vehicle.

Salamander looked out of the window at the haunting woodland. The last six hours of driving were done in complete silence. He was only given a bottle of water to last him the journey and he could feel his stomach growling for attention.

The soldiers both got out leaving only him and the driver alone in the vehicle. He too wanted to get out and stretch his whole body. He could hear muffled greetings and conversation but could not see who it was with.

Hearing footsteps, his door opened and instead of being grabbed, he was invited out. Where could he run to anyway, he didn't have a clue where in the world he was.

Climbing out he stretched hard and high trying to loosen his cramped body. Looking towards the front of the vehicle taking in his environment, was a man he had never seen before. The man had a presence about him that put Salamander on edge, a similar unwanted fear he had when around Jafar and Max. He stood at least a foot taller than Salamander, his uniform represented authority and he held a distinctive grin.

Major Sokolova stood, legs shoulder width apart, hands clasped behind his back, his body language reflecting his intent to intimidate and show him who was in charge.

Two of his soldiers stood behind Salamander, their AKMs relaxed but held across their bodies. The driver that had brought Salamander was now leaning against the Tigr observing. The only noise that could be heard was the sway of the treetops on either side of the road.

Dusk was coming.

"Welcome to Russia." the Major said, his arms now spread in a welcoming gesture.

Salamander understood his English but remained silent.

"So, Jafar has sent you all this way to deliver my precious cargo to me. You have succeeded in your task I hear."

Salamander dared himself to speak, "I've done what I was asked against my will, and now I want to return to my family."

The Major walked up to him and placed his hands on his shoulders. "Of course. Which way do you want to go?" he gestured jokingly to the forest.

The Major enjoyed the concern that spread over Salamander's face and broke into laughter, slapping the sides of his arms, "Come," he said putting his arm around his shoulder and walking them both to the rear of the vehicle, "Let's look at the gifts you have brought me."

One of the soldiers trotted ahead to open the back door displaying the two blue sports bags.

The Major stood looking at them briefly before smiling and stepping forward to open them.

Salamander stayed quiet and still, again in a predicament he was unable to know or see any way out of.

Chapter Sixty

As Tanner drove along the tree lined road of the forest, the woodland became denser. He drove slowly, as he and Nina looked around for the slightest hint of movement.

Suddenly to his right, he saw vehicle brake lights illuminate, through the trees. He grabbed Nina's attention and disconnected the hotwire, switching the engine off into a free roll. Tanner pulled slowly on the handbrake bringing the car to a stop, avoiding the brake pedal to prevent the glow of lights.

They could both hear car doors opening and closing, and in the distance, an inaudible conversation was taking place.

He whispered to Nina, they were going to deploy and move through the forest using the trees as cover, to get as close as they could. She nodded in agreement.

Tanner brought his assault rifle round off his shoulder, eased back the cocking lever to check a round was in the chamber, thumbed the fire selector to three round bursts, and grabbed his bag with extra magazines.

Nina checked the MP5K under her coat then brought her pistol to hand.

Reaching up he adjusted the internal light switch so the inside of the car wouldn't illuminate when the doors opened.

They both opened the doors as quietly as they could, leaving them ajar to avoid the noise of closing them.

They moved slowly through the dense trees, the light fading once they were under the canopy of the branches.

The floor was covered in pine needles which cushioned their footfalls as they crept closer.

Reaching the tree line edge, they stopped in cover next to

the road to see two Gaz Tigr 4x4s parked nose to tail.

Nina was six feet to his left. Both had lowered onto one knee ready to advance. Tanner removed his rucksack to improve his agility. He assessed the situation.

A younger soldier leaned back on his hands against the left side vehicle, he was facing their direction, pistol holstered, he wasn't an immediate threat. At the rear of the vehicle were two large men with AKMs in a relaxed posture with a third person looking inside the back. They would be his initial targets, extinguish the biggest threat, it wouldn't take them long to bring their weapons to bear.

As the third person came into full view Tanner realised it was the man he had been chasing across three countries and a sea… Salamander. Tanner doubted he had any weapons, and determined he would be the least threat initially.

Tanner then saw a pair of legs, wearing black combat boots below the rear vehicle door that was open. The top half of the person Tanner could not see so could not assess the risk of the individual. He surmised the man must be inspecting the weapons so could in all probability be Major Aaron Sokolova.

Tanner was fuelled for the moment, the adrenaline tap fully open. He could feel the blood pumping through him, and his senses heighten. The butt unfolded; the SR-3 tight against his shoulder muzzle three quarters raised - right index finger resting on the outside of the trigger guard, safety off.

His eyes met with Nina's… his open palm held up, signalling to wait.

Chapter Sixty-One

Salamander was a bag of nerves as the Major unzipped the bags. He just wanted to go home. Surely there can't be more for him to do. He felt a shiver grow over him and his knees nearly knocked together.

The Major pulled back the sides of the bags and stood back to admire each metal box. Placing a hand on each, he spoke to himself in a low tone, "Good, the time is coming, father."

There was a minute of silence, no one moved, and nobody spoke. Then, the Major removed a screwdriver from his inner jacket pocket and set about removing the screws, holding the topside of the metal box in place. Like a surgeon at work, he moved quickly from screw to screw. Lids removed, the recognisable components that Salamander had been witness to in Istanbul, now stared him in the face once again.

The Major inspected the internal workings and made a switch inside. Each weapon powered up, the digital readout and keypad illuminating red. A disturbing smirk had remained on his face throughout the process. Returning the switches to their previous positions the red glow from the electronics faded, then re-securing the lids, he zipped up the bags, returning everything as he had found it.

The Major turned and indicated with his arm for Salamander to walk with him. After a few steps, they were standing on the open road, the light fading fast.

The next question caught Salamander off guard, "You want to return to your home in Tehran?" The Major faced him.

"Of course," he stuttered, "It's all I want."

"You have indeed, exceeded everyone's expectations by

delivering these two biological weapons, that hopefully, will kill thousands of Ukrainian people. I take it Max told you what pain and death they will cause - and all delivered by your hands. You should be proud of yourself." He chuckled.

Salamander nodded, he didn't know how to answer what was starting to look and sound like a madman.

He wasn't remotely proud, he felt sick to the core.

The Major's tone changed in an instant. "But you are a traitor. You turned against DOTA and my friend Jafar."

The other soldiers remained where they stood, not moving, only listening to the Major's words.

"I've paid penance for my mistake." Salamander threw back, feeling an anger rising in him.

The Major switched his personality again and made a half-hearted laugh, "I suppose Jafar did promise you a return to your family, and I, promised I would return you to them."

Salamander felt hope explode throughout his body followed by sharp breaths of relief that fell from his smiling lips. Then as quickly as hope came, it disappeared, when Major Sokolova drew his pistol, aiming it at full stretch. He froze in abject horror at the executioner now stood before him.

The Major's aim was centred to Salamander's face, and he felt the surge of power as he witnessed the traitor's terror.

Salamander knew death had come for him, and there was nothing he could do about it.

"You will return to them," the Major declared sadistically, "In the afterlife - to which Jafar will send them to you!"

The Major felt the pressure on the pad of his finger as he prepared to pull the trigger.

Chapter Sixty-Two

Now!" Tanner projected forward bringing his weapon to the firing position. Moving at a tactical pace, weapon up, he stared down the iron sights of the Vikhr rifle bringing the centre mass of the first soldier lazily carrying his AKM.

From this range Tanner's weapon was effective. The loud triple crack of the three round bursts left the barrel with a flash of orange, striking his target's chest. In Tanner's sight, the body jolted backward. Surprise followed by death in quick succession spasmed across the soldier's face.

The gunfire smell hit Tanner's senses. He continued forward through the muzzle smoke. By the time Tanner had his aim on soldier number two, soldier one was already down in the dirt never to rise again.

Tanner had the scent of the kill but remained composed.

Centre mass number two flowed into his iron sight, his weapon rising toward Tanner. In the automatic setting, the soldier wasn't ready for AKM kickback, and sent an upwards arc of 7.62mm rounds into the treetops. It provided Tanner the opening he needed, *crack, crack, crack*, another three round burst tore through his target who twisted and collapsed to the floor. The echoes of the gunfire bounced around the trees before slowly fading.

In seconds Tanner had extinguished the initial threats and now held aim at the Major from twenty feet away, an easy target. His breath was controlled but his body and mind buzzed as the adrenaline surged.

Nina was to his left, pistol drawn, pointing in a similar direction. He hadn't heard any shots from her direction, but then again, he hadn't given her any warning and already had the advantage in the situation.

Incredibly, the ice-cool Major still had the barrel of his pistol firmly pointed at Salamander, a wicked smile still spread across his face.

The driver in the background was frozen against the vehicle, pistol still holstered not attempting to draw it, he knew he wouldn't stand a chance.

"Drop the weapon!" Tanner demanded.

He looked at Salamander, the expression of horror replaced by utter confusion. 'No surprise there,' Tanner thought, he probably never expected me to turn up and save his arse.

To Tanner's surprise, the Major started to laugh almost uncontrollably, "You have no idea, do you?" His aim remained on Salamander, but he held Tanner's stare.

"Drop it or I drop you!" Tanner demanded, "This is your last chance, Major."

The Major turned to Nina, "What do you think I should do?"

Tanner saw Nina slowly move in his peripheral vision...

Then felt the barrel of her MP-443 Grach pistol press against his temple.

"Good to see you, Maxine," the Major chortled.

"You too, brother." Max replied.

Chapter Sixty-Three

Maxine Sokolova aka Nina Rosewood hadn't been completely dishonest with Tanner when they spoke during their car journey. Her mother was English, and her father was Russian. She was fluent in both languages and studied Russian Politics at Oxford University.

It was also true how MI6 approached her.

But she had lied about the rest of her life, especially about her twin brother Aaron, the Major.

They were very close and completely relied upon each growing up when their father was banished from their home. Maxine idolised her father, and along with Aaron, their world was shattered when he no longer returned home, after their mother had moved her Ukrainian lover into the home.

She as well as her brother, built a hatred for the Ukrainian that grew even stronger over time.

Maxine never could, and never did tell anyone, about the times the monster used to creep into her bedroom in the middle of the night. It started with him just laying with her his hand slipping under her nightie, the smell of tobacco and whiskey on his breath. He had threatened her that if she spoke of it to anyone, he would beat her brother to the edge of death.

As time went by her mother started drinking more as her relationship strained with the Ukrainian, often going to sleep at night in an alcohol induced coma.

As Maxine grew older, his visits became more frequent, she tried to pretend to be asleep but that didn't put him off. She would just squeeze her eyes tightly shut and take herself to a different place, until the pain stopped. The hatred for him and all Ukrainian men could be no greater.

Even when she heard he was dying of cancer, it wasn't justice enough for her, nothing would pacify the nightmares that still haunted her at night. A secret never to be revealed.

When their father passed, both she and her twin brother made a pact to avenge his death by raining hell on all Ukrainians. Unlike Aaron, she did not take up a religion, there was no God in her eyes. She only had belief in herself.

The last time her father had come to Russia to speak to them, he confessed his religion and his reasons for not returning and remaining in Istanbul. Her father had taken a quiet moment with Maxine.

He wanted her to meet a friend of his the next day.

The meeting was arranged, and she was introduced to a suited man of similar age to her father. He wore a long thick trench coat and a traditional Russian hat.

They met in Sokolniki Park in central Moscow and strolled talking for over an hour. It was there she was recruited by the FSB. After months of hellish training, she was to become a double agent, to be recruited and infiltrate MI6.

Using her mother's maiden name, she became Nina Rosewood. The FSB had the ability to alter Maxine's past, while creating a new history for Nina. She was then sent to Oxford. As a Russian who possessed a remarkable intellect with a part English bloodline, the FSB were confident she would soon be of interest to the British Intelligence Services.

Once recruited and working for MI6, she would regularly pass information to the FSB, keeping them one step ahead in the spy game as a double agent.

While helping her brother put their plan together, with the

help of Jafar, she was stunned when her MI6 boss, Ed Boden, directed her to investigate Major Sokolova, and in doing so unwittingly tasked her to investigate the dealings of her own brother. She was in a perfect position to keep the biological weapon plan intact and ensure there were no disruptions.

Then Tanner came along.

Her next steps were simple, keep close to him, work with him, and try to keep him at distance from reaching Salamander and the weapons… until now.

*

The cold steal of Nina's pistol remained pressed against his head. Tanner looked at her from the corner of his eye.

Her usual frosty exterior had altered slightly, her lips pursed, allowing a small smile of satisfaction.

She had completely fooled him, and she felt good about it.

He could now see the similarities between them both.

His mind was on fire, spiralling as he tried to understand what was happening. No one's weapons had moved, they were in a three-way standoff, all aiming at different targets. Maxine to Tanner, Tanner to the Major, the Major to Salamander.

Something needed to give. Tanner was certain the first to back down would probably be the first to fall, "You're a double agent?" Tanner spat the question out.

"Well done, Mr Tanner," Maxine sneered, "I knew there was more to you than brawn and keeping me warm at night."

"She was the one forcing me to bring the bombs here." Salamander blurted out.

"Shut up!" the Major shouted, adjusting the pistol in his

grip seeing Salamander cower.

“So, are you going to enlighten me on what the fuck is going on here?” Tanner demanded.

“Are you going to lower your weapon?”

“No. Are you?” Tanner knew the answer.

“Of course not.” She paused. “I am MI6 that is no lie, but I was a plant, I work for the FSB. But that is beside the point. My main purpose was to ensure you didn't ruin the plan my brother and I put together. You are like a dog with a bone Tanner, but you're so focused on getting the bone that you are blind to your surroundings.”

“Well, I certainly got the bone with you.” Tanner tried for a small victory, but it was ignored. He decided to try and rattle the situation - he needed to find an opportunity to react. “Have either of you thought of the devastation you are about to inflict on a ton of innocent people?” He knew the words would fall on deaf ears, but he needed time.

“Fuck you!” the Major replied, “You have no idea why we are doing this.”

Tanner took the Major’s angry reply as his cue to rattle him further, “Of course I do, you’re Jafar's little bitch, and he is getting you to do his dirty work.”

“Jafar is DOTA, I am DOTA, we serve the same purpose.”

Tanner was pleased at how quickly the Major was losing his cool, “Oh, so Jafar turned you into a disciple too. He likes to prey on weak minded people.”

“Your mouth will get you killed.” Maxine said calmly.

Tanner could feel the situation heating up, it could give him the opening he needed, “Did you fuck Jafar too Nina?” he emphasized her false identity.

It didn't work, instead she just gave out a single laugh. There was no risk of her losing control, a fact he already knew.

“This isn't about DOTA, for me it never was. I'm not a follower, this is for our father.” she said.

“Your Father? He abandoned his country I heard. Another weak soul for Jafar to take advantage of.”

Tanner's last comment blew the lid off the Major who on hearing words against his father saw red, quickly turning his pistol toward Tanner. “My father was not a weak man, he was a great man, watch your infidel mouth!” he raged.

It hadn't quite played out as Tanner had hoped, he now had a second weapon pointing at him.

Two verses one, not the best odds he mused.

“Brother. Calm it, he is just trying to rattle you.” It was clear she had control of her brother too.

“Well as lovely as this reunion has been for us all, we have some business to attend to.” The Major’s tone was instantly calm once more, and Tanner noted that as quickly as the Major’s anger had built, it had just as rapidly started to ease, suggesting to Tanner he might well be unhinged.

“Well, what can I say, I'm clearly outnumbered.” Tanner composed himself and took a check of everyone around him. He began lowering his weapon, then causally, and somewhat unexpectedly, threw the rifle to the floor in front of him.

As the weapon clattered to the ground it momentarily averted the gaze of the others, giving Tanner the split-second he needed - then it all happened unpredictably at once.

His training brain kicked in and all other distractions were frozen out, his only mission now, was to survive.

In a single movement he dropped his head out of Maxine's

line of fire, swinging his left arm up and back knocking the MP-443 pistol out of her grip and into the undergrowth.

At the same time, he drew his pistol at breakneck speed.

Surprisingly, Salamander was the next to move. He saw the chance to escape toward the trees. This movement drew the Major's attention, and he brought his weapon around to the fleeing man and away from Tanner.

Tanner's target was the Major, but as he drew to shoot, the forgotten driver in the background chose the wrong time to become a hero. Tanner saw the weapon raise in his direction and altered his aim beyond the Major, squeezing the trigger at the exact same moment as the driver. The soldier's shot was loose and ended in the trees behind him. Tanner's Sig Sauer clunked twice, followed by the ping of the brass jackets as the rounds ejected from the chamber. With the lick of flame leaving the muzzle he watched the double tap thudding into the driver's chest, their exit decorating the side of the vehicle behind him.

The Major fired a volley towards the running Salamander, who dived headfirst into a ditch at the side of the road.

Two targets left.

Tanner needed to move - with Maxine to his rear and her brother turning towards him, he was a sitting duck.

He started to move backward and to the left when he collided with Maxine, who was trying to retrieve the MP5K from under her jacket. Tanner used his weight and knocked her to the ground then stamped on her.

Her brother was close to reaching the vehicles for cover. His aim was up, the only thing that had stopped him from firing was the thought of hitting his sister.

Tanner fired wild shots in his direction. They were off target, with one shot going for a tour in the forest, and the other hitting the side of the vehicle with a metallic thud.

Stepping over the *grappling bitch*, Tanner moved toward the tree line to gain cover. As he left the road he looked to the right and could see Salamander crawling in the ditch.

He continued into the shadows and dived to the ground as Maxine finally lost her cool. Enraged, she let out a volley of shots in Tanner's general direction. The rounds were so close he felt the path of heat as the bullets whizzed past him, showering him in splinters of bark.

As her magazine expended, she threw the automatic to the floor and picked up the pistol that Tanner had earlier disarmed her of, before firing it into the nothingness of the dark trees.

"Maxine!" her brother shouted.

Following his voice, she sprinted towards the Gaz Tigr with the new art deco blood pattern seeping down the side.

Tanner remained on the deck until he heard a pause in the chaos. He then moved into a kneeling position and returned fire toward Maxine as she clambered into the passenger side doorway. She was almost in when one of Tanner's rounds stuck her left upper arm - she let out a cry of pain and wrapped her other hand over the entry wound to protect it. Even after the door was shut, Tanner kept firing into the bulletproof glass, each 9mm round making a small spider web with the impact.

His last round was spent as the Tigr roared up the mud road, leaving a cloud of dust in the dusk light. The smug grin on Maxine's face was now replaced with pain and fury.

Tanner watched the 4x4 disappear down the road and rounded the junction… taking the biological weapons with it.

Chapter Sixty-Four

Tanner stood within the arena of the gunfight, the light rapidly fading. Muzzle smoke drifted in the air, the metallic smell of sulphur filling his nostrils.

The high pitch ring still buzzed his ears, and the adrenaline *come down* hit him like a junkie going cold turkey.

Tanner's breathing felt rapid, in tune with his accelerated heartbeat. He took some deep sulfuric breaths to try and get his body under control. Standing amongst the brass casings scattered like confetti, he heard a groaning noise emanating from beyond the line of trees... Salamander.

Tanner rushed to where he remembered last seeing him in the ditch. He was no longer there. Instead, there was a trail of blood and depressed grass leading into the trees. He quickly followed the bloody path to find Salamander sitting upright against the trunk of a tree. His face looked grey and clammy, his hands covered in blood and holding his gut, trying to apply compression to extend what little life was left in him.

Tanner knelt beside him and moved his hands to assess the wound. When his hands were removed, a spurt of dark blood shot out from the entry point of the bullet.

Tanner replaced Salamander's hands over the hole and gently pressed them down.

He let out a painful grunt.

Salamander's hands felt ice cold, his breathing short rasps.

Tanner reached behind Salamander's lower back.

He felt a sticky mess pooling in his palm and knew he was in the last moments of his life.

Between breaths, Salamander tried to speak.

“Hunter. I'm sorry, I didn't know what they were going to do,” he struggled, “My family - they had my family.”

Tanner gave an understanding nod and placed a hand on his shoulder. At that moment, he felt sorry for the man dying in front of him. It appeared everything he had done was an attempt to save the ones he loved. Tanner would have done the same thing, and he found an unexpected sense of respect for Salamander. “It will be okay; we’ll get you fixed up and back home soon.” Tanner knew the reality but at that moment didn’t want to remove any last element of hope from a dying man.

“Promise me you'll save my wife and daughter, Anahita and Daria, she's only six years old.”

“I will.” Tanner made the promise not knowing if he could keep it, he didn't even know if they were alive.

No more words left him as his body became lifeless.

Tanner ran his thumb and forefinger over Salamander’s eyelids to emulate a look of peace upon his face.

He sat and leaned against the same tree looking up.

The sky was almost as dark as the shadows in the dense woodland. He had a moment of reflection. It was time to switch his mind to combat mode, pushing everything negative out and refocusing to achieve the mission at hand.

‘Track the twins, stop the biological attack, kill anyone in my way, be the fucking hero.’ He exhaled, then sprung up to look at what equipment he could utilise.

First, he gathered up the weapons on the ground.

2 AKMs each with full magazines and Vortex Venom red dot scope. Spare AKM mags from the two dead soldier's belts.

Dead driver's MP-443 Grach pistol, plus two mags.

MP5K - empty.

Tanners' SR-3 Vikhr compact assault rifle.

Tanner checked the abandoned Gaz Tigr - no keys, and he was unlikely to be able to hot wire this one. A quick search found another AKM and a couple of mags on the passenger side. In the rear, a small grab bag stored a couple of flashbangs, other than that, the vehicle was useless. He headed to where his attack had begun to retrieve his backpack.

Tanner decided his armament would consist of an AKM and all the 7.62mm round mags, his Vikhr, and his Sig P229.

He filled his bag with the ammo and the flash bangs.

He didn't risk running through the woods and picking up an injury in the dark. Instead, he ran in the direction he saw the twins speed off in, following the road before looping back to where he left the Lada Niva.

Tanner hoped in their haste to get away, they had not thought about stopping and making the Lada inoperable.

Chapter Sixty-Five

The camouflaged Gaz Tigr accelerated down the dirt road, the tall trees on either side looking like rows of guardsmen. The deep gripping tread of the tyres tore into the surface, tearing up chunks of mud and discarding them in the air, leaving plumes of dust in its wake.

Maxine looked in the wing-mirror at the shadow of Tanner growing smaller, left standing in the middle of the road, fading behind the clouds of dust.

She gripped her upper left arm and looked at the blood oozing between her clenched fingers pressed on the wound.

Tanner's initial attack had been launched against her brother's men so quickly it had caught her off-guard. He had then got the jump on them, on her, and had gifted her an injury with a 9mm round. Not quite as the plan was supposed to go. Tanner was supposed to be dead.

She remembered his face as he fired at the glass toward her. The determination of the dog had returned, and she was the bone. If it wasn't for the reinforced glass, she would have a few additional holes in her right now.

He wanted to kill her.

If her secret hadn't already been revealed, with Tanner alive, it soon would be. She would now become a target not only for MI6 but the FSB once they were made aware of the biological attack she and her brother were planning.

The FSB would and could not be part of that.

The political backlash would be immense.

Maxine would now be running and hiding for the rest of her life, and her hate for Tanner in that moment burned from her very core.

While Maxine sat silently tending the bullet graze wound, her brother was the opposite, and was acting like a crazed madman. Major Sokolova was so pumped that even his driving became erratic. He couldn't sit still in his seat.

He realised how close he had come to death before his escape. He began letting out 'whoops' while laughing hysterically, his eyes wide as he focused on the road.

"We did it sis, we have the bombs."

"We also didn't clean up, and now have two liabilities on the loose." she snapped back.

He heard her tone, but he wasn't going to let it dampen him.

"Who gives a fuck, we have the bombs, and my men are waiting for us." He shouted, "Death to Ukraine!" and began punching the ceiling of the cab.

She knew there was no point in calming him - that would soon follow once the adrenaline faded, then he would slump. Maxine had torn the sleeve from her good arm and using her teeth to aid her, tied the material tightly around her bicep, covering the wound.

She grimaced as the pressure was applied.

When they reached the main road, they turned right onto the E58 and sped off to the west - towards the border.

Chapter Sixty-Six

Tanner reached the Lada. His eyes had adjusted to the lack of light and his natural night vision had established itself.

He checked around the vehicle - all tyres still inflated, no bullet entry holes on the front grill and the doors were still ajar. Just the way Tanner had left it.

He threw his backpack onto the rear seat, and his loaded weapons next to him on the passenger side.

He had to hotwire the car again, but it was simply a case of re-tapping the naked battery wire on his previous work and the Lada flashed into life again.

He turned the car about and gunned it towards the E58, his mobile gripped in his hand waiting and hoping the reception would remarry with the phone.

Turning right onto the main road, the bumpy countryside lane gave way to a smooth tarmac road, paralleling the Sea of Azov toward the Ukrainian border.

Tanner's eyes flicked between the road ahead, his phone, and the map. He estimated thirty-eight minutes to the border, or what resembled a border in these times of conflict.

The phone screen lit up as it drew on the signal, and three bars showed up. He quickly punched the 'S' contact in his phone, representing Stones. All contacts in their phones were letters or abbreviations, to protect their identities, in case the phones ever found their way into the wrong hands.

It hadn't even rung once before Stones answered, "Tanner?'

"Yeah, it's me. I have some important news."

"It's good to hear your voice, I have some urgent information for you too," before Tanner could speak Stones continued urgently, “Are you alone, can you talk?”

“Yes.”

“Before you go any further watch your back, the Firm agent Nina, isn't who she says she is.”

“No shit,” he retorted, “She's FSB. Her name is Maxine Sokolova. The dead twin of Major Aaron Sokolova who I can assure you is very much alive as she just tried to kill me.”

“I was updated by Ed in the last hour,” Stones pressed on, “They lost comms with her in Istanbul, and have been trying to track her. GCHQ linked her and the Major's phones and as they dug deeper the rest started to become apparent.”

“Salamander's dead,” Tanner updated, “And they still have the weapons.”

“What's the plan?”

“Can you track my phone?”

“I'll get GCHQ onto it ASAP.” Stones had Palmer with him, and she was already making the call.

“If you can track any of the Sokolova twin's mobiles that would be an idea. I'm currently heading west toward the Ukraine border. I'm going to need as much help as I can get to find them. I think they have an hour on me.”

“We are on it - we have the drone back up to assist,” Stone’s tone edged toward concern, “You, ok?”

“Don't worry about me, just get me to those weapons before they have time to set them off.”

“Ed's team has assessed the target to be Mariupol. A highly populated area housing many Ukrainian soldiers,” Stones informed, “That's where the weapons would have maximum impact and sustain the most fatalities.”

Tanner recognised the familiar brief silence which meant

more ‘good news’ was inbound,

“Tanner, you are still on your own with this one. Sorry, but NATO cannot conduct any strikes as it would be seen as an act of war against Russia- and with Putin's itchy trigger finger, we don't want to risk that.”

“Understood.” That's how Tanner liked it anyway, he worked better on his own, with no one to get in his way or hold him up, “Get a message to the soldiers in Mariupol. Tell them to get everyone the fuck out of there.” Tanner ended the call and looked down at his map - keeping to this road should take him straight into the heart of Mariupol.

Chapter Sixty-Seven

Maxine and Aaron drove in silence, both coming to terms with what they were shortly to inflict on the Ukrainian people. Men and women, young and old… children.

They had come too far now to turn back.

They had endured a childhood of abuse and torture at the hands of a Ukrainian, and a father stolen from them. Nothing could heal them of the deep emotional and psychological scars that cut deep into their souls.

Having finally calmed down from his childlike excitement when escaping the woods, the Major was going over the plan in his head, while driving as fast as he could in the armoured vehicle. “I don't think we have time to meet the troops as per the original plan.”

“Because of the loose ends we didn't deal with?” Maxine was physically sore from the gunshot, and mentally pained because Tanner got away.

“It could compromise things of course, what is done is done - but it does not mean we cannot still achieve the mission and unleash hell on these fuckers.”

“What have you got in mind?” she didn't have her brother's enthusiasm at present.

“I'm going to call my 2iC and get him to reposition the troops to Pikuzy. It's a small village with a route into Mariupol, they can meet us there. It's out of the way for us, but easier for them as the convoy will be slower. Once regrouped, we will have the support and firepower to re-enter the city and set the bombs.”

Maxine agreed with her brother, and he made the call to get

his men repositioned.

Soon, they were approaching the border.

Crossing in this zone wasn't a problem for the Major, his rank and reputation were enough to let him pass through with no questions asked.

The border checkpoint was held by Russian troops. It was a small checkpoint lit up by the orange glow of floodlights that resembled large heat lamps. It was manned by six soldiers, who took turns on watch at the barrier hut. No doubt the others were in one of the three builds parallel to each other, either drinking vodka or watching porn - probably both.

He almost wanted to stop and drag them with him, but he needed men with desire, men that had a purpose to fulfil.

As he approached the checkpoint the barrier into Ukraine was left open, but the one into Russia was closed.

Winding down the window he glided slowly past the hut.

At first, the soldier just waved him past, but then caught sight of his insignia and jumped from his seat into a position of stiff attention. He saluted as the Major continued by.

The Major wound up his window and started to accelerate while muttering some annoyance under his breath.

They were now in Ukraine.

The E58 had now become the M-14 and the headlights carved their way into the blackness of the lamp-less road.

The clouds were low and heavy in the sky, blocking any moonlight from shining through.

It was getting late, and as they drove around the fringes of Novoazovsk, the roads were empty.

Few people ventured out at night for fear of being mistaken for a soldier of the opposite side by a sniper of the opposite side. It was like an invisible curfew had been put in place.

The Major wasn't bothered about the occasional stray round hitting the armoured vehicle, his speed coupled with the armour was enough deterrent for most not to bother wasting the shot.

He tried to assess what time his troops would arrive in Pikuzy, close to midnight he imagined. It would be best to hunker down there for the night and advance first thing in the morning. Some military strategists would say attacking at night would give you the advantage. The Major, from experience, knew that it also led to uncertainty and higher blue-on-blue contact.

Turning off the smooth tarmac of the M-14, he took a road heading northwest, cutting across to the new meeting point. The heavy Tigr bounced around on the track which had more holes than a fisherman's net, kicking up stones and lumps of tarmac that had been used to fill the pots.

He reduced his speed.

Rain had started to fall hard, reducing his visibility, and hitting the roof of the cabin, sounding like gravel was being poured over the vehicle from a height.

He felt tired.

Maxine was already asleep using her blooded-sleeved jacket as a makeshift blanket.

He continued to drive into the night.

Chapter Sixty-Eight

With everything that had been happening over the last few hours, Tanner hadn't thought about the Russia/Ukraine border crossing. He had seen it up ahead bathed in an orange glow, a Russian guard sitting at his post in a small hut.

Tanner had received another call from Stones updating that the Reaper had been pulled off task due to the heavy cloud layer - they had no visibility and so once again, he was on his own. He'd pulled over keeping the engine running and switching off the lights to observe the activity of the checkpoint through the Vortex Scope taken from the AKM sitting next to him.

It was late, and the sky outside was black, accentuating the warm glow of the hut. The rain had come, a few drops at first, but soon it felt like he was in a car wash. The window wipers gave him a few seconds of clear view before returning his line of sight to a watery blur.

He had assessed that the only threat would be the one soldier sitting in the box. No other person seemed to be around, they must all be camped in one of the larger buildings that occupied the crossing. There were three structures, all grey unrendered blocks, with corrugated metal sloped roofs, the rain cascading down like a waterfall.

Tanner thought the rain hitting the roofs must be deafening, a huge advantage if things got noisy, delaying any reaction.

There were two roads that ran between the buildings. The one entering the Russian route seemed to be closed but the pole barrier for the road Tanner wanted to take, was raised.

A quick scan did not identify any security cameras.

Tanner planned to approach and slow down as if to speak to the guard, then floor it at the last minute if no obstacles blocked him. If necessary, he would give the guard a bad news delivery with the 9mm. He unholstered his pistol, checked a round was in the chamber and tucked it under his leg nearest his window. Switching on the headlamps he pulled back out into the road and brought the car up to speed.

As Tanner approached, he kept his headlamps on high to dazzle the guard for as long as possible. He slowed as he drew nearer the checkpoint box - the rain still hammering down. The guard stood and raised his hand to shield his eyes from the headlights, allowing Tanner to see he had an AKM strapped across his body. Everywhere had a tangerine glow to it.

Tanner crawled closer to the guard, who didn't want to leave his box for fear of getting wet. The tyres made popping sounds as they rolled over the odd loose stone. He was almost level with the doorway, and impulsively made a strategic decision, raising the Sig from under the fold of his leg.

He didn't need to sight it; from that range it would be effective enough. He squeezed the trigger. Firing a single shot. He felt the top slide jolt back and forwards with a smooth metallic 'clunk-click', and the cartridge expended to the other side of the car. The guard didn't have time to react, he stood frozen to the spot as the round impacted the middle of his face, turning it into a bowl of flesh and bone. The glass window behind the soldier shattered, as the bullet passed through the guard's head. His body slumped in the chair like a ragdoll.

Tanner didn't even stop, he just cruised by pulling his weapon back through the window, and slowly accelerated away down the M-14. He checked his mirrors for a response to what had just happened. Nothing.

His decision to take out the soldier was made at the last second. If he was to stop, he had no documentation and a car full of weapons, he would have been taken into custody.

Driving away at speed could have been achieved, but it would allow the guard to raise the alarm, the fallout of which could escalate quickly. So, he'd decided to gamble on the heavy rain against the metal roofs and send the guard to meet his maker, allowing him to get away with no witnesses.

The quick fix of adrenaline kept his focus in check, pushing the tiredness to the back of his mind.

With the map on his lap and the internal light on he tried to work the plan. What were the Russian *Pinky and Perky* up to?

It would be guesswork and assumptions at this time, so he decided the best plan was to take the most direct and fastest route to Mariupol, in the hope of either catching them or getting ahead if they had taken an alternative route. Anything else that cropped up he would have to deal with on the ground.

The M-14 followed the coastline of the Sea of Azov and would take him directly into the city. Tanner knew this was a risk, the area had pockets of Russian and Ukrainian forces and coming across either could be hazardous to his health. He hoped the night would allow his presence to go unnoticed.

He pushed the Lada to a comfortable speed, the lights barely breaking the darkness even when switched to full beam.

With so much going on in his head, his mind for reasons of its own took him back to the time he had spent with Nina.

Chapter Sixty-Nine

The night was pitch black as the Major and Maxine arrived in Pikuzy to wait for the Major's convoy of troops.

Located twenty-three kilometres to the north-east of Mariupol in Eastern Ukraine, the small village appeared lifeless. No rooms were lit, and as the light beams from the vehicle lit up the streets it appeared the village was abandoned.

Pikuzy had been hit hard by the conflict, most buildings were riddled with bullet holes and broken windows, others were little more than a pile of rubble. The village had been caught in a tug-of-war between two sides, a struggle that had seen no-one triumph especially those that called Pikuzy home.

The Major reversed back and parked between two derelict houses off the main road. The rain had eased into a drizzle, and he cracked his window open so he could hear his troops rolling in. He didn't wake Maxine and decided he would try to get some shut eye himself.

A few hours later the Major woke to a low, distant rumble. He checked his VOSTOK Komandirskie Russian Army Commander wristwatch - the white glow of the face with its red star emblem highlighted the luminous hands that showed the time: 0136hrs.

He got out, careful not to wake Maxine, and stepped into the road. He watched his men approach, the BTR-80 armoured carrier leading with its turret manned.

He felt triumphant before the battle had even begun.

He spoke to his 2iC, passing down orders for the men to move the vehicles out of sight then to bed down in whatever shelter they could find. They were to be ready to roll in the morning. In good military fashion, everyone dispersed without question, happy to make the most of a few hours rest.

*

As dawn broke, the daylight confirmed Pikuzy's status as a ghost town. It appeared not a single resident inhabited any of the buildings, the abandoned residential properties peppered in bullet holes and decaying paint. Homes had seen their windows smashed, doors kicked in and contents looted.

The road that ran through the centre of the village on a direct route to the city had received its own makeover courtesy of a barrage of large calibre rockets.

Abandoned cars had been used as a canvas for graffiti artists to voice their political views while others had been burnt out, their frames and form buckled and twisted.

No one would be returning any time soon.

The rain had stopped and everywhere was damp, the overcast sky adding to the gloom.

*

The Major held a bonnet top mission brief on the Tigr. Attending was Maxine, his 2iC, and three squad leaders. Between them they commanded twenty-two men, having lost three of their number during the skirmish in the woods.

The Major started to brief.

"It's a twenty-minute drive into the city from here to the old bridge," he pointed at the location on the map, "We will dismount and deploy on foot from there. Crossing the bridge, we will move across open ground over the railway line, making our way to this point." His finger moved across the map. "2iC and one squad leader will take two units of five men, and push down Fontanna Street, making your way to Mariupol City Hospital and secure there. The hospital is your target. Lieutenant Colonel Maxine Sokolova will plant and set the biological weapon. You will provide her with cover fire." The Major used his sister's FSB rank to give her authority and respect from the men around her.

"Once the weapon is set, return to the RV and wait. I and the two other squad leaders with their units will follow the exact route until here." He indicated a junction on Kundzhy Street where Maxine and her units were to split. "We will then move down both sides of the street to the open area. Here at the fountain, we will hold using the green areas for cover. Once the area is secure. I will set the second weapon. Then we will bug out returning to the RV. Once we have all regrouped, we will head east as a convoy at speed, to put distance between us before the weapons go off. Any questions?" He looked around at the faces studying the map.

No one had any questions.

"Expect resistance, anything that moves against us, shoot. He smiled, "Mount up, we leave in 15 minutes."

Aaron noticed Maxine had been quiet. When they were alone, he felt he needed to question her commitment.

He was happy with her response.

It was cold, calculated and she was angry.

Tanner getting away was still grinding at her. She had given herself to him and now she wanted him dead. His escape meant she'd been exposed, and she wondered what other tricks he had up his sleeve that he'd no doubt be determined to play. She rubbed her aching arm.

More so, her childhood nightmares had been haunting her. She hoped this attack would go some way to blocking them out. Revenge for her and her father had been a long time coming.

The Major found a quiet spot in the living room of a deserted house. He rolled out his prayer mat. He needed to pray, to ask Allah for protection, to see him complete his mission against the infidel - striking a blow for DOTA.

It was a good day, he was blessed, and the wind was blowing in a westerly direction.

The convoy had mounted up and was ready to roll.

The Major and Maxine led the troops down the road.

He had two whip flag poles added to the front of his Gaz Tigr nudge bar. One bore the Russian flag… the other the Tawheed, used to represent Islam.

Chapter Seventy

By dawn the weather had improved and the Reaper was back on task high above the patchy cloud, watching Mariupol and the surrounding areas from high in the sky.

Satellite imagery had shown the movement and relocation of Major Sokolova's forces overnight from Kuznetsi to Pikuzy.

GCHQ had tapped into the few cellular towers still operational, to triangulate the RF signals from both Maxine's and her brother's mobile phones. This confirmed they had now met with the Major's troops and were camped in the small village of Pikuzy, with the biological weapons.

GCHQ also tracked Tanner's phone signal, and the Reaper had eyes on his location. The drone's live stream was being broadcast and observed in several places - the Polish Air Force base in Miroslawiec - MI6 headquarters at Vauxhall Cross - Northwood Bunker, Head of British Military Operations with NATO representation - and the briefing room in Tanner's unit compound, Tehran.

Stones had fed all the information through to Tanner as soon as they found out where the weapons were located.

Tanner had arrived on the outskirts of Mariupol city a little past midnight, not knowing if Maxine and her crazed brother had already arrived and set the horror of their attack into motion. Tanner felt relieved when he heard they were waiting to regroup outside the city and had bunked down for the night. This gave Tanner time for some rest - he was running on fumes and the adrenaline had burnt out. He had made it into the city and found a railway yard, with hundreds of freight carriages, it looked like they had not been used for a while.

In the dark, he hid the car, unloaded the weapons, and found a carriage to hide out in until the sun rose.

Before bedding down for a few hours, Tanner searched the ground outside, until he came across what he was looking for.

Climbing up the ladder at the end of the carriage, Tanner climbed onto the roof and with the piece of stone chalk he had found, he marked a big 'X' onto the top of the carriage.

Stones would now have a visual lock on Tanner's position.

He woke at 0600hrs confused at first by his surroundings and had to orientate himself. Tanner was cold as the daylight had started to creep through the cracks of the freight carriage. He slid the side door open a crack, to let the fresh air in, it felt frosty, and the mist came off his breath.

After a couple of deep breaths and feeling the icicles in his lungs, he started to feel awake.

Chapter Seventy-One

Ed Boden and his MI6 team had worked through the night to formulate a plan to support Tanner. They'd recalled all their known sources in Ukraine, hoping for a contact in the Mariupol region. The message they tried to send was for people to evacuate the area, both civilians and soldiers.

Satellite imagery had picked up small droves of the city's population leaving, but not as many as they had hoped.
Ed understood the mammoth task. How do you convince a person who has grown up in conflict to abandon their home and few precious possessions? Unfortunately, these people were not afraid. Most would rather run the risk or fight back, it was in the Ukrainian DNA.

The second part of the plan was to find someone amongst the Ukrainian forces who could command a platoon of soldiers and assist Tanner in stopping the weapons from detonating.

It was high risk, a possibly fatal task for all involved if they could not stop the Major's forces.

An unlikely source in Kyiv had suggested a cousin, Volodymyr Shevchenko, who was fighting in Mariupol.

His feelings against the Russian invasion were equally as strong as the source's. The Kyiv contact had been run by MI6 for the last three years and was reliable. The source had since contacted his cousin Volodymyr to gauge his interest in taking a call from some 'friends'. It had been explained it would be to protect the people of Ukraine and he had not hesitated to volunteer his services.

Before daybreak, the call had been made to Volodymyr. He was briefed on the full facts - nothing was held back from him.

Ed needed him to understand the stark reality of the situation.

If Volodymyr was willing, he was needed to lead a group of as many men as he could muster, to go up against a known Russian attack. Potentially in the next few hours. In addition, they would need to bring Tanner into the fold, as he had the intelligence that might give them the advantage to defeat the enemy. Volodymyr was onboard, the thought of this weapon being used against his country fuelling him to defeat this Major and his men. He was given the position and train carriage in the railyard where Tanner would be waiting.

Ed contacted Stones with the update.

The rest was now down to fate.

*

Shortly after Tanner had woken up, his mobile phone vibrated. He noticed the battery had one bar left.

"Tanner," he answered.

"Stones here, how are you doing?"

"Cold, tired, hungry, and wanting a beer."

Stones recognised the humour in Tanner's tone, "Well not everyone gets to holiday in Ukraine nowadays, you should make the most of it, do a city tour."

The military humour didn't fail to bring a smile to Tanner's face, it was much needed. "So, what's the plan?"

"Ed has made a contact for you in the city."

"Ed!? Can I trust this one?" it was a cutting statement. Stones understood Tanner's lack of faith in Ed's operators, "His name is Volodymyr, not much is known about him so be careful. He'll lead a squad alongside you to get the job done."

"Does he know what we are up against?" Tanner asked.

"Yes, he has been briefed, no holds barred. He is a passionate Ukrainian and the opportunity to defeat a Russian attack on his country is welcomed."

"Sounds like a loose cannon," Tanner shrugged, "Perhaps that's what we need."

"They are on their way to you now, so keep a watch out. It wouldn't be a good start if you shot one of them by mistake."

Tanner's mind went back to the guard he'd killed the night before. He would have been found by now, and the shit would certainly be hitting the fan somewhere. "Stones, if," Tanner corrected, "Sorry, *when* we defeat the Major and I have the weapons in front of me - how am I going to disarm them?"

"When you're at that point, call me, I have someone from the bomb disposal unit already in the next room waiting to assist."

Tanner heard some noise outside, "Got to go, I think someone is here."

Chapter Seventy-Two

Tanner retreated into the shadows of the carriage and hid behind the remnants of the last cargo hauled.

From his chosen angle, he could still see through the gap in the side door he had opened earlier. It gave him a viewpoint along the track of anyone coming his way.

He had picked up the AKM and pressed himself back into the corner, rifle butt tight into his shoulder. He looked through the sight enhancing the limited outside view.

The sound of footsteps crunching on the stones of the surrounding tracks grew closer. He could hear snippets of conversation in a language Tanner didn't understand. They were not cautious with their volume, and sounded like they were on a causal stroll around the yard.

Two figures came into the sight's view reaching the end of his carriage. They were both wearing old-style combats, not the new digital camouflage the larger western world forces had adopted. They both wore open-face black balaclavas, their weapons casually tucked across their smocks.

Tanner thumbed the safety off his weapon as they moved closer. With the pad of his index finger, he applied a tiny amount of pressure to take up the trigger slack.

He took his gaze away from the red dot sight as the two armed men were in close quarters. As they closed, he could see both wearing homemade blue armbands around their left upper arms. When you have two forces wearing similar Army fatigues it helps to identify which side you're fighting for to avoid your oppo shooting you in the rear.

They stopped at the farthest end of the sliding side door.

The larger one with an overgrown beard, gently knocked on the wood side of the carriage, and attempted in English, "Tanner, you are here?"

Tanner waited and the man knocked again "Tanner? I'm Volodymyr."

Taking a sigh of relief, Tanner reverted his AKM to safe, and called out "Hey, I'm in here."

Tanner slid open the carriage door and jumped down.

Volodymyr was a few inches taller than him and wider. A smile beamed from his bearded face. In his best English, he offered, "Tanner my friend, I hear we have-mutual problem to deal with?" His voice was deep and hearty.

"It's good to meet you Volodymyr. Yes, we do, where are the rest of your men?"

The big man-made Tanner feel at ease, and appeared genuinely pleased to meet someone who could help. "We based further in city; we came to pick you up. We will go back and join others, and you can brief us on what you know."

"Sounds good, let me grab my stuff. I don't think we have much time before the Major rolls into the city."

Tanner grabbed his gear from the carriage, and they left.

*

They drove into the city in a metallic blue Mitsubishi double cab pickup, it had a UK registration plate. It was explained to Tanner that the 'Brits' had sent a load of second-hand 4x4s over to help the Ukrainians on the front line. He thanked Tanner as if he had personally delivered the vehicles.

The once beautiful city in southeastern Ukraine was

situated on the coast of the Sea of Azov, at the mouth of the Kalmius river. Steeped in history, it was but a shell of its former stature. Gone were the thriving, bustling streets of city life. Many that had stayed remained hidden in their homes hoping when the shelling started it would not be them receiving the unwanted gift from above. Others tried to go about their lives, and Tanner was surprised to see there were still plenty of people on the streets.

Many of the grand buildings of historic architecture and vivid colour had been redecorated by war and destruction. Some buildings had completely collapsed into a mountain of rubble. A few boarded-up shops remained open selling the essentials for living. The city had fallen victim to ruin and everywhere Tanner looked the buildings were full of various calibre holes like a dot-to-dot artist had suffered a seizure.

Tower blocks of apartments had large areas missing and from the outside you could view people's homes, now ripped open and exposed for the world to see.

They had not been driving long before they arrived at Spartak Hotel just off Myru Avenue, close to the centre just a few blocks from the Donetsk National Academy Theatre.

The hotel was Volodymyr's base camp. There were plenty of beds for the soldiers and all the amenities they needed.

The various models of UK 4x4s used to transport the troops, were scattered amongst the side streets so as not to lose them all if taking fire.

The Spartak hotel was in the commercial zone of the city, close to banks and restaurants once vibrant with business.

This once genteel hotel was situated on the corner. The external walls were painted clay brown, topped with arched magnolia windows that stretched around the hotel on all four levels, with a domed roof on the corner section.

They parked and dismounted.

The entrance was modern looking, with large glass windows and a doorway, under a red pillar canopy. The large letters of the hotel name 'SPARTAK' in Russian were hung on the front of the canopy. The style of the letters gave Tanner a vague recollection of Caesars Palace in Las Vegas.

Walking through the hotel doors they were greeted by guards in the reception area, all the men acknowledging Volodymyr with a nod while looking upon Tanner with curiosity - the fact he was the only one wearing civvies made him stand out all the more.

Volodymyr never wore any rank, but they all seemed to look to him for orders and to command them.

They walked through to a conference room once used for discussing the latest trends in business or self-help courses. It was now an Operations Room, crammed with Volodymyr's army - nearly fifty armed men from various backgrounds.

Some were officially recognised soldiers; others were everyday tradesmen who decided to take up arms and protect their city and country from the onslaught of the Russians.

Volodymyr walked to the front of the conference area and the respect was apparent as the room fell immediately silent, with all attention on him. He addressed the room, explaining how time was a critical factor and that the brief would be short and to the point. He expressed the importance of the role they were about to play and that some would not be there at the end to celebrate victory, but they'd be honoured and never forgotten.

Although Tanner could not understand the brief when it dipped from English into Ukrainian, he fathomed by the demeanour and tone the unusual way of motivating the troops, which ended with them singing celebratory war cries.

To die for Ukraine was an honour to these men.

Volodymyr then introduced Tanner and invited him up to the front to brief the group of the grim reality.

The soldiers fell silent with all eyes on him.

The congregation was a mixture of young and old, some faces already weathered and hardened by years of conflict. Others were still fresh from their mother's milk but they all had the cold exterior expression he often saw in Maxine.

It must be an eastern bloc trait he imagined.

With the help of a translator, he began, "There is no easy way to say this, you don't look like the type of men I need to soften the blow for. Sitting twenty minutes from your city in Pikuzy, a squad of approximately thirty highly trained Russian soldiers, led by a very determined Major and a member of the FSB, want to attack this city, and kill as many Ukrainian people as possible. They are both operating under their own agenda. They have not received any orders from Moscow to do this. They are here to send a message on behalf of an Islamic terror group called, Disciples of the Afterlife, and for other personal reasons unknown." Tanner felt some of the detail to be irrelevant. The room remained still as he delivered the sucker punch, "They have two biological weapons that they plan to detonate within the city. The toxin they plan to release is called Botulinum. It will cause many fatalities. Evacuating the city might save a few. When the toxin is released into the atmosphere it will spread where the wind blows it, it could spread far beyond the limits of Mariupol. Thousands of innocent Ukrainian people will suffer a prolonged, agonising death. Our job is to stop these bombs from being triggered." If there was another level of silence that was even quieter, the room had just found it.

Not one person removed their eyes from Tanner as if waiting for a punchline that was never to come.

Volodymyr took over, using a large map of the city covering the wall behind him and a long stick to point.

He named each of his seniors who were to lead a squad of five men. Their grouping would be spaced out across the centre of the city at the predetermined positions. Volodymyr used his stick to indicate how this would cut the city in half, enabling them to react to whatever presented itself.

He continued briefing as Tanner's phone started to buzz.

It was Stones with a Reaper update - Major Sokolova's convoy had started to move towards the city.

Chapter Seventy-Three

Major Sokolova's convoy held a steady 50kph along the direct road, weaving in and out of holes created by heavy artillery. His Russian and Tawheed flags flapped proudly in the wind. The sun had decided to join them for the attack, the sky bright blue with only patches of cloud, but still with a chill to the air.

Maxine and the Major had taken a moment to themselves before mounting up. A brief sibling embrace, then words of encouragement for a successful mission.

They now sat in silence going over the plan in their heads playing out any eventuality. Maxine particularly played out the version where Tanner would turn up to disrupt the party. 'Where is he right now?' She anxiously wanted to know.

The road from Pikuzy to the outskirts of Mariupol was straight. The flat open area of unkept fields on either side had not been harvested for some time and nature was slowly clawing its land back.

After ten minutes, they reached the outskirts.

The Major's body was starting to pump, feeding itself slow drips of adrenaline as they got close to the dismount position. He had to control it, wait for the moment to release it fully to when and if the attack was met by resistance.

Maxine was quiet, as the Major knew all the soldiers would be, it was how the human brain worked when knowing it might not be alive by the end of the day.

The road joined the M-14 that cut through the heart of the city. The open fields gave way to the residential district of Livoberezhnyi. There were still several Ukrainians out on the streets, some ran when they saw the Russian flag others just watched. The Major wondered how many people were still hiding in their houses. They passed a large cemetery, and this brought a smile to the Major's face, as he thought how he intended to fill it further.

Maxine guided her brother with the map, through the streets crossing a bridge over the railway tracks. She gazed out of the window to her right at the rail yard and all the freight carriages lying in wait to be used again. It had a depressing feel about it. It reminded her of the industrial period of the 1800s wherein she had seen pictures in history at school. The tracks ran on the left and the Kalmius river on the right.

They were approaching the dismount position.

At the bend in the road leading to the Post Bridge, they had reached the point where they'd continue on foot. The Major pulled over to the left in front of a boarded-up grocery shop with a 'temporarily closed' sign painted on the front.

The men left the vehicles and fell into their smaller units, each charged by their commander. The Major and Maxine moved round to the rear of their vehicle, out of view from the rest of the troops. Standing looking at the two bags concealing the bombs. Their eyes met and they smiled at each other, they didn't need words - they both knew the moment was now.

They unzipped a bag each and armed with a screwdriver, the lids were removed again. The Major powered up both weapons, and the digital counters came to life, a small red line rotating clockwise where each numerical figure would be visualised. Once the electronics had finished the functional checks, the two digital displays showed five rectangular zeros.

The Major punched in the passcode via the illuminated

keypad and the two weapons displayed a digital clock showing 0:00. They had already agreed on the time.

One hour was to be set, giving them enough time to get in and out - putting distance between them and the bombs before the toxin was released. The wind was in their favour.

They synchronised their watches, and with timers set, the countdown began.

The lids were quickly secured and with bags in hand, they started to move at pace. Once the Major was happy, he nodded to his 2iC, no words were said, it was comms silent unless necessary. They proceeded over the Old Bridge.

The Major made a last-minute change of plan before they left Pikuzy. The BTR-80 armoured vehicle with the turret mounted fifty calibre machine gun would roll at a snail's pace over Post Bridge into the city. It would meet them at the junction he and Maxine would separate from. The BT-80 was planned to act as a distraction allowing the foot soldiers to move in unnoticed, and to add extra firepower if needed.

They moved as a single unit covering their arcs for any potential threats. The only noise was the dull patter of the rubber-soled boots meeting the concrete bridge and the slight metallic taps coming from their webbing.

The Kalmius river below had a strong current and gave a continuous roar as it passed underneath.

Chapter Seventy-Four

Tanner, Volodymyr and his men dispersed from the hotel like a football team running out of the tunnel to start a game. They had listened to the plan intently, a fact evident as Tanner watched them separate into squads to their ordered locations.

Their points were at least two hundred metres apart covering a good stretch of the city centre to enable them to watch and respond.

Civilians still walked around conducting their business.

On seeing the soldiers moving quickly, some decided to find shelter understanding something was about to happen, while others, continued about their day, hardened to reality.

Tanner joined Volodymyr with five of his soldiers.

He had positioned himself and his men almost in the centre of the defensive line he had planned. They double-timed two blocks over, reaching the Donetsk Theatre.

The theatre was a large, impressive construction with a neoclassical architectural style. Until recently, a tiled bright red roof had adorned it, but it had collapsed in on itself from the persistent bombing. At its fore, the white stone building had what remained of several huge pillars enhancing the approach from its location within the inner-city garden island, moated by a ring road. Once a place of joy and laughter it was now a devasting reminder of historic loss - a building that showed the remnant of war and abandonment. When they arrived at the fringes of the theatre park the decision was made to keep watch from the south side in the streets as the park did not provide adequate hard cover. From their position, they could see the approaches from the east and the west.

Tanner received a call.

Stones informed him the Major and his men had dismounted and were on foot - they were moving into the city crossing the Old Bridge. He also informed that an armoured vehicle was moving across the Post Bridge. Both the Major and Maxine had been identified carrying blue sports holders, the biological weapons. All personnel were armed.

Tanner passed the news over to Volodymyr who repeated it to his soldiers in their native tongue. At that moment, Tanner noticed the battery die on his phone, “Fuck!”

Volodymyr turned, “What is it?”

Tanner explained he’d not had chance to charge his phone and how a bomb disposal expert was awaiting his call to help disarm the weapons if necessary.

Volodymyr grabbed one of his men and handed Tanner's phone to him. He delivered the man’s new orders with a tone that expressed how the mission's success now relied upon him.

Before the soldier left, Volodymyr grabbed him by the scruff of his jacket, and at an uncomfortably close distance, told him to return the mobile to Tanner and Tanner alone.

The soldier met his eyes and nodded, and was then running up the street, weapon and webbing bouncing in all directions.

The morning was still cool, the roads and pavements wet from the previous night's rain. Tanner looked up at the cloud speckled sky hoping the Reaper was over them.

The younger soldiers had gone quietly into themselves, contemplating the choices they had made - would they be drinking to the fallen later - or be one of fallen? They remained watching and waiting for any signs of the enemy.

Chapter Seventy-Five

Major Sokolova's unit moved swiftly off the bridge onto Shmidta Street passing farm warehouses. A few workers saw them and ran out of sight. The men had been given orders not to fire at anyone until fired upon or given the order. The last thing the Major wanted was to alert any enemy soldiers of their presence over a couple of quick kills.

The soldiers moved across a railway track through the coverage of trees into the edges of the built-up area of the city.

The Major looked across to his right and he could see the BT-80 keeping pace with them. It crossed the bridge over the tracks at the same time as him.

They continued into the built-up suburban area zigzagging their way toward the centre… Torhova St, Kafais'ka St, Hrets'ka St, until they were finally on Fontanna Street moving northwest towards the split point - patrolling both sides of the road, taking cover and moving in a staggered pattern.

They arrived at the corner of Kundzhy Street.

Maxine was surprised at how many people were still around in the city. Most just stood aside and watched the Russians pass, there was nothing they could do but let the invaders stroll into their home.

Before moving onto the main street, the Major waited until he heard the low rumbling of diesel engines and hard rubber cruising up the street. The steel-bellied warrior had arrived.

It was time for the brother and sister to go their separate ways. Both armed with a ticking biological weapon filled with a fatal toxin.

The BT-80 continued down the middle of the road, the

Major walking behind it, the weapon counting down at his side. The two units of men had pushed either side of the street in a cover movement. Moving southwest they were three blocks from the city park.

Maxine with the 2iC and her units peeled off and continued down Fontanna Street. Her pace was a little quicker, so she could reach Mariupol City Hospital at the same time as her brother's target location.

Forty-three minutes until weapon detonation.

Chapter Seventy-Six

Maxine and the Major's movements were being watched from above - with each of their movements broadcasted to the live streams in four locations.

Stones had been trying to contact Tanner with updates, but the call kept going to the answering machine. He felt a surge of panic. Not only could he not inform Tanner and the men supporting him of the current locations of the inbound Russian troops - he also didn't have a link to him when, and if the time came, and the bomb disposal advice was needed.

He contacted Ed Boden with his problem.

Ed was watching the feed from Vauxhall Cross, London.

He had an idea.

Volodymyr's mobile phone broke the silence. Looking at the illuminated screen it was another number he did not recognise. He was contemplating hanging up, due to being on stag for a very imminent attack, but remembered his early hours call from an unknown number, Ed Boden.

"Pryvit?" he answered in Ukrainian - Hello.

"Volodymyr, it's Ed Boden we spoke earlier about our mutual friend."

"Ah yes, what is it can I do for you?" his accent was thick.

"Is he with you? Can I speak to him?"

Volodymyr tapped Tanner on the shoulder with the phone. Tanner looked at him quizzically then took it "Hello?"

"Tanner it's Ed." He sounded relieved Tanner thought. "Stones has been trying to get hold of you on your mobile."

"It's dead. It's getting recharged as we speak."

"Heads up, the drone has spotted the Major and half his forces heading straight for you on Kundzhy Street. Looking at where you are that's the street right in front of you that leads to the theatre area. They have an armoured vehicle with them."

"Where have the other half gone?" Tanner asked.

"They have continued in a northwest direction, target location unknown. Looks like they are separating the bombs for maximum effect."

"Roger, I'll contact Stones when I have the weapons." Tanner ended the call and handed the phone back to Volodymyr then, pointing in the direction of the enemy, Tanner back briefed Volodymyr on the situation. "What's in that direction? Why have they split?" Tanner asked.

Volodymyr quickly passed information to two of his men before sending them with messages to his other troops on the ground. He then looked at Tanner, "The only thing I can think of is the Hospital is that way."

Tanner paused, "Is it still in use?"

"Very much so, brimming with casualties of war, my bet is that's where they are targeting." Volodymyr's face paled.

'Probably has many friends in there,' Tanner thought.

"One more thing I forgot to mention. I need Major Sokolova alive, injured at worst, but able to talk. We might need his assistance in disarming the weapons."

The two messengers returned. The one from the East brought with him an RPG - Rocket Propelled Grenade, and two rounds. Just then, automatic fire pierced the air with loud cracking from one of the units to the west.

Chapter Seventy-Seven

Maxine left her brother behind and continued between the high-rise blocks down Fontanna Street. They moved double time past an immigration centre and a grocery shop.

There were a few customers on the street that quickly moved inside and locked the door when they saw her and her armed men moving at speed in their general direction. She didn't blame them, but she knew it wouldn't save them.

They continued down the street, flagged by trees on either side. As the first block came to an end, they continued straight over the crossroads. Maxine was third in line.

They moved across the open junction just as the sound of rapid gunfire rang out. She took cover, hearing cries of pain from one of her soldiers. She spun around, weapon ready. The soldier had taken a bullet through the knee. He'd dropped his weapon and was rolling around the road clutching his wound in agony, his combat trousers ripped by the impact, with a mess of bone and cartilage protruding the now red material.

Maxine saw a second soldier fall. He was standing like a zombie, arms dropped at his sides. The life had gone from his body that seemed to be waiting for gravity to drag it to the floor - another round joined the two already in his chest seeing a spray of blood exit his back - as gravity finally won.

The other screaming soldier was trying to drag himself across the road when he was hit with the fatal blow, taking out the side of his face, leaving his jaw hanging from a hole where his upper mouth and nose once were.

Return fire was sent back down the street to no avail.

The gunmen were at least three-hundred metres away and

with no visual, the rounds Maxine and her men laid down were a means of suppression to allow them to keep moving.

The unit was back up and on the move.

Before Maxine started moving, she took a risky glance down the street and saw soldiers starting to move tactically in her direction. She upped the pace.

Thirty-nine minutes until weapon detonation.

A small unit of Volodymyr's men were on stag, watching downrange along the street. They were using the walls around the Staraya Tower for cover.

They had received the message that a group had splintered off and could be coming their way - their weapons were readied, and they used the wall to steady their aim.

Three blocks ahead, armed figures started to cross a junction in front of them. By the time they reacted and started to lay down fire, only the rear markers of the group took hits. One was a direct kill the second was trying to crawl to safety. An ordered second volley of AK-74 firepower ended his attempts to crawl any further.

Two Russian kills, they wanted more and started to move down the street towards them, signalling to one of their fellow units two hundred metres to their left to move forward too. That message was passed further to their left and again to another unit, seeing twenty Ukrainian soldiers start to move on Maxine's troops from three different directions.

Chapter Seventy-Eight

Tanner looked across to where the engaged firing emanated but was unable to see any of Volodymyr's other units from his position. He could hear shouts, then more cracks of the AK-74. The Major must be close.

Tanner heard the rumbling through the trees over the width of the theatre park. He then saw the top of the turret from the BT-80 armour vehicle as it came to a halt at the opposite side of the square. The turret-mounted machine gun was manned.

Tanner looked at Volodymyr, he too had seen the turret between the trees looking round like a dragon waiting to breathe fire at its enemy. Everyone's alertness had increased.

Tanner could see some of the men lined up a few metres apart, clutching their weapons, massaging the wooden barrel stocks with sweaty palms - their brains choosing whether to fight, flight, or freeze. The moment the first rounds go down their subconscious would decide for them. Tanner held up his hand telling them to hold. The message was visually passed to the other men at the east end of the park then passed over once more. Tanner wanted to wait until the Major's men were within sight, at the moment there was too much foliage between them, and they would be firing blind. Better to get your enemy to expose themselves before giving away your location. They held their position as a spread of shadowy figures emerged through the brush two-hundred metres from their line of sight. "Standby! Standby!" Tanner steadied himself, his AKM already focused on his target. Tanner controlled his breathing.

When he was steady, he squeezed the trigger, and a burst of three rounds exploded from his barrel and met his target.

Chapter Seventy-Nine

Major Sokolova strolled behind his armoured mobile shield, his AKM poised, ready to be raised to any target that presented itself - the biological weapon ticking away in the bag over his shoulder. It was an uncomfortable shape and awkward to carry. The thought had crossed his mind to put it in the back of the BT-80 but he refused to part with it.

This was the final act and what better place than Mariupol Theatre Park.

He watched his soldiers move slowly down each side of the street, some behind him watching their six. The street had emptied of civilians, they knew trouble was here, and they didn't want to be caught up in the crossfire.

The Major had heard the exchange of gunfire from the direction in which Maxine had gone.

He rolled questions around in his mind.

Were the Ukrainians waiting for them?

How could they know they were coming?

Tanner? Salamander? He was certain he hit Salamander back at the forest, but never had time to confirm the kill.

He hoped all was well with Maxine. He knew she wouldn't fail him, she was like him, a winner, a fighter.

The firing had stopped. He felt certain it was not a large enough exchange to have seriously impacted the mission.

One block closer to the target area.

The streets were partially sheltered on either side by high-rise buildings. Some still stood, many had seen sections knocked out like Jenga blocks, left as piles of rubble mixed with the fragmented elements of people's lives.

Most of the shops and eateries were closed after being raided. Above them sat several floors of apartments.

The BT-80 slowed in front of the Major as the street ended and the park opened - an island with a sea of tarmac around it.

The vehicle crossed the ring road and came to a stop on a cobbled open area of the park. The men filtered out of the street, quickly crossing the open road and taking up positions in a line at the park's shrubbery edge.

Major Sokolova walked to the front of the wheeled block of steel, the turret man panning left and right.

He surveyed the area, all seemed quiet, too quiet.

Maybe Tanner didn't get to intrude on his plan.

The Major knew where he wanted to plant the weapon. Right next to the fountain, inside if it was dry. His sick sense of humour against Ukraine's dominant religion of Eastern Orthodox Christianity - He was to make a mockery of the bible proverb 13:14 'The teaching of the wise is a fountain of life, turning a person from the snares of death.'

The focus of this proverb is ‘the teaching of the wise,’ representing what he already knew, had practiced, and was willing to pass along to others. Their abusive Ukrainian stepfather was not wise, he knew what he was doing was wrong, but he still practiced it, he was most likely abused as a child himself, but he was still willing to pass the pain and torture on to them. The Major knew what had happened to his sister, but he never spoke of it. He had heard her tears of pain in the night, all he could do was press the pillow to his head tighter. The Ukrainian bastard's people will pay.

The Major gave the order to advance and secure the park, and the soldiers started forward through the bushes and trees.

Suddenly, a burst of gunfire reverberated off the buildings surrounding the area. Twenty metres to his right one of his men jerked back as if being pulled by a harness. His weapon dropped to the floor as the rounds hit him ripping into his flesh his knees bent as he hinged backward, before slamming into the ground. Hell had opened the floor to war.

Thirty-four minutes until weapon detonation.

Chapter Eighty

Maxine's squad pressed forward, the loss of the two men already forgotten. The mission is what mattered, and for the soldiers… survival.

High-rise tower blocks lined the road, with trees that her soldiers used as cover. The 2iC stayed close by her, his role to ensure her safety in delivering the weapon to the chosen target site. They approached a hotel on the corner of the next junction. Instead of running out into the open crossroads as before, the 2iC brought the men to a halt.

Maxine peered around the corner of the hotel to see ten or more soldiers moving quickly up the street in their direction. Were these the same ones that fired upon them in the last street, or were there others following up from behind them? She had to prepare for the worst. She briefed the 2iC on the situation and they quickly split their men into two groups.

On her mark, she brought her AKM to aim and started to lay suppression fire down the street toward the enemy - the signal for the other troop to move quickly for the other side.

The deafening firepower echoed throughout the quiet streets, the soldiers on the receiving end either hitting the floor or leaping to find protection.

With half her men now on the far side they could cover the others set to make the crossing.

Maxine's magazine ran empty, and the smell of cordite filled the air. She pressed the mag release button and it hit the pavement with a dull clatter as she swiftly replaced it with a full one. Her eye was back on the sight and training across the street, falling on a soldier who was trying to press himself as flat as he could to the road. Lining up the crosshairs, she unleashed a volley of controlled rounds. The first fell short striking the surface in front of him in puffs of dust and dirt.

A small adjustment of her aim, and the next rounds hit home, killing the target, the blood oozing out of him, painting the road in dark crimson red.

There was a lull before a barrage of enemy fire returned, seeing the walls of the buildings surrounding the junction blasted into fragmented chunks of brickwork. One of Maxine's men had failed to find sufficient cover, and he paid the price as a wave of bullets hit him, his death instantaneous.

Her men on the other side returned with a sustained wave of fire giving Maxine and the others the cover to join them. She made a break for it, taking a glance down the street as she went to see it now littered with bodies.

The planned route was to head northeast up the very road on which the enemy was now advancing - Now regrouped, they would instead reroute and continue through the hospital's medical college complex to reach the main hospital building. She gave the order to move and after more suppressing fire, they advanced. As they ran, the two men covering the rear had to turn and take the knee to lay down more fire. As more enemy soldiers then rounded the junction, Maxine's worse fears had come to light - there were now two Ukrainian units descending on them.

The road ahead bent to the right at a forty-five-degree angle, moving them out of shot, but not before she lost another man at the rear. In the distance, she could still hear the attack that was no doubt aimed on her brother.

Thirty-one minutes until weapon detonation.

Chapter Eighty-One

The drone looked down, observing the two attacks as it circled high above the city. The watching audience witnessed the two Ukrainian units moving up on FSB Lieutenant Colonel Maxine Sokolova - Target Bravo - their visual showing she was still in possession of the bagged biological weapon.

The body count on both sides was piling up. The screens showed dark shadows of dead men lying in the road, limbs pointing in all directions like squashed flies.

What target Bravo couldn't see at this time was a third Ukrainian unit moving up to the northwest on the outskirts of the medical complex out of sight.

The smallest adjustment to the Reaper optic and Target Alpha - Major Aaron Sokolova - came into view, the battle all around him continuing to rage.

*

Tanner's initial shots had opened the floodgates seeing automatic panic fire unleashed from every angle of the park. The rounds ricocheted off the buildings, fencing them in, the sound making Tanner's ears ring out.

As Tanner saw the latest target in his sights drop, the guy manning the BT-80 DShK .50 Cal, took his cue to join the party. Squeezing both hand-triggers, the steady rhythm of fury took over, drowning out all other gunfire.

The dispensed hot casings rained down the side of the vehicle, jumping around the cobbles. The muzzle looked like it was breathing fire, round after round spraying over the heads of his fellow soldiers across the park.

As plants, trees and hedges were scattered like confetti, the veterans amongst Volodymyr's men knew to find cover, just as some of the younger guns became cannon fodder.

Tight in cover, Tanner looked to his right and saw a trio of blue-arm-banded soldiers. They hadn't registered what had started and were all standing, firing erratically.

Tanner shouted in their direction to take cover, but the noise and echoes of the DShK overpowered his voice.

The first soldier had his leg blown off and half his ribcage removed - the second saw his arm torn from his shoulder and his chest cut away as if he'd been bitten by a shark - the third had his head removed by a single round, his decapitated body joining the pile of mangled corpses that moments earlier had been his comrades. The 0.50 calibre rounds had cut them down like a knife through butter.

They had the firepower advantage, but Tanner had the numbers. He focussed his attention back on the enemy.

The big gun ceased, either a reload or stoppage, or the fact its targets were now hidden from view or annihilated.

Now was the time.

Leaping over the wall towards the Russians, Tanner proceeded at a quick, controlled pace, the AKM shouldered, his upper body moving as one with the weapon. Each time a shadowy figure appeared in his sights through the foliage, he released a three-round burst, his movement slick and accurate.

The other blue-banded soldiers took his lead and started to move forward laying down fire. Some lost their heads and rushed forward, their bursts of automatic fire only striking the stone walls behind the Russian troops.

Several charged past and overtook Tanner.

They entered the park only to receive an instant lesson in combat control, as while the Major's men fired from their cover, the .50 cal rejoined the game.

The weapon once again gave them the advantage, sounding like a rapid steam train as it tore across the park disposing of more of Volodymyr's men. The large park had plenty of cover behind trees and the occasional abandoned kiosk.

They had to be smarter, they were losing men needlessly.

Taking cover with Tanner was Volodymyr. Tanner instructed how they needed to focus their fire on the BT-80. Tanner would get in a position where he could take out the turret man as at the same time Volodymyr could hit the wheels of the vehicle with the RPG.

The turret gun had ceased again, and the ground troops of both sides were on the move toward each other.

Using the trees for cover, Tanner, Volodymyr together with three of his men, fired and manoeuvred in an attempt to get a clear shot at the armoured BT-80.

As Tanner took out another target, his rifle emptied.

He took cover, releasing the empty magazine. In an instant he had another mag push home with a click, and with a slight assist, had the bolt release forward, ready to re-engage. The movement took moments, his actions as if on autopilot thanks to the hundreds of hours of drills, drummed into them time and again by their SAS instructor, *'Smooth is fast, fast is smooth.'*

As Tanner was set to advance, the soldier next to him came under Russian fire, the blood splattering Tanner's face as the bullet exited the Ukrainian's back.

Tanner wiped the blood from his face then advanced with

haste, Volodymyr and the two remaining soldiers following quickly at his rear.

They were soon in position, with a clear line of sight through the trees to the BT-80.

The two soldiers gave cover fire, their weapons firing single shots to conserve ammo. Tanner could tell they had more experience in the field, they were more composed.

Tanner looked across at the turret man, trying to line him up in his optical sight. The shooter had once again paused his firing, and was now behind the metal plate, fumbling with the big gun. Tanner could see the muzzle smoking, its empty shells covering the top of the vehicle. He had a quick pan around to see if he could see the Major, he couldn't lose sight of the primary objective.

As he scanned the terrain, two Russian soldiers passed into his scope seeing Tanner dispatch them with short-controlled fire, watching the puffs of red mist through the lens.

Again, Tanner was waiting for his clear shot as Volodymyr loaded the RPG. The bobbing of the man's helmet was all that was exposed behind the steel plate in front of the DShK, giving the firer some protection.

He needed to get his shot off before Volodymyr fired the RPG otherwise, the .50 cal would be coming their way and the opportunity would be lost.

All around them, the few remaining features of the once tranquil city park were being destroyed, with round after round tearing through the decorative walls, benches and kiosks.

The noise of the intense exchange was relentless, and Tanner's adrenaline gauge was at maximum, his body and blood pumping.

Volodymyr nudged him in the direction of the gunner. The turret guy had sorted his problem out. As he readied himself to re-engage the weapon, he was now exposed over the parapet of the gun shield for Tanner to take the shot.

Range 150 metres, breeze blowing into his face. The butt of the rifle pulled firmly into his shoulder not too tight - not too loose. His right knee was on the ground - left foot planted in front, giving him a stable firing platform. He brought the gunner's face into the sights, the red dot of the scope to the bridge of his nose. There was no need to adjust for range or wind. Tanner slowed his breathing and pushed back the excitement. When he was true… he squeezed the trigger.

The features of the gunner's face disappeared inwards and out the back of his head as he slid down the turret into the vehicle.

Volodymyr took his chance to get a better side angle of the BT-80 and lined his RPG sight at the front two wheels - the vehicle needed to sustain enough damage to one side to have any chance of preventing it from moving.

He crouched, aimed, and fired.

Chapter Eighty-Two

WWWhhhhhooossss was the last sound Major Sokolova heard before a blast force took away his legs and sent him to the floor. He quickly regained himself and reached out for the bag carrying the weapon. The explosion vibrated through him and shocked his ears to deafness. Luckily, he was standing on the other side of the BT-80 when the RPG hit.

The Major got up and slammed his fist on the side shouting to the driver to man the turret. He could see the advantage slipping and his anger began to build. 'Had Tanner been waiting for them?' That could be the only explanation as to how and why this resistance was here.

The Major surveyed the terrain when to his right he saw a second RPG being lined up. Gripping the bag, he sprinted as hard as he could when a second *WWWhhhooosss* came from behind him, followed by a loud explosion.

He turned to see the BT-80 listing to the side, and still no man at the turret. Filled with rage he slung the bomb over his shoulder and started firing his AKM in the direction of the RPG firer. One mag down, he reloaded and set about emptying the next one. He shouted orders for his men to move forward, he needed the park secure to get the bomb in the fountain. He had been obsessed with this part of the plan for a long time.

The men were making slow ground into the park, and a few had already given their lives for his cause, but he didn't care.

The soldiers had made a good baseline in the trees at the edge of the paved area twenty metres from the fountain. In the middle was a four-tiered stand like a giant wedding cake. That was his target - on the top like a masterpiece on display.

He looked around and counted - he only had six men left, but it was enough to achieve the aim.

Bits of bark hit him in the face as bullets whizzed past him and into the trees, he kept low.

Major Sokolova ordered the four soldiers furthest away on either side of him to lay down continuous fire, whilst he pulled in the closest two to run the open ground protecting him.

He raised his assault rifle and had a quick scan around. He saw two soldiers wearing the blue band running into a new position. He fired two rapid bursts, taking one out by the legs seeing him drop to the concrete. His oppo made the mistake of turning to help him, and the Major took the shot.

'Killed by kindness,' he laughed. The Major's mood was verging on madness as all around him the world seemed to be falling apart - his men dying in droves for his cause.

He checked his watch, twenty-four minutes to detonation.

Readying two soldiers to provide him with close protection, he shouted a command and they started to sprint toward the fountain. The Major's other men let out volleys of automatic fire providing the cover he needed to make the walled edge of the water feature. The two soldiers adopted firing positions using the low wall for cover - then took over the firing from the others in the trees, allowing them to reload.

Major Sokolova carefully unzipped the bag and removed the metal box with its black nozzles protruding from the sides.

He held it close to him.

The top of the fountain was four small tiers away - over the wall and a few steps up, and he could place it on the top.

He raised his head ready to go when a bullet struck the top of the fountain wall, exploding stone chips into the left side of his face and eye. He recoiled behind the wall, grabbing his face as he let out an enraged roar.

The Major's palm pressed against his face. It was warm with blood, and he could feel the punctures in his skin that now housed minute pieces of shrapnel. He blinked his left eye and felt a scratchiness, it hurt, and he could not see out of it.

He shouted an order for cover and the moment his men's rounds started taking control, he stepped up, exposing himself over the fountain wall. With a few quick steps, the biological weapon was placed on the top tier.

He stepped back to look upon his creation. Everything around him seemed to pause for a few seconds as Proverb 13:14 was read out in his mind. With the crazed grin returning he started the sprint back to the tree line across the cobbles.

He heard a loud groan over his right shoulder as one of his soldiers was bought down. He did not stop, there was no time for mercy. Back in the relative safety of tree cover he looked at his watch. Nineteen minutes to detonation.

There was only one thing left for him to do, get the fuck out of there. Shouting a retreat, however, was easier ordered than done. The Major's primary escape, the BT-80, was now disabled and the only option left was to move back on foot to establish a baseline then get back to the RV.

He looked around, five men left including himself, and by the looks of it not much ammo. He could see the Ukrainians trying to move around to flank them, 'They would not be moving for much longer,' he thought. The only route out was back up the street the way they had just come from. Working as a team they started to fire, cover, and manoeuvre backward.

Chapter Eighty-Three

Maxine heard the two explosions and the gunfire intensify. She was sure her brother wasn't expecting the resistance he was currently facing.

If all else fails, the bombs were on timers.

The bag over her shoulder was heavy and cumbersome, the edges of the box dug into the side of her ribs and back. 'It's not far to the hospital,' she thought, 'Then I can ditch the bag and make a run for it.'

They followed the road around before taking a hard right. As a unit, they had to stop at the corner and turn to face the rear. Finding cover they waited for the chasing force to round the S-bend road they had come from. The 2iC ordered the men to hold until his signal. Hiding from view he waited for the numbers to increase in their line of sight.

Maxine counted approximately twenty men moving towards them, all wearing blue armbands. She looked around, eight men plus her. They were outnumbered.

"Fire!" The order came from the 2iC and the noise of nine AKMs firing at once exploded into a monstrous sound.

Her breathing became heavy as she watched the front row of Ukrainian soldiers drop to the floor as a wave of 7.62mm rounds hit them. The enemy soldiers quickly diverted through the carnage to take any protection they could find.

The men on the ground were a mixture of dead and wounded, some still moving with groans, but her men soon picked them off and ended their misery.

With the Ukrainians hiding, it was time to move toward the hospital. Her unit turned to move out of firing points, up the street between the medical academy's three storey buildings. As they did so, the four soldiers in front of her were suddenly down in a hail of bullets. They collapsed like puppets having their strings cut, never to rise again.

Ahead of them, was another unit of blue-banded soldiers. Outflanked, Maxine and her four remaining men were cut off and surrounded, 'fuck!' she thought. She was never going to make it to the hospital target. The only way for them to move was into a courtyard littered with trees and walled on every side by buildings with no escape.

It was a dead end.

Now under constant fire, they had no choice but to start backing into the courtyard. Bullets whizzed by way too close for comfort, and Maxine could feel the heat in the air as they passed her. She didn't want to die but the choice was out of her hands. At least she would go with a purpose when the toxin would start to release. They would go down in the history books. She would save a bullet for herself - she would never allow another Ukrainian man to ever touch her again.

They took cover behind various trees, the bark splintering around them by the relentless fire.

Maxine could see the only way out was cut off and that none of them would survive.

The 2iC was close by and she shouted to him.

She would push further back and set the weapon down in a safe place if he could give her cover. He nodded and she quickly zig-zagged between the trunks until there was nowhere left to run, the tree-line coming to an abrupt stop at the foot of a walled building.

The 2iC and his men were quickly in tow, firing in the

direction of the approaching soldiers.

Maxine removed the Botulinum weapon from the bag and placed it into the brush at the base of a tree.

Her watch told her there were only sixteen minutes to detonation. With the weapon hidden, she stood only to see another of her men hit the dirt after being struck by close fire.

The 2iC was no longer in eyesight, but several of her enemy were and Maxine fired a wave of rounds at the incoming targets until the rifle emptied.

She reached into her assault waistcoat. It was her last magazine. Ramming it home she selected single shot mode.

Suddenly, an enemy soldier appeared in front of her but as he set himself to shoot his gun clicked, his ammunition spent. Understanding his time had come he threw his weapon to the ground and drew his long commando knife. He let out a war cry, deciding in that moment how he would meet his end. He charged at her; the graphite blade extended toward his enemy. Maxine was set to fire when he was brought down by a rain of bullets courtesy of the 2iC reappearing at her rear.

An honourable death.

The 2iC ran to her and grabbed the scruff of her jacket. He pulled her along the wall of the building, and soon it became clear where he had disappeared to a moment earlier.

He pointed up at the structure, his words steady and clear, "Get the fuck out of here." He pointed up at a high window.

He then stepped back to fire a single round, the glass fragmenting into a shattered pattern.

Maxine looked at him, a moment of warmth spreading over her lips as she said, "Thank you."

"Go!" He leaned against the wall, bent his knees, and cupped his hands, creating a step for her to use so he could bunk her up onto his shoulders.

Using the 2iC as a ladder, Maxine didn't hesitate, and quickly dragged herself over the broken glass and through the window. As she dragged herself through, a shard sliced through her clothes into the flesh of her stomach.

She lifted herself off the glass with a grunt, the wound was not fatal, but it was enough to slow her down.

She suddenly had the notion she might be able to reach down and pull up the 2iC, but as she leaned to look out of the window, she witnessed her saviour below, his back against the wall as a wave of bullets flew into him as if in front of a firing squad. Holding her side in pain she made her escape, the countdown on her watch reading eleven minutes to detonation. She needed to move fast.

As she ran through the building the gunfire had silenced. Her men were now all dead.

Chapter Eighty-Four

The Reaper continued circling the city, a spectator of the two battles below. They had a predicted location of the two biological weapons, but currently no firm eyes on them – lost under the tree canopies of both target areas.

The optics had been switched to thermal imagining in the hope to see the body heat of Major Sokolova and his twin sister, Maxine. With the continuous movements of the people on the ground and the heat from the battle raging, it was proving difficult to pinpoint either of them for more than a few fleeting moments at a time.

Stones watched. He'd been unable to get through to Tanner but understood while engulfed within the fight he'd struggle to keep tabs on his phone. He had to trust that Tanner would reach the weapons and call him if assistance was needed.

From the air, the viewers watched the gunfight move toward the hospital, leaving a trail of dead and wounded behind it. Earlier they had seen the Ukrainian units giving chase and a third unit moving around to intercept the Russians.

Their plan had worked, and they had the Russian troop surrounded, forcing them into a dead end, with no way out. The action taking place could not be watched through the blanket of trees, and still they struggled to identify Maxine.

After a while, the gunfire ceased, and the Ukrainian soldiers moved forward disappearing under the canopy.

Had they won?

The city park square battle had seen the armoured vehicle disabled by a couple of rounds from an RPG. The devastating power of the .50 calibre removed from the fray.

The firefight was ongoing when from out of a tree-line three figures had sprinted out toward the fountain.

The Reaper controller had zoomed onto the figures, and they were able to identify one as Major Sokolova, and confirm the weapon was with him.

They watched him unload the biological bomb and place it on top of the fountain before sprinting back to cover.

They now had eyes on one of the weapons, sitting in the open for all to see. For the people watching, two questions needed an urgent answer.

Where was Tanner?

Who had, and where was the other weapon?

The second question was answered, a few moments later.

Chapter Eighty-Five

The BT-80 sat sloped on one side with smoke and flames licking up from where the wheels once stood.

Tanner and Volodymyr remained in their covered location holding back any attempts from the Russian soldiers to circle to their side of the park.

Out of Tanner's peripheral he caught sight of three soldiers making a mad dash across a wide-open section of paved area, near the fountain to his right. He hadn't recognised one as Major Sokolova, it was only when he moved his scope around for a shot, that he saw the large blue sports holdall.

Bringing up his AKM sight, he then had a clear recognizable view of the face, wide eyed and grinning like a maniac, just as he had been when they'd met in the woods.

Tanner's eyes focused on the bag, which suddenly disappeared from his view as the Major ducked below the wall skirting around the fountain.

"The bomb." Tanner pointed.

Volodymyr waved over a couple of his men.

"I need the Major alive." Tanner reminded him.

"Why?" Volodymyr hurled back.

"He might be the only way of stopping the weapons."

He looked upset but understood.

Tanner humoured him, "He's all yours afterward."

Volodymyr gave a cold smile.

Tanner trained his optic back onto the fountain. As he did, Major Sokolova appeared above the wall, stepping over it into the dried-up water feature and climbing the short tier steps that once produced its waterfall effect.

He placed the metallic box that housed the weapon on the top, like an angel topping a Christmas tree. 'More like Azrael,' Tanner thought, *the Angel of Death*. The Major then stood staring at it, 'The guy is a fucking lunatic!'

Then, the Major was gone.

Tanner brought his eye away from his AKM to get a wider view of the situation. He caught the Major now sprinting back to the tree cover. One of Volodymyr's men fired in the direction of the runners - luckily, he missed the Major, but instead took down one of his soldiers.

Tanner turned to Volodymyr who had just been joined by another of his soldiers with radio comms.

"They have the other bomb." he told Tanner excitedly, "Found hidden at the base of a tree."

At that moment, it was the last thing Tanner expected to hear. "Get them to bring it here." He pointed, "The other weapon is over there on top of the fountain. Get them both together so we can work on them at the same time."

Volodymyr relayed the message before instructing his men to take the rest of these fuckers out.

Tanner knew there couldn't be too many left.

"Secure the weapon - I'm going after the Major." Tanner said and was up and gone, heading to the position he last saw Major Sokolova disappear into.

The Ukrainian forces rapidly descended on the area park where the few remaining Russians took cover. The gunfire that followed fell quickly silent; the Major's men defeated, the majority dead with only three choosing to surrender.

Tanner looked across to see Volodymyr reach the bomb then continued his pursuit.

He soon caught site of the Major running away.

As he came into the open road, Tanner knew he had to slow him down. The sky had started to darken bringing with it the rain, it was only a drizzle but enough to make his shot more difficult. He took a knee and leaned against the rear of the BT-80 to steady his aim. He felt the heat of the bodywork through his clothing from the fire damage on the opposite side.

He brought his weapon up to engage, the running figure of Major Sokolova falling into the crosshairs. He could see the drizzle falling between them, misting his view.

He couldn't afford to deliver a fatal shot.

His breathing was steady, range one hundred and fifty metres. The sweat from the recent firefight was running down his brow, it blurred his vision as the salt drops mixed with the rain stinging his eyes - he blinked it out.

Tanner squeezed the trigger.

The rifle kicked back into his shoulder, his sight remaining firmly on the target.

Missed.

He adjusted. Range two hundred metres away.

He took the second shot and knew instantly it was true, watching as the splash of red ran up the Major's left upper leg.

He flopped to the floor but quickly got to his feet, dragging himself down a side street.

Tanner was already running to make up the ground. He could hear cheers of celebrations behind him in the park, but the time to celebrate was far too premature. Sprinting up the street the rain hit his face feeling like needles against his skin. His adrenaline was close to maxed out, the only thing keeping him going. He neared the corner of the side street.

Slowing his pace, he brought his rifle up to his shoulder and he stepped back from the wall to peek around with his weapon at the firing position. Leaning his body slightly to the left, he looked to see Major Sokolova some fifty metres ahead dragging his leg as he went. “Stop, Major!” Tanner demanded, his shout so loud it made his throat hurt.

“Stop!” Tanner repeated, firing a warning shot that saw the Major stop in the middle of the street.

He limped slowly around to face Tanner, his pistol drawn at his hip and pointing at him. Tanner slowly side-paced towards him, still in firing position.

“You're too late Tanner.” He laughed. His hair was matted with sweat and rain, the blood still leaking from his leg, “There is nothing you can do; the time is counting down.” Looking at his watch he heckled, “Eight minutes until they go boom with no way to turn them off!”

“This doesn't need to happen, Major, you can stop this.”

“I don't want to fucking stop this!” he screamed.

Tanner could see he wasn't right in the head, that he was a madman. “People don't have to die like this, come back with me and stop the toxin from being released. I promise, no one will hurt you.” It was like trying to talk to someone who should be committed to an asylum, and the Major began to laugh uncontrollably in Tanner's face - he didn't give a shit; how could he reason with a man like that?

“These aren't people Tanner, they are infidels, they are Ukrainians,” the Major emphasised the last word with hatred through his teeth. “You'll never know what my sister and I have been through. This is our payback.”

Tanner was trying to find an angle, but seconds were

ticking by. "Jafar doesn't care about you, he is just using you to carry out his work, he uses everyone."

"Jafar and I are the same, Disciples of the Afterlife will thrive after we have sent our message. Allahu Akbar." The Major kept repeating the last two words as he raised his pistol.

Tanner put one into the shoulder of his firing arm.

The Major jolted back, but continued to laugh as he staggered, dropping the pistol. Tanner moved towards him closing the distance. He didn't want to kill him but neither did he have the time to drag him down the street.

"How do I shut the bomb down, Major?"

"Fuck you, Tanner." He bent over picking up the pistol with his remaining good hand. "Six minutes Tanner, tick, tick, tick."

'CRACK.' the sound of the shot vibrated between the buildings. Tanner watched as the top of Major Sokolova's head flipped open, the impact of the round sending fragments of skull and flesh up into the air.

The Major was dead in an instant and laying in the road, the contents of his brain leaking out in a pool of blood.

Tanner released his trigger and breathed in the cordite smoke that left the barrel.

He had no time to waste listening to a man that was never going to help him. Tanner just decided enough was enough, the world was better off without Major Sokolova, and he needed to get back to the bombs.

So, Tanner took the shot.

Chapter Eighty-Six

Tanner had turned on his heels and was moving as fast as the energy inside him would allow his legs to go. He pumped his arms to keep the momentum, running hard as if his life depended on it.

It did… As well as many other lives.

His breathing was burning his lungs and throat, the exhaustion threatening to overwhelm his body. But that was not the way he'd been trained, people like him never knew when to give up, they could close out the pain and the emotion, take charge of their body, while putting the rest in a box, filing it deep in their mind for another time.

He closed in on the theatre park where he had left Volodymyr and the dead Major's creation. He hoped the other weapon would be there too. He briefly wondered what had happened to Maxine, was she dead, or had they kept her alive? Would she be at the fountain held prisoner when he got there?

He passed the now smouldering BT-80, the rain having cooled it off and ran between the trees towards the fountain.

Volodymyr had answered his prayers and had both the biological weapons lined up, side by side.

His men had gathered around to watch the show with three Russian captives, but no Maxine.

Volodymyr handed Tanner his semi-charged mobile phone that had been brought back from the hotel base. Tanner held it in the air for the drone to see as he called out, "Screwdriver?"

"Vykrutka!?" Volodymyr shouted to his men.

A man came forward responding "Tak, Tak," pulling a multi-tool from a belt pouch and handing it to Tanner.

Tanner began unscrewing the lid of the first weapon housing, peeling it off and handing the tool to Volodymyr to remove the other. He looked down at the digital countdown.

One minute and twenty-four seconds remaining.

"Tell your men to run, tell them to run now, and don't stop." Tanner ordered Volodymyr to repeat the order to his men.

He started shouting at his troops, but they were reluctant to leave, perhaps not understanding the gravity of the situation… more likely simply wanting to see the job through, to know they had saved countless countrymen - as was their mission.

They stood looking at one another then back to the biological weapon the cylinders of Botulinum waiting to feel their lungs and penetrate their bodies.

Volodymyr shouted at them again and this time fired his pistol into the air. One started slowly moving away. Another shot fired with a violent threat emanating from Volodymyr, and the others soon followed, dispersing slowly at first, but then upping their pace as they fled, the Russian POWs heading in the opposite direction, their hands zip-tied behind their backs.

Both lids were removed, the clocks were synchronized, both read less than a minute.

Tanner's phone rang - Stones. "We have less than a minute, what should I do?" It wasn't Stones' voice he heard. The man was short, sharp, and to the point, with no bullshit. The bomb disposal expert. "First, step back so the drone can zoom in and give me a visual, at the same time tell me what you can see?"

They both stepped back.

Tanner kept it as brief as he could with an eye on the seconds remaining, "Both weapons look identical. Two glass cylinders containing the toxin, violet in colour. At the cap end of the bottle is a piercing instrument, which goes into a black box. On top of the black box a digital read, reading thirty-nine seconds. Digit keypad and a battery pack below, wrapped in a thick blue film. Black nozzles sticking out the sides."

The nerves in Tanner's voice were audible.

The expert responded with urgency, "Tap the keyboard, what does the screen read?"

Tanner could hear the concern in the expert's voice, who was also watching the countdown from the Reaper feedback.

"It displays five stars and then returns to the countdown. Twenty-two seconds." Tanner's voice quivered slightly.

Volodymyr was frozen next to Tanner, staring at the clocks.

"It needs a five-digit passcode to be stopped. Does anyone have any notion what it could be?" the bomb disposal guy put the question to all that were listening.

Hearing the expert at a complete loss, Tanner understood. He looked up, knowing they were watching down on them. He ended the call and put his hand on Volodymyr's shoulder.

Tanner didn't know if he was ready to die, but his fate was no longer in his hands. He had tried his best.

At least he'd found the answer to Hunter's killer.

They watched the digital readout tick down - five seconds.

There was a moment of peace as the rain seemed to stop to allow a ray of sunshine through.

"I'm sorry." he said to Volodymyr who remained silent. Both counters hit zero, and in unison, the Botulinum weapons made a whirring sound, followed by a loud click…

Tanner pictured the faces of his four children for the last time.

Chapter Eighty-Seven

Kuzma Belenchuk was the engineer onboard the Kalinovka fishing vessel. He had seen Maxine on a few occasions over the past few years, employing the services of the captain and his crew to do her dirty work. He had heard rumours she might be FSB, but nothing was ever proven, all he knew was he didn't like her and that she was bad news.

When he first saw Salamander boarding the vessel with two conspicuous bags, he knew she was involved. When he knocked on Salamander's door the first time, he could see the fear on the man's face and noticed how he kept gazing at the holdalls with trepidation. It sparked his interest.

Kuzma was a proud Ukrainian man who had served with the 703rd Engineering Regiment of Ukraine's Armed Forces, up until four years ago. He'd had to escape his homeland after a drunken argument got out of hand and he accidentally killed another man. He had no choice but to flee his country and family to avoid prison.

He had been hiding on the vessel in the four years since.

It had become a place of safety for him.

He believed he was still a good man and a patriot.

He felt sorry for Salamander who looked lost to the world. After he had broken the ice with a few shots of the powerful vodka, Kuzma confided in Salamander that he knew Maxine must have a hold over him and offered him his ear.

The vodka had oiled Salamander's trust, and as the drink drowned his senses, he'd blurted out how people were holding his family and forcing him to help them unleash a biological weapon against Kuzma'a very own Ukrainian people.

More of the vodka was poured and at one point Salamander was in tears. Kuzma had placed a strong hand on his shoulder, giving him reassurance that everything was going to be ok, followed by yet another shot.

Eventually, Kuzma got to see what was in the bags.

He'd convinced Salamander to let him prise open the lids to see the liquid waiting inside. Believing the Iranian's story, Kuzma informed a now barely conscious Salamander that he was going to do the 'right thing' and make both bombs inert.

Salamander had agreed, nodding his head with his eyes half closed, his words slurred. He was a good man, Kuzma had decided, but had also decided he would get more of the moonshine vodka into Salamander to ensure he could never remember such a bargain.

Using his training from the 703rd Engineering Regiment he made the invisible changes to allow the weapon to be activated without the release of the Botulinum toxins.

It was a subtle action, unlikely to be seen unless somebody investigated the weapons thoroughly.

He could never return to his country and fight against the Russians, but he would do what he could for his countrymen and claim a victory from afar.

Kuzma hoped he might see Salamander on a return journey one day to rejoin his family in Tehran, but when he saw the Russian soldiers waiting for him on the jetty in Kerch...

He knew he would never return home.

Chapter Eighty-Eight

Things started to move quickly from that moment. Tanner closed his eyes tightly as the countdown hit zero, squeezing Volodymyr's shoulder. The whirring noise spun and the weapons both gave a click before winding down to a stop. After which, the only noise Tanner could hear was his own heartbeat and the distant sound of birds tweeting in the park.

After a few seconds, he forced his eyes open and looked down at the opened biological weapons. The clocks flashed all the noughts, and the liquid stained with the gentian violet colour remained level inside the glass cylinders. No bubbling and more to the point, no hissing noises of the toxin releasing.

The drone above just looked down at the stillness.

It witnessed as the two men standing before the weapons suddenly embraced each other. It was like watching a silent movie as an overwhelming sense of relief swept over each operation room that had watched events play out.

Tanner was lost in emotion while having the life squeezed out of him by Volodymyr. Once free of the squeeze, he found himself laughing - It felt surreal how quickly he had come to terms with dying and was overjoyed the grim reaper would not require his services that day. 'Fate'' he thought, 'When it's your time, it's your time, don't fight it, don't predict it.'

News quickly spread and soon after, some of Volodymyr's soldiers returned and started celebrating in the park.

The inert weapons were put in one of the donated British 4x4s and guarded while a removal plan was being generated.

Tanner had the use of Volodymyr's blue Mitsubishi pickup, and with the guidance of one of his men he went to where the last-stand gunfight had taken place with Maxine's men.

As he drove, he passed both Russian and Ukrainian casualties of war. A tragic waste of life.

Tanner arrived at the location. Already the bodies had been collected and lined up side by side. He walked down the body line, looking at each face expecting to see Maxine but secretly hoping not to. Once he had seen them all and her face wasn't there, he started to wonder what had happened.

He walked around the dead-end area where the Russians fought to the last man. Empty ammo cartridges splayed all around the grassed ground, between the splintered tree trunks and bullet-pitted walls of the buildings that surrounded him. No way out he thought. But where was Maxine's body?

He elevated his searching eyes to the windows of the buildings, all at least ten feet from the ground. As he walked around the wall line, he heard a crushing noise under the sole of his boot. Stepping back, he saw shards of glass on the ground. Moving away from the building wall for a better view, he noticed the window had been broken above. Looking at the other windows, it was the only one that had been shattered. He stepped further away from the building and using the sight of his AKM that was slung across his back, took a closer look. No figure of Maxine was standing in the window frame but a shard of glass sticking up from the bottom had a red glistening of blood covering the peak on it. 'She must have been helped through the window,' Tanner thought, 'That's why she's not dead on the ground with the rest of them.'

He let out a chuckle - Maxine had escaped.

Chapter Eighty-Nine

Shortly after returning to the SPARTAK hotel base, Tanner had reported his findings to Stones knowing it would swiftly be passed on to Ed Boden.

He would certainly now have a shit storm to deal with.

A plan had been put in place at prime ministerial level.

The biological weapons were transported by Tanner, Volodymyr, and a few men to Mariupol International Airport.

Although closed, a NATO C-130 Hercules had come in high and carried out a rapid dive and landing. On board were bomb disposal experts and UN officials for chemical weapons. The weapons were sealed in airtight explosion-proof boxes, and soon the Hercules was reaching for the skies again, heading for the NATO Air Base Geilenkirchen in Germany.

Tanner was also onboard after a hearty farewell with his new Ukrainian friend Volodymyr.

The past week's events had caught up with him once more, and his mind was still fighting to find certain answers. Why did the weapons not detonate? Was it a poor design? Weapon failure? Or did Salamander play a part?

With no answers found, he drifted off to sleep for the short flight, the low drone of the C-130 propellers becoming hypnotic through his ear protection.

Chapter Ninety

Before returning to the UK, Tanner headed back to Tehran, to the compound at the British Embassy.

The final parts were already in motion, and Tanner wanted to be there to finish the job. A joint strike operation was being mounted to hit two locations simultaneously.

Strike One, would be in Fujairah, UAE. At the row of businesses which included ATYAF Gents Salon and the Food Store. The HUMINT team had been watching the area since they deployed there. The Pattern of Life had been established and the key players identified. The Elder and the Barber Saad were priorities amongst many other low-level faces. The planned strike was to take place at 2000hrs local time, during the DOTA weekly meeting in the basement of the food store.

This would be Hunter's justice.

Strike Two, Jafar Malik's compound. The satellites had been taking regular images of the numbers and types of people inside the compound. It seemed that a woman and a child were often seen in the open. At ground level, SRR had been keeping watch, to ensure the target would be in the compound at the same strike time of 2000hrs.

Tanner would be present at the compound strike.

He had grown a sense of respect for Salamander since he'd witnessed his death. A man forced to carry out desperate deeds, blackmailed with threats of harm to his wife and daughter, who were held captive in Jafar's compound.

A man who may have even played some unlikely part in seeing the biological weapons nullified.

This strike would be justice for Salamander.

Since landing in Tehran, the inspection reports from Germany were both biological weapons had been made inert. They would look and run like they were going to detonate but never could. Whoever did it knew what they were doing, and no one would ever know who it was.

1959hrs, stacked up ready to raid, the two strike teams set PE 4 charges on both the compound and shop doors in two different parts of the world.

At 2000 hours – BOOM!

The two teams were moving in.

Tanner followed the Special Forces strike team specializing in compound clearances into Jafar's residence. Flashbangs went off with thunderous claps, bright flashes, and smoke as they cleared the many rooms. There was some resistance from Jafar's men, but they were extinguished quickly.

Those not armed were all plastic cuffed, searched, and brought to the middle of the open area in the compound and laid face down, guarded so as not to become a threat.

Jafar was found in his prayer room still on his knees when the door was kicked in. The two soldiers looked at him to confirm he was Jafar Malik, and once satisfied, killed him where he knelt. A double tap to the chest and then a single shot straight between the eyes.

Kill order complete. DOTA disbanded for now.

Tanner heard over his comms that Strike One had also been a success. The two priority kill orders on the Elder and Saad had been carried out.

'Don't fuck with British forces,' Tanner smiled.

After the commotion had died down, Tanner found his way to those being temporarily held for processing, asking the woman in charge for those he was looking for.

He was pointed in the direction of a woman sitting on a step with what could only be her daughter - a local interpreter standing next to them.

“Anahita and Daria?” Tanner asked.

They both looked up at him.

He knelt, looking to the interpreter to translate for him, then back to face them. He spoke with the echo of their native tongue in the background.

“I was with your husband when he died. He told me to tell you he loves you both very much and will be waiting for you when the time comes.” Tanner felt he had to give them more. “He didn't die in vain; he gave his life and saved hundreds if not thousands of people. Although it will never be spoken of, he was a hero, and you should both be proud.”

He could see the tears falling from Anahita’s eyes, but she kept her composure… her beautiful daughter seemed to understand some of what was happening and started to cry.

As he got up to leave Anahita reached out and grabbed his hand… “Thank you,” is all she said.

Chapter Ninety-One

A few days later back in the UK, Tanner had left the crematorium after Hunter's funeral, and got in his car to drive back to the base for the wake.

She watched him. He looked the same, but cleaner cut. Unlike her, he'd probably had time to rest. As she shifted in the seat, she reached for her side as the stitches across her stomach snagged on her clothing.

The man she looked upon was the cause of why her life was now in pieces. She had nowhere to turn. He would pay for her losses - she was just waiting for the right moment.

Watching him drive off she was set to become his shadow, when an older gentleman in a long dark overcoat appeared and knocked on the passenger side window with his gloved hand. He was looking in at her pointing to the door as if for her to unlock it. 'Who was this crazy old fool?'

She was set to drive when another man was at her driver window. She could not see his face as he was standing too close, but she could see he was holding a PPS silenced pistol. She recognized the weapon and who carried them. She looked back at the old man and reluctantly clicked-open the doors.

The suited gentleman got into the passenger side removing his trilby and placing it on his lap. The other got into the back seat and sat behind her, his face filling the rearview mirror.

"I think you have caused enough problems without following this man. The FSB has decided you have become a liability to the state of Russia," the older man said in a controlled tone, "Let's go for a drive, Maxine."

Grant Spencer was born in Hertfordshire in 1976. He joined the Royal Navy Submarine Service in 1994. During this time, he conducted Top Secret covert missions on Hunter Killer submarines in the latter years of the Cold War - and engaged in global Special Forces operations.

in 2006…
Grant became the first Submariner to successfully complete Special Duties Selection, Operation Samson, becoming a Human Intelligence (HUMINT) Advanced Operator – conducting overt and covert operations handling CHIS's (Covert Human Intelligence Sources) during both the Iraq and Afghanistan wars and domestically within the UK.

Returning to Submarines in 2014, he spent his final years on covert Trident missile patrols that act as the UK nuclear deterrent.

Grant is now an author…
His first book, *Trust No-One* was released in July 2023.
The book is the first in his *Frank Tanner* series.
Although fictional, the series draws on real-world experiences faced by Grant during his Armed Forces career.

Grant's ambition is to create a varied genre of stories and books in conjunction with the Tanner series.

Printed in Great Britain
by Amazon

29068466R00165